In the Shadow of Love

SALLY JOHN

CROSSWAY BOOKS • WHEATON, ILLINOIS
A DIVISION OF GOOD NEWS PUBLISHERS

In the Shadow of Love

Published by Crossway Books
     a division of Good News Publishers
     1300 Crescent Street
     Wheaton, Illinois 60187

Cover design: D² DesignWorks

Cover illustration: Tony Meers

First printing, 1998

Printed in the United States of America

Library of Congress Cataloging-in-Publication Data
John, Sally D. 1951-
   In the shadow of love / Sally John.
     p.   cm.
   ISBN 0-89107-983-1
   I. Title.
PS3560.0323I5   1998
813'.54—dc21   97-43172

11	10	09	08	07	06	05	04	03	02	01	00	99	98
15	14	13	12	11	10	9	8	7	6	5	4	3	2	1

In the Shadow of Love

Dedicated to our military families
whose sacrifice touches us all.

With special thanks to:
Rod and Bridget Nesseth
Jeff and Patty Frost
Linda Murphy,
widow of Navy pilot Tim Murphy

Keep me as the apple of the eye;
hide me in the shadow of thy wings.

PSALM 17:8, KJV

Prologue

1971

The two boys stood in a backyard, tossing a baseball back and forth. Under an azure sky, pines towered over a stone wall that bordered three sides of the spacious, close-cropped lawn. Nearby two tiers of flagstone patio led up to a broad, white-shingled house. Only the rhythmic smack of the hard ball hitting the boys' gloves broke the silence.

The older one, apparently about nineteen, was shorter and stockier than the lanky, younger one. After a time he spoke. "Wanna pitch, kid?"

"Nah."

"Well, I'll let you off this time. You know you gotta practice every day. Every single day, rain or shine, year round."

"Told ya I would."

The older boy snapped his wrist, slinging the ball into the other's mitt. "You're gonna be great. College scouts get wind of you, bet they'll be coming to your games this spring."

The boy snorted. "They don't watch freshmen."

"Phenomenal pitchers like you, they do. You're headed for the pros, kid. Just remember, I got dibs on being your agent when I get back."

The young one held the ball, squeezing it in his right hand until the knuckles whitened. "What if you don't get back?"

"Then we go to Plan B. Somebody with better credentials

will handle your career. And I'll . . ." He shrugged. "I'll do whatever it is I'm supposed to do."

The late-afternoon fog rolled slowly toward them, up from the bay, sweeping away the sky's blue. "You don't have to go."

"Yeah, I do."

"But they didn't draft you." The boy pulled the baseball cap down low over his eyes.

"That's true." He hooked his thumbs in his back jeans pockets. "You'll understand someday. It's one of those things. I just know I have to do it. I don't know why."

The boy turned toward the house and began his pitcher's windup. He paused, then wildly hurled the ball. It slammed into the wall with a loud thump, narrowly missing a window.

The other came over and quietly reached up, placing his arm around the young one's shoulders.

— One —

1991

"WITLESS DRIVERS." Tori Jeffers muttered the words as she glanced over her right shoulder and floored the gas pedal of the station wagon. With the agility of a Le Mans contender, she swerved across two lanes of bumper-to-bumper, rush-hour traffic.

"Tori!" yelled Linda Peterson from the passenger seat next to her. "Your belligerent attitude does not belong on the freeway!"

"Now, now, honey. You'll get my hackles up talking like that." Her subtle southern drawl was in sharp contrast to her quick jerk of the steering wheel as she pushed the car onto the exit ramp. Ignoring Linda's gasp and the blaring horn behind them, she nonchalantly added, "And this is not a belligerent attitude. It's just my usual take-the-bull-by-the-horns approach toward life."

"That may serve you well on the job, but your bull needs some time out. Put him in the pen!"

Tori smiled. "What exactly does that mean?"

"It means . . . Hey, that light's yellow. You'd better slow . . . Tori!"

Continuing at full speed toward the stoplight, she veered left at the bottom of the ramp. The tires squealed through the intersection.

Linda exhaled sharply. "Good grief! Does it really matter if you're ten minutes late to a Little League board meeting?"

"No, but I have to spend those ten minutes at the gas station, not on the freeway." She grinned at her friend. "We've been flying on fumes."

Linda shook her head. "Honestly, Tor. This is just what I'm talking about! You never let up. You're always rushing because you have something to do or somewhere to be because you belong to every organization in San Diego County, not to mention being a single mom and reporting for the *Gazette*." She took a breath. "At this rate you'll burn out before you're thirty!"

Tori braked behind several cars at a stoplight and looked at Linda. Her friend's large brown eyes were wide open, staring back at her. Wisps of blonde hair had escaped her ponytail and dangled along jaws that now worked furiously as she chewed a piece of gum. Tori smiled. "You look a little frazzled, sweetie."

"I'm serious."

"I'm fine! You know my philosophy: life is too short to sit back and wait for anything."

"If you don't wait for this red light, I'll never speak to you again."

Both young women burst into laughter. They'd been threatening each other with that phrase through fifteen years of friendship and had never once stopped talking to each other.

As they drove toward the gas station, Linda resumed her lecture. "You're not fine. Either that red suit has grown or you've lost weight. Your violet eyes now have matching circles under them. And honestly, that haircut!"

Tori fingered the short, black strands above her ear. "What about it? You said you liked it."

"I changed my mind. I'd like it better on our little boys!"

Accepting her friend's honest appraisal, she shrugged while turning into the gas station. "Well, I admit it's a little, oh, severe." She glanced at Linda with a smile. "But with the time I save not fixing my hair, I can join—"

"Look out!" Linda cried.

From the right a silver Jaguar shot across their path. Tori slammed on her brakes. The other car screeched to a halt at the pumps.

"Of all the nerve!" she yelled, her heart pounding in her

throat. "What does he think he's doing? What an idiot! I almost hit him!"

"But you didn't. We're okay, Tori."

They watched the door of the Jag open. A long, white cast emerged.

"Oh, look, he has a broken leg," Linda observed.

"The fool almost had a broken car!" In one swift motion Tori shut off the engine and jumped from the car. With determined strides, heels clicking across the concrete, she reached the driver of the Jaguar as he shut his door. "Just what do you think you're doing?" she demanded.

The man turned to her. "Uhh, excuse me?"

Hands on hips, she lifted her chin to make eye contact with him. "You almost caused an accident!"

"I did? Where?" His brows furrowed.

Tori gestured with her thumb over her shoulder. "Right there." The blank look on his face exasperated her. Her voice rose an octave. "Just now!"

He looked over her head. "With that white Taurus station wagon?"

She nodded.

Palms turned upward, he shrugged and smiled at her. "What can I say? I didn't see you. I apologize."

She noticed his eyes then. They were the deep blue of a midsummer sky. There was a dancing brightness about them that thick, dark lashes could never subdue. She'd seen eyes like that only once in her life. Stray locks of wavy, mahogany-brown hair fell across his forehead. His wide mouth softened broad cheekbones and a square jaw.

She blinked. The man's smile was lopsided in a mocking sort of way. He was laughing at her! "Well," she huffed, "I would appreciate it if you would drive a little more carefully in the future." She turned on her heel.

"Why don't I move my car so you can go first?"

"That won't be necessary," she called out.

"But you must be in a hurry. Didn't I see you pass me on the freeway, doing about eighty near the Camino Heights exit?"

She jerked her head back toward him. "Which just goes to prove that I was here first and should have been at that pump first!"

Laughter burst from him.

She clenched her teeth, attempting to halt the spread of an unmistakable warmth about her ears, and strode to the car.

"What did he say?" Linda asked as she climbed in. "I could only hear what *you* said."

"He saw us go by on the freeway." Tori pulled a nail file from her purse and began sawing it across a fingernail.

"Oh." She chuckled. "So, is he married?"

"Linda Peterson!" Tori's hot temper flared again. "You're a happily married woman! Why would it even cross your mind—"

"We've had this conversation, my dear. I just keep looking for your sake. I guess since all of the other pumps are full, we'll just have to sit here and look at him. He is handsome, don't you think?"

"He's rude and dangerous."

"He could probably say the same about you, Tor. Do you think he lives here in Rancho Lucido? I can't see from here if he's wearing a wedding band. You really didn't notice?"

"Oh!" She slumped down in her seat. "I am perfectly happy the way I am." Through the windshield she watched the stranger. While gas pumped into the Jag, he cleaned the car's windows. He wore a long-sleeved, burgundy T-shirt. Fringes of cutoff blue jeans dangled above the cast on his left leg. Balancing on his other jeans-covered leg, he turned and disconnected the gas hose. With a barely noticeable limp, he strode into the building.

"He kind of looks like a jaguar, doesn't he?"

Tori grimaced at her friend.

"Sleek. Lithe. Broad. Powerful. Confident."

"You're reading too much fiction again."

Linda shook her head, still gazing through the window.

"Oh, it just seems that you need help noticing men. It's perfectly natural. God made us this way."

"Linda, God made me single, and it really is okay. I have a good relationship with Allen. We care a lot about each other. He's the perfect male friend for me. I have absolutely no need for another man to date. My life is full. I don't know why you have to—"

"Oh, look, he's waving." Linda waved and grinned through the windshield. "Wave, Tor. You don't want him to think you're totally senseless. Want me to go ask him if he's married?" She reached for the door handle.

Tori started the engine. "Now that would be totally senseless."

After filling the car, she went inside to pay.

The attendant, a young man in grease-stained coveralls, grinned at her. "You're already taken care of, ma'am."

"No, I haven't been in here yet."

"The guy in the Jag gave me enough money to pay for your gas too. He said, 'I owe that lady in the white wagon an apology.'"

"How much did he leave?"

"Enough. He figured you were on empty, so we guessed at what it'd cost. Left me the change. I made almost five dollars."

"Thanks." She walked back outside. The stranger had just dropped thirty dollars for her tirade. The question was, was that a gentleman behind the lopsided grin, or just some rich hotshot who always paid his way into looking good?

Tori rushed through the gate of the neighborhood recreational club to the Little League board meeting. The California sun had already dipped behind the high hills that bordered the western boundary of the community. A glance at her watch confirmed her tardiness, but she paused in the deserted patio between buildings. The dull pain threatened to burst into a full-fledged headache if she didn't pause for a moment.

Water trickled lazily from a fountain set amidst a miniature

Japanese garden in the center of the walkway. She plopped her soft attaché bag that served as purse and catchall onto a nearby wooden bench, then sank beside it. Closing her eyes, she gulped a lungful of crisp March air heavily laden with the aroma of sycamore trees.

Linda was the best of friends. Tonight was the third out of the past five that she'd fed the twins dinner. That probably wasn't right, although Danny and David didn't seem to mind. They were just as much at home at the Petersons' as in their own house. They got along well with Matt, who was also ten years old, and thirteen-year-old Kelsey referred to them all as her triplet brothers. Linda and her husband Tim were the extended family that Tori depended upon since her own lived in the East.

And when this best friend voiced an opinion, she listened because she knew it was offered in love. Today's appraisal of her condition was on target, though she didn't want to admit it. Her fast-track life suited her high-energy, take-charge personality. But some revamping was probably in order. The slight weight loss, recent headaches, and dark circles under her eyes indicated that her annual bout with exhaustion might be making an early appearance.

She sighed aloud. If she skipped next week's—

"Well, we meet again."

Her eyelids flew open. The words came from across the garden, in the shadows. Where had she heard that voice, that odd mixture of husky and soft? Uneven footsteps approached.

Good grief! It couldn't be . . . "What are you doing here?" she demanded.

"Looking for a meeting room." He stopped near her, resting his cast on the stone edge of the low fountain. "Do you happen to know where the Little League board meets?"

She stood, hoisting the heavy bag to her shoulder. "Funny, you didn't have to wait at the gas station, but you're as late as I am. The room is this way."

He walked next to her. "Perhaps I should try racing on the freeway."

"Touché." She unsnapped the bag. "I'll pay you for the gas."

"No. It was a gift, to compensate for my rudeness. You can just accept it and thank me."

Tori paused outside the door. "Well, thank you."

"You're welcome. Texas, right?"

"What?"

"Your accent."

The hair on the back of her neck bristled. "No. Tinnissee."

"Is that the same as Tennessee?" He reached around her and pulled the door open.

Light illuminated his face, exposing the grin. That crooked, mocking grin. She marched ahead of him, hot anger flooding her.

Twelve pairs of eyes turned toward them from a long table at the other side of the large room. Bill Jenkins, the exuberant, balding president and permanent Little League fixture, rose to greet them with a smile. "Welcome! Welcome! Everyone, I'd like you to meet our newest board member." He extended his hand behind Tori as she passed him.

That new guy is certainly getting quite a reception, she mused.

"Oh, glad you could make it, Victoria."

She bit her tongue and sat down. Bill's formal use of her given name could usually be ignored, but tonight it irritated her. While his solicitations toward the stranger continued, she rummaged in her bag for a pen.

"Did you have trouble finding the place? Need an extra chair for that leg?"

"No, no. This is fine."

Through lowered eyelids Tori watched him sit in a corner chair across the table from her, stretching out his cast-covered leg. Bill was still talking.

"Erik Steed has graciously stepped in at the last minute to serve as a division agent and to coach a team in the Minors A League. You'll find his name included in the new board member list that is attached to tonight's agenda."

Tori looked up. Directly across the table the man lounged, tilting back his chair, smiling through introductions, totally at ease in a roomful of strangers. His tousled, thick brown hair created a nonchalant youthful image, but its neat, executive trim above the ears and those creases around the eyes hinted at years. Thirty-five? Thirty-six?

He glanced at her. She averted her gaze to the paper on the table. "Erik Steed, 487-2815." *That should be spelled with a* c, she thought. *It doesn't look right with a* k.

She figured he must have a son about the same age as her boys if he was coaching Minors A League. She stole a glance at his left hand resting on the table because Linda would ask again. No ring. But then he appeared that carefree type who, while not hiding the fact that he was married, would not announce it by wearing the telltale gold band.

He and his family had probably, like many others, transferred to the area for career reasons. No doubt they lived in the more exclusive west side of town and, remaining true to the mores of yuppiedom, had immediately jumped into community activities—

"Victoria."

She started. "Yes?"

"Your report?" There was an edge to Bill's voice.

"Report?"

"The golf tournament. You remember, that little detail you've been working on for six months?"

"Oh, sorry. My mind hasn't caught up yet with the rest of me."

One of the men interjected, "Bill, you know Tori belongs at the end of the agenda."

She chuckled along with the board members. "Thanks, but you have to remind him before he types these things up. Uhh, the golf tournament."

Across the table the handsome stranger watched her. She cleared her throat, shifting her attention toward the others. "Well, everything is progressing on schedule. We expect more entrants before the deadline next week. The dinner-dance should be a lot of fun. We've hired a popular group that plays six-ties music. I think they're good."

"But how would you know, Tori?" another member teased. "You're too young for that era."

Above the laughter she retorted, "My grandmother told me they were good! I do want to keep all you old folks happy."

She enjoyed the bantering. At the age of twenty-nine she was accustomed to being somewhat odd in a community that boasted a majority population of college-educated, career-minded couples who hadn't begun their families as early as she had.

Not many people intimidated her, and she eagerly explained to anyone who cared to listen that she had earned a high school diploma at the age of seventeen, married a Navy man just before her eighteenth birthday, given birth to twins at nineteen, and in between feedings interviewed people by telephone and wrote articles for the local newspaper.

Bill held up a hand. "You've done a great job of promoting the tournament, but Erik probably isn't aware of what it's all about. Why don't you give him a brief synopsis?"

She took a deep breath and spoke directly to the new member. "Well, it's rather obvious. The purpose is to raise money for the kids. We sponsor it every year. The entry fee is $200, which includes dinner. First-place prize is $1,000, second $500, third—"

"Where do I sign up?" Erik asked.

She raised her eyebrows. "With me, but it takes place two weeks from Friday."

He shrugged a shoulder. "The cast comes off tomorrow. May I give you a check tonight?"

She nodded.

He addressed Bill. "Do you mind if I make a suggestion?"

"Go right ahead."

"Wouldn't more funds go directly to Little League if you low-ered the purse?"

Tori responded, "I think we attract more players by offering large amounts."

She listened as others voiced opinions. Her fingernails dug into her palms, and she wondered at the nerve of the newcomer. His manner wasn't exactly haughty, but somehow it didn't seem quite right.

His suggestion was voted down. To her it seemed he questioned everything after that. Why not an all-star team? Why not run the concession stand this way? Why not draft teams that way?

"It's always been done this way, Mr. Steed." She never hesitated in adding her opinion. "It won't work any other way."

"Change can be good, Mrs. Jeffers." His deep-set eyes held hers.

Some changes were made, and the interminable meeting adjourned. She noticed that the first to begin conversing with Erik Steed were the other two women in attendance. *Figures*, she thought. *He's that type. Mothers of the boys on his team will dote on him—*

A distasteful realization dawned on her, and she dashed toward Bill, cornering him. "Listen, Jenkins, I need to be at the draft," she whispered.

"You know I can't let you do that. Only coaches are allowed."

"Then you've got to promise me you will not allow my boys to be placed on that man's team."

"What man?"

She looked at the ceiling. "That new one."

"Victoria—"

"I swear, I'll quit. I'll quit the board and you can take your golf tournament and—"

"I can't promise—"

"What do you know about him? Is he qualified?"

"Now, now, Victoria, you know I go by the book." His patient tone sounded as if he were explaining something to an uncooperative child. "Yes, Erik is qualified. He was an excellent pitcher at the University of Arizona, so he knows the game. He's a bachelor, but he'll have a nephew on the team. He's living here temporarily, helping his sister through a divorce. That tells me he's quite concerned about the boy's welfare."

"Who's his sister?"

"Stan McHenry's wife."

"What does he do for a living?"

"His family owns an international trading company, and he's taking a leave of absence. The League is very fortunate to have him."

"Don't let him choose Danny or David. Please."

"That's not my job."

"Oh honestly, you can be so dogmatic!" She turned on her heel and left the room, pursing her lips as she marched along the darkened sidewalk toward the exit gate. The stranger was not the sort of influence she wanted for her sons. They needed the role model of a respectable, local father, not some hotshot out-of-town bachelor executive. Perhaps she could call another coach and suggest—

"Mrs. Jeffers . . ." The low, husky voice was becoming familiar.

She stopped under a street lamp in the parking lot.

"Unbelievable. You walk the same way you drive." Erik stepped around to face her. "I can understand why your mind needs extra time to catch up with the rest of you. Is there anything you do slowly?"

His face was hidden in shadows again, but she heard the grin in his voice. "No. It's just the way I am. Always have been, always will be."

"I see. Here." He handed her a check. "I'll trust you to fill in the correct name."

"If I can trust you for sufficient funds." She squinted at the paper.

"That's my San Francisco address. I don't have a local account."

"I'll add your name to the list, Mr. Steed. Thank you. Someone will call you about your tee time." She walked toward her car.

"See you!" he called out.

"Not if I see you first," she mumbled to herself.

"Last and least of the matter, he's single." Tori folded her arms, holding her jacket shut against the chilly evening.

"Wonderful!" Linda exclaimed.

"I don't like him."

The friends stood in the dark outside Linda's house, watching Danny and David run along the sidewalk, past three houses to their own at the end of the cul-de-sac.

"You don't even know him, Tor."

"I know enough! He drives a Jag, has the ability to take months off from work, has a snob for a sister, spells his name with a *k*, wears this mocking grin, charms his way out of being rude at the gas station, charms his way into making Little League changes." She paused to take a breath. "And his teeth are too straight. That all adds up to being a jerk."

"How about confident and successful and enjoys people?"

Tori pursed her lips. "This subject is closed. I'd better go tuck in the boys."

"Hold on a minute." Linda ran into her house.

Tori sighed, looking up at the black sky dusted with stars. The day had been too long, too full. And it was only Monday. When would she trim her schedule?

Linda emerged with a plastic-wrapped plate. "Dinner. I know you won't eat otherwise."

"What would I do without you?" Tori took the plate and gave her friend a hug.

"I don't know. Maybe you'd let this Erik Steed character take you to dinner."

"I'll ignore that." She looked down at the dish. "Since your Navy man is out on cruise, I'll bet this is one of your special experimental recipes. Thanks, sweetie."

"He reminds you of Joe, doesn't he?"

"Oh, Linda, just drop it."

"Listen to me for two minutes. You have just described Joe at a board meeting or in any situation. How do you always say it—something about changing the world?"

"He's not like—" A tightening in Tori's chest cut off her words. "All right, the man's disposition tonight did resemble the personality of a whirlwind, an unrelenting persistence to rearrange the entire world."

"To make it a better place. That's it. I think this guy's perfect for you."

"You just think he's cute."

"He is that. And he's younger than Allen."

"What do you have against Allen?"

"Nothing. He's a wonderful man. A Christian, solid, dependable, successful real estate agent. He'd make a great uncle. Tor, I've told you this before. I don't think he has enough energy to hold your interest."

"That's probably just what I need to slow me down, which is what you always say I should do. And I'm beginning to agree with you!"

"Golly, you must be tired. Go home!"

"Good night, Linda. Thanks again for taking care of the boys." With a wave, Tori set off toward her house at a brisk pace. She retrieved her attaché case from the car in the garage, then entered the house, tapping the automatic door button to close up for the night. The boys had already turned on lights in the combination kitchen/family room. A long counter ran the length of the kitchen, separating the two areas. She kicked off her shoes, strode across the dark tan carpet, and set the plate on the white tiled countertop near the answering machine. Its red light flashed. It could wait.

She turned, breezed around the dining table, through a doorway, across a corner of the living room and headed down the hall. "I'm on my way, guys! Did you brush your teeth?"

"Yeah!"

"Nope."

"Get with it, Daniel! It's 9:15. The school bell rings in

eleven hours!" Without a sideways glance, she passed the bathroom on her left, David's room on her right, Danny's on her left. The smallest of Rancho Lucido floor plans, the house had always felt perfect. Safe. Controllable. At the end of the hall she entered her bedroom.

Just inside to the left, she deposited her bags on the desk. The sight of the blank computer screen and typed pages, covered with red scribbling and spread around the keyboard, nagged at her. *Later. It's not due till noon.*

She shut the door, pulling out earrings as she stepped to the dresser. Her eye caught the 5 x 7 photo framed in beige porcelain. Linda had snapped that one, perfectly capturing Joe in all his glory. Laughing. Wearing his favorite piece of clothing, the dark blue flight jumpsuit. Holding aloft his helmet. Legs apart, the stance daring the world to stop him. Eyes the color of a midsummer sky, sparkling through dark lashes. Golden hair reflecting the sunlight. Or did the sun draw its brightness from that golden head?

Tori turned and quickly undressed, tossing her suit and blouse onto the single bed. A few moments later she opened the door with a shout, "Ready or not, here I come!" Flannel nightgown and red terry cloth robe flowing behind her, she bounded into Danny's room. He was hurriedly pulling on his pajama shirt. "Gotcha!"

He laughed. Although the twins were identical in looks with white-blond hair, blue eyes, and cherubic cheeks, their personalities revealed definite uniqueness. "Hey, sweetie, did you know the draft is Wednesday night? Baseball practice could start this week."

"All right!" Danny held up his hand for his mother to high-five. They climbed to the top bunk. "Will Dave and I get on the same team?"

Tori sat cross-legged next to him and shrugged. "Don't know. I didn't request it." She frowned, remembering what she *had* requested. "So, how was your day?"

"At recess I won handball every time."

"My little athlete."

His eyes widened. "Mom, quit calling me little!"

"Sorry."

Danny looked at his hands. "Ummm, I only got my name on the board twice today."

Tori groaned.

"The teacher said I was talking when she was."

"What do you say?"

He hesitated. "Yeah, I was. But she talks so long, Mom!"

Tori hugged him. "Well, let's see, this is March, so you've only got about three months left. How about you choose something special to do Friday night and then don't talk while the teacher is talking again this week?"

"Okay. Can Matt sleep over and go to the new ice cream shop with us?"

"It's a deal." Tori kissed his cheek. "Good night."

"'Night, Mom. Love you!"

"Love you, too."

She walked across the hall. David sat reading in the lower bunk. She plopped down at the foot of the bed, folding her hands behind her head, looking up at the springs of the top bed. David didn't seem to require the energy she expended with Danny.

"This book is awesome, Mom."

"I thought you'd like it. Sorry I haven't seen you since breakfast." Her usual habit was to leave the newspaper office at 2:30 when the boys came home from school, then write while they did homework and played.

"That's okay. We got along fine. How'd your interview go?"

Where had this child come from? At times he was more friend and mentor than young son. "It went well. Linda took the photos."

"Mom, I've been thinking."

"Umhmm."

"Maybe you should get married."

Tori cleared her throat. "Oh?"

"Yeah, then when you had meetings our dad could take care of us. Or else you could stay home and he could go to the meetings."

"Hmmm." She turned her head to study him. His smooth, round cheeks made him appear too innocent for these concerns. She really had to change her schedule if the boys were feeling neglected. "What do you think of Allen?"

"He's wimpy, Mom!" Danny said from the doorway. "He doesn't know anything about baseball!"

"Daniel, that's an extremely disrespectful thing to say!"

"Mom, he's okay," David interjected his opinion, "but he just seems a little, uh, old for us."

"Grandma might like him," Danny added as he climbed onto the bed next to his brother.

Tori stood. "Have you two been discussing this subject?"

They glanced at each other and nodded.

She sighed. "Well, what's the first thing I would tell you to do about a problem or a decision?"

"Pray," they answered in unison.

"So, pray."

"Mom, you always say it's good to pray together," David reminded her.

Tori stared at her sons, waiting for the lump in her throat to move. They resembled their dad too much. How in the world could she pray with them about marrying another man?

"Well, okay," she breathed. "Dear Father . . ." The boys bowed their heads. She closed her eyes. "Danny and David think we need a dad and husband. We ask that You'd help us find the right one. We pray in Jesus' name. Amen."

"That was quick."

"God hears short and long ones. It's late, guys. Go to bed."

Alone in the kitchen she slid onto one of three stools beside the counter, stretching across it to push the message replay button.

"Hello, Tori. This is Allen. I'm assuming you're at the PTA

meeting and it'll be too late to talk when you get home. Would you like to have dinner Friday? I'll call you. Good-bye."

Elbows propped, she buried her face in her hands, massaging her forehead. Allen. Why couldn't she remember what he looked like? He wasn't as tall as Erik Steed, was he? His smile as frequent? His eyes as intense?

"Oh!" she exhaled, grabbing for the telephone. Why was that man entangled in her thoughts? She punched Allen's number.

"You've reached 451-0151. Please leave your name and—"

She slammed the phone back onto its cradle. "I need to talk to you! Why are you asleep already? And it was Little League, not PTA! Oh!"

Tori jumped from the stool, her mind racing as she prowled about the room drawing the draperies over the patio door, gathering newspapers, plumping pillows.

Allen is a nice man. A good man. The most thoughtful I've ever met. Solid. Settled in his real estate job. Not given to chasing flights of fancy. Always in town. Widowed for ten years. A son and daughter in college.

The orderly contemplation of Allen continued as she strode around the counter into the rectangular dining area.

On the church board. Respected. Wears glasses—horn-rimmed. Soft, brown eyes. Salt-and-pepper hair. Friendly face. Friendly kisses on the cheek.

She shoved the dinner plate into the microwave oven.

Not the goosebump-raising, adrenaline-pumping, I-can't-remember-my-name kisses. But those only come around once in a lifetime, don't they? When you're seventeen. Before real life strikes. If it's just his age and lack of baseball knowledge . . . he's only fourteen years older. Maybe he could lose a little weight, look younger. And anybody can learn about baseball.

The phone rang, and she dashed to it.

"Allen?"

"Sorry. Only me."

She'd recognize that voice anywhere by now. Tori leaned back against the counter, tapping her foot.

"Erik Steed."

"Yes, I know."

"I can tell you're delighted. Which is why I'm calling. I was just studying the Little League board roster—"

"You study rosters?"

"Well, yes. I like to be familiar with names and positions—"

"I'm sure you do."

"I feel at a disadvantage joining at such a late date—"

"You certainly seem to know your way around a board meeting."

"Do you mind letting me complete a sentence?"

She smiled at the exasperation in his voice. "No. Go right ahead."

"Thank you." He noisily expelled a breath. "Anyway, I ran across your name and thought that perhaps my apologies were inadequate."

"Why would you think that?"

"I saw you smile at the meeting, which proves you're not an ogre, but ever since we met at the gas station this afternoon I haven't seen your smile directed my way."

Her smile faded.

"I've only seen lips pursed and nostrils flared."

"My nostrils don't flare."

"Yes, they do, but your nose is petite, so it's not unattractive."

Tori rolled her eyes.

"Are you still listening?"

A smile tugged at the corners of her mouth. "Yes."

"I'm on my knees right now—well, on one knee anyway—and I humbly apologize for frightening and offending you."

She grinned. "Okay, okay. Third time's a charm. I accept your apology."

"I think I detect a smile in that voice. By the way, do you prefer to be called Victoria or Tori?"

"Mrs. Jeffers."

"I take it back. You are an ogre."

The microwave beeped loudly.

"Is that your dinner, Mrs. Jeffers?"

"Yes, it is, Mr. Steed."

"What are you having?"

The long telephone cord stretched behind her as she crossed the kitchen. "Umm, actually I don't know. My neighbor gave it to me. Whenever her husband is out of town, she whips up these marvelous concoctions that he would never touch." She opened the oven door.

"Well, I'm sure you're aware that real men don't eat marvelous concoctions. Although I must admit it sounds more appetizing than my peanut butter and jelly sandwich."

"Aww," she sympathized. "Try adding potato chips and banana slices."

"Inside the sandwich?"

"Yes. It works wonders."

"Hmm. I don't know. It's beginning to sound like a marvelous concoction."

"And you wouldn't want to tarnish your image."

"Definitely not."

"I promise not to tell anyone."

"All right. I'll try it. Good night, Mrs. Jeffers."

"Good night, Mr. Steed."

As if rooted to the floor, she stood contemplating the phone in her hand. How had that happened? Chatting like old friends? His low voice familiar, managing somehow to get on her good side?

She shook her head and replaced the phone. He was too smooth, too charming. *I really don't like him,* she repeated to herself.

Erik pushed the Off button of the cordless telephone and set it on the end table next to the couch. *Phase one accomplished,* he thought wryly. If that difficult woman by the name of Jeffers was the mother of Daniel and David Jeffers, he needed to be on her good side.

He had arrived in town last week, too late to attend the baseball tryouts. Therefore, in order to prepare for the draft, he had requested copies of notes from other coaches who had watched all the boys hit, run, field, and pitch. The Jeffers boys, obviously twins from their birth date and name, scored consistently higher than everyone else. To field a winning team, he would need them. He couldn't afford the possibility of interference by a pushy, disgruntled mother.

Phase two would be the draft itself. Negotiating first pick shouldn't be an insurmountable task. Not knowing anyone placed him at a definite disadvantage. That would help his case for requesting first choice. And he'd offer to take on the five weakest players as well as his nephew Nick, who, unbelievably, had never even played the game.

Stretching his arms above his head, he laughed out loud. Here he was, the chief officer of operations for his family's international trading company—on a first-name basis with many U.S. Congressmen—feeling an adrenaline rush while plotting how to coerce a group of sleepy, southern Californians into seeing things his way. And all because he was determined that his team of wishful nine- and ten-year-old baseball players would be number one.

His sister entered the living room. "What's so funny?"

"Oh, just life in Rancho Lucido." He shifted on the couch, easing his cast from the glass-topped coffee table. Susanne was fussy about such things, and at the moment his concern for her prompted him to go along with her silliness.

"Well, I find it pathetic." She lowered herself onto the love seat, rested her head against the back, and closed her eyes. "The sooner you can get me out of here, the better."

Erik watched her. Mixed feelings of love and contempt constricted in his chest. His sister, two years older, had been his friend since childhood. A feminine version of himself, she was commonly mistaken for his twin. She was tall and well-proportioned with thick, deep brown hair that covered her shoulders. She had a model's high cheekbones and wide mouth. Her blue eyes, though, had more often than not been full of tears since his arrival last week.

But it seemed she had only herself to blame for that. Sure, Stan had dumped on her by his tawdry affair, but what had she done to prevent it? Had she nurtured their marriage by insisting on the most expensive house on the block—one that must have pushed him into working seven days a week at his law firm? Had the extravagant no-touch, plush white carpets, white walls, and white furniture enticed him into her arms? No, her demeanor for years had signaled the message as clearly as if she carried a flashing neon sign: "Do Not Touch."

She resembled the friends who had surrounded her this week. They all appeared to have an abundance of time, jewelry, and disparaging epithets directed toward men. Even Susanne's beauty had been compromised. Drawn lines about her mouth gave her face a pinched look, similar to that of her divorcée comrades. Similar to that of the nightmare at the Little League meeting tonight. Come to think of it, that woman could join his sister's group. Certainly no man was married to her?

"Suse, do you know Victoria Jeffers?"

"No."

"I believe she has twin boys Nick's age."

"They probably don't go to his school." Her eyes remained shut. Her voice sounded as if speaking required much effort.

"She's about five-six with short black hair. Petite frame. Attractive. Until she opens her mouth. She talks a lot. Gestures a lot. On the obnoxious side. Probably tries to run every committee in town."

"Umm, sounds vaguely familiar."

"Are her kids good ball players?"

She looked at him. "Erik, how in the world would I know that?"

"Just thought you might know something. I'm doing research for the baseball draft."

"You're not really going through with that, are you? My life is a shambles, and you're concerned about baseball!"

He stood. "Listen, Susanne, we start picking up the pieces by taking care of Nick. You signed him up. You promised him he could play this year."

"But I thought his father would be here," she pouted.

"Well, I'm here. And the doctor says I'm to stay here for three months without one business thought in my head, or my next health problem will make this fractured femur incident look like a hangnail." He hobbled over to where she sat. "I plan to follow his advice, but I need some definable goal other than getting you through the paperwork and moved to San Francisco. Teaching Nick baseball fits the bill." He bent, hooking a finger under her chin to lift it. "So, let's pick up our pieces together, okay?"

She nodded, tears filling her eyes, and asked, "Is my Jag fixed?"

"Yes, it's fixed." A weariness settled on him like an old, heavy cloak. He straightened. "Good night."

—*Two*—

"MOM! MOM!" Danny yelled as he burst into the bedroom where she was working at her desk on Wednesday evening. "Our new coach is on the phone. Dave and I are on the same team! He talked to both of us, and now he wants to talk to you. His name's Sta—, Ste—, Steel or something . . ."

Tori's heart sank. This was just what she had prayed would not happen. She picked up the phone on her desk. "Hello."

"Hi! It's your new coach."

"So I heard." Maybe she'd never have to see him. The boys could bike to the club for practices without her—

"Your boys certainly sound enthusiastic about baseball."

"It's their favorite sport." She could watch the games at a distance, from the bleachers—

"They were rated high at the draft. They must be good players. I feel fortunate to have both of them on the team."

"They'll work hard for you." She'd just remain uninvolved, a bystander—

"Actually, you were rated high, too."

"What!"

Erik Steed chuckled. "Coaches are concerned about other things besides players—evenly distributing scorekeepers and cooperative parents—and of course the good team moms."

Tori knew what was coming.

"I was told you were the best team mom in the county."

Flattery? She smiled to herself. "Mr. Steed, I've really

31

overextended myself lately. I won't be able to be team mom this season."

"Hmmm. It must be difficult to keep mind and body together, what with a full schedule of committee meetings, luncheons, and shopping."

She jumped from her chair. "Mr. Steed, you have absolutely no idea what I—"

"Mom!" The twins stood in the doorway.

"What do you want?" she yelled, not bothering to cover the phone.

"You gotta be team mom!" Danny pleaded loudly. "Remember when Mrs. Evans did it? We never had any good parties. And the treats were gross!"

"Mom, there was no team spirit," David added. "We need you!"

She sighed loudly. The boys were asking her to do something for them. It wasn't their schedule interfering with hers. Rather, hers was too full to include theirs. What was the priority?

"Well, Tori?" His voice was soft. "I do need someone who knows what's going on since I'm new here. And my sister refuses to do it."

"I think that makes it four against one." She rubbed her forehead. "All right."

The boys whooped.

"Thank you. Now, I've been instructed to have a parents' meeting . . ."

She looked at the grinning faces before her. "Mr. Steed," she interrupted, "what did you offer my sons?" The boys scooted out the door.

"What? Oh, umm," he faltered, "a—a Padres baseball game. I think it was the field level seats that closed the deal."

"Well, at least now I know what I'm worth."

Erik Steed recovered quickly. "Not at all, Tori. It's merely a token of my gratitude for the favor. Your experienced help will be priceless. Now, I understand our first order of business is to hold a team meeting."

"Umhmm."

"I have in mind Friday night, so we can all meet before my first practice on Saturday morning."

"You do move quickly, Coach. All right."

"How about your house, seven o'clock?"

Tori did some mental calculations. Team mom's house was acceptable. Cleaning. Baking. Dinner with Allen. "Seven-thirty."

"Seven-thirty it is. See you then. Thanks again."

"You're welcome." *I guess*, she added to herself.

Friday evening at seven o'clock Tori sat at the rectangular oak dining table in her kitchen/family room and stared at the bouquet that covered half the tabletop. Its thick floral scent permeated her nostrils, which were, she admitted to herself, indeed flared. Relieved only by the delicate white baby's breath, every single blossom was a shade of purple. Orchids, statice, tulips, carnations, irises, lavender, and daisies all gathered artfully in an enormous cream-colored earthenware vase.

Of course, it wasn't the beautiful arrangement that struck a discord within her, but the accompanying card. "Thanks for volunteering to be team mom, Mrs. Jeffers!"

The audacity of the man was becoming insufferable. She couldn't remember exactly volunteering. Coercion better described that phone call.

Tori blinked. The flowers, delivered this afternoon, were gorgeous. She looked across the room. The boys and Linda's son Matt lounged on the floor watching television. Allen sat in a chair reading the newspaper.

Why didn't she feel satisfied that all the planned activities had been successfully combined? As promised, Matt was spending the night. Allen had sweetly rearranged their dinner date to accommodate three boys, pizza, ice cream, and a team meeting. Parents of nine other boys would be arriving shortly—and one uncle named Erik Steed. Groaning, she laid her head on the table. She suspected it was he who didn't fit in the picture. There was something about him that grated like nails down a chalkboard.

"Mom, the doorbell!" All three boys raced to answer it.

The impact of Erik Steed stepping into her front room was immediate, and it was total. Her house felt too small.

"You're early," she greeted him.

His grin was in place. "Thought I might be of some help. Well, you two are obviously the twins." He held up a hand. "Don't say anything. I want to figure out which one is which."

In silence they watched him kneel and study their faces.

"You're Daniel, and you're David." He shook their hands.

Matt whispered in awe, "Wow, mister, nobody can do that except their mom."

Erik laughed. "It's simple. You two sounded so different over the telephone, I knew there had to be something in your faces, something about your eyes that says, 'Hey, I may look like that guy, but I'm Dave' or 'I'm Dan.'" He shrugged.

The boys stared at each other. Tori knew he had won them over in less than two minutes with a lucky guess. The man would not have even needed the promise of a professional baseball game.

He turned to Matt. "Are you on the team, too?"

"Yes, sir. I'm Matt Peterson."

They shook hands. "You're my shortstop, right?"

The grins on the boys' faces matched their coach's. Tori looked at the ceiling.

"Hi. I'm Allen Miller. Friend of Tori's."

She hadn't heard him come in. Erik straightened to greet him. "Erik Steed."

As the men shook hands, involuntary comparisons jumped through her mind. Erik was very tall. Cast removed, he was casually dressed in jeans and a V-necked, pale blue cashmere sweater that did nothing to hide his muscular physique. Unruly, deep brown locks brushed his forehead.

Allen wore a white dress shirt and navy blue pants, both still neatly pressed after ten hours on the job, and a nondescript tie, still neatly knotted. His salt-and-pepper hair remained brushed back from his round face. Spotless glasses rested atop his nose right where they should be.

"Excuse us, Coach. We're supposed to stay out of sight during the meeting."

"Okay, guys. See you later."

Tori spoke to the men. "Why don't you two have a seat and talk about baseball or business while I make the coffee?" She hastily retreated to the kitchen, wincing. Talk business, not baseball! Allen doesn't know anything about baseball.

While the coffee brewed, she lost herself in hostessing details. After her third rearrangement of mugs and platters of cookies, she realized the stalling techniques were pointless.

She stood at the sink, tapping fingernails on the countertop, gazing at shadowed kitchen reflections in the dark window but seeing only three long months of baseball with Coach Erik Steed. There was nothing to be done. The boys obviously liked him and she didn't. For their sake she would just have to make the best of an unpleasant situation.

Another shadow entered the window. Pasting a hostess smile on her face, she turned. "Mr. Steed, thank you for the flowers." She gestured toward the table. "They weren't necessary."

In one graceful movement of familiarity, Erik strode into the kitchen area, leaned against the counter, folded his arms, and smiled. "You're welcome, Mrs. Jeffers." He tilted his head. "I hope they didn't cause a problem with your friend Miller."

"No, of course not," she bristled. Allen hadn't even noticed them.

"Good. I came out to see if I could help you with anything."

"I'm just waiting for the coffee."

They glanced at the quiet coffeemaker, its pot full.

He raised an eyebrow. "Looks like it's done. Do you always hide in the kitchen while your guests arrive?"

Perplexed, she frowned at him.

"You didn't hear the doorbell? Matt's mother arrived. Linda, correct?"

"I'm sure you have your team roster memorized by now, players and parents." Tori bit her lower lip. She'd have to control this incessant urge to snap at him. At least she could be polite. She reached for a plate and held it out to him. "Have a cookie, Mr. Steed."

"Thank you, Mrs. Jeffers. Are these really honest-to-goodness homemade chocolate-chip cookies?" He took a bite.

"Yes." She set the platter down and turned to pour coffee.

"Delicious. I'm impressed. Now I know my instincts were right."

She looked up at him. "Instincts?"

"About choosing you for team mom." He popped the remainder of the cookie into his mouth.

"I thought you said other coaches advised you on that point."

"I just said you were rated high." He shrugged and reached for another cookie. "Besides, I never base my decisions on anyone else's opinion alone. Even if I do ask for it and they just happen to be your sons."

The corner of her mouth lifted involuntarily. So he hadn't talked about her with the other coaches as she'd imagined.

He took the coffee mug from her hands. "Don't smile too much. It might crack your pixie face." With that he took a handful of cookies and left the room.

She heard the doorbell but remained still. Linda would take care of introductions. She needed a few moments to digest Mr. Steed's words. *Crack my pixie face? What did that mean?* Probably that he found her as difficult to get along with as she him. Fine. She needn't exert herself beyond common courtesy.

Allen walked in. "Coffee smells good. Erik seems like a nice guy. Did you know his family owns an international trading company?"

"Yes." She turned to pour coffee for him. Good, they had discussed business. "Sounds fascinating."

"It is." He didn't catch her facetious nuance. "Thank you." He took the mug from her. "He's involved right now with negotiations concerning the Vietnam trade embargo."

"Tori!" Linda stuck her head through the doorway.

Allen laughed. "I think your guests are calling, Ms. Hostess."

Reaching for a platter of cookies, Tori gritted her teeth. "Guess it's time." She followed Allen toward the door.

Linda grabbed her arm. "What's wrong?" she whispered. "That grin looks like you plastered it there."

Tori grinned even more widely, shrugged, and went in to greet her guests.

A short time later Erik Steed stood before the fireplace and conducted the parent meeting in the same manner as he seemed to do everything. Smoothly, comfortably, efficiently. She caught a glimpse of the international businessman. If his tennis shoes and casual jeans didn't make him look about twenty-one, his polished, succinct mannerisms would be intimidating.

"Well, if no one has any more questions, I think we're finished. I hope you'll stay around and visit awhile. I'm sure our gracious team mom has more coffee and cookies."

Their eyes met across the room. She pushed the hostess smile back into place. "Yes, of course. That is, if our coach hasn't devoured them all."

As everyone rose, Allen caught her attention near the front door. "I'm leaving," he mouthed.

She walked over to him. "Working tomorrow?"

"Yes." He gave her a peck on the cheek. "Bye. I'll see you Sunday."

As he left, Linda stepped in front of her. "Erik is staring at you," she murmured in a singsong tone.

Tori narrowed her eyes, keeping eye contact with Linda, her back to the noisy room. "He is not."

Linda's eyes widened. "He is! I have to go."

"No! Don't you dare leave me alone!"

"Goodness, Tori, what is your problem tonight? Kelsey's got

three other thirteen-year-old girls spending the night. I can't leave them alone any longer. Good-bye!"

"He said I have a pixie face!" she whispered.

"Well, now that you mention it . . ." Linda laughed her way out the door.

Erik Steed remained until everyone had gone. "I'd like to tell the boys good night."

Tori pointed down the hallway. "Second door on the left." She looked up at him. "See if you can figure out whose room it is," she challenged.

He grinned. "Care to make a bet?"

She shook her head. "Nope. I'm sure I'd lose."

A few moments later Erik entered the kitchen, where she was loading mugs into the dishwasher. She noticed he wasn't smiling as he stood near the table.

"Thank you for being the perfect hostess, Mrs. Jeffers."

"You're welcome, Mr. Steed. I enjoy entertaining." *Well, I usually do*, she added to herself.

He leaned over to study the bouquet. "You have two great kids. I look forward to coaching them."

"I'm sure the feeling is mutual. I can tell they're already impressed with you."

He pulled a bloom from the arrangement. "Too bad their mother doesn't agree with them," he murmured. "Here, this is it." Straightening, he held up the flower. "What is this called?"

"Statice." In hopes of ushering him out, she strode past him into the front room. "Or sea lavender."

He followed. "It has the deepest hue, almost the color of your eyes. But it's all dried up. Kind of prickly around the edges."

Hand on the doorknob, she paused, pressing her tongue against her upper lip. Who did this guy think he was? She pulled open the door and turned to him, smiling sweetly. "That's just the nature of statice."

His mouth twitched as he studied the flower. "Hmm. Nothing to be done about it then, huh?"

"Absolutely nothing. Good night, Mr. Steed."

With a nod of his head, he sauntered out. "Good night, Mrs. Jeffers."

To say that Tori Jeffers enjoyed entertaining was an understatement. She relished the entire process, from the planning to bidding guests adieu. Serving as chairperson of the Little League committee in charge of the annual golf tournament fund-raiser ranked as leisure-time activity in her book.

She stood now, hands on hips, surveying her handiwork in a banquet room of the exclusive Rancho Lucido Inn. "Hey, Linda, thanks for coming early with me."

"You did it again, didn't you? Delegated the entire committee to take care of the golf segment while you organized the party."

Tori grinned. "How does it look?"

Twenty-five white linen-covered tables were arranged in a horseshoe shape, the wooden dance floor placed in the center with a low platform at the other end. A buffet table ran the length of a side wall.

"It looks wonderful. But I still think you should have used purple flowers rather than red for centerpieces."

Tori grimaced. "Just for that I'm not going to tell you how great you look in that black dress. I'm sorry Tim isn't here to see you in it."

Linda's husband, a Navy pilot, was serving duty on an aircraft carrier in the Pacific. "Oh, well," she sighed. "Only eight weeks to go. You're a knockout in that red silk."

"Thanks." She looked down at the straight, knee-length dress and pushed up the long sleeves. "It's still my favorite."

"It's your color." Linda giggled. "Well, right after purple, that is."

"You're worse than the boys. Oh, gee, there's a flower out of place." Tori walked past her friend. "Guess I'd better go fix it."

The thought of Erik Steed continued to nag persistently at the back of her mind. She had successfully avoided seeing the man again, but the boys spent three afternoons a week with him at baseball practice, which of course resulted in endless references to "Coach Steed this" and "Coach Steed that." They thought he was the greatest, but she couldn't shake her dislike of him.

Guests began arriving, and Tori's attention was soon diverted to more pleasant thoughts as she personally greeted friends and consulted the staff about last-minute details.

She turned as an arm came around her shoulders.

Allen smiled. "Hi. How's my favorite gadfly?"

"Preoccupied!" She laughed.

"And you love every minute of it! Say, did you grow?" He adjusted his glasses and peered into her eyes, level with his own.

She laughed again. "New shoes. Aren't they great?" Turning slightly, she bent her knee and pointed a four-inch red heel toward him.

"Wow. How can you walk in those things?"

"It's a secret, Allen," she whispered in his ear. "Only women are privy to it." She resisted the urge to ruffle his neatly combed hair. "How was your golf game?"

"Not bad. Nowhere near as good as Steed's, of course. That guy could have been a pro at one time."

"He was in your group?"

"Yeah. I really enjoyed talking with him. The guy's got some depth to him."

"Depth?"

"We discussed things like the meaning of life. I told him about our men's Bible study. I wouldn't be surprised if he shows up sometime." He glanced behind her. "I think Bill Jenkins is looking for you. I'll let you get back to work."

"I saved seats for us at that far table, Allen." She pointed. "But I don't know if I'll be able to sit for long."

He squeezed her shoulders. "You forget, I've seen you at functions like this in the past. Have fun. Linda said she'll keep me company. See you."

Bill Jenkins caught her eye and beckoned her to meet him

at the buffet table. "The room looks great, Victoria. It's time for the official welcome. Are we ready?"

"Yes, I think so." She looked at the chef in the tall white hat behind the table. He picked up a carving knife and nodded toward her. "We'll do the awards at 8:30." She walked with Bill to the platform. "By the way, who won?"

"Steed. By four strokes."

"Steed? He had a cast on his leg two weeks ago."

Bill nodded. "I know. The guy's amazing. I'll meet you up here at 8:30 then."

"You don't really need me with you to hand out the checks and trophies—"

"Of course I do! You add that feminine touch of class. And besides, you're responsible for all this." He stepped up onto the platform and reached for the microphone. "Ladies and gentlemen . . . ."

As Tori watched, a group near the patio doors dispersed, and Erik Steed came into view, laughing, talking, and looking devastatingly handsome in a black tuxedo. She smiled ruefully to herself. *Devastating* was the operative word. Those women hanging on his every syllable were not what one would call avid golf fans. She turned her back and mingled with people she found far more interesting.

Some time later Tori joined Bill on the low stage and presented trophies while he regaled the crowd with golf stories. The last participant to be introduced was the winner.

"Congratulations, Mr. Steed." Tori handed him the trophy and thousand-dollar check with a cold smile.

"Thank you, Mrs. Jeffers." Erik leaned toward her ear as Bill continued talking into the microphone. "I'm giving this back," he whispered, holding the check in front of her.

She stared at him. "Have you been drinking?"

"Water."

"You can't do that."

"Why not?"

"You just can't," she sputtered.

"Watch me." He grinned, tore the check in two, and tapped Bill's shoulder. "For the kids."

Amidst the cheering, Tori slipped off the platform and hurried through a side door, then followed the open-air walkway around to a flagstone patio outside the banquet room's main entrances. Indirect lighting cast shadows throughout the surrounding lush foliage. She took deep breaths of cool night air.

Of all the nerve! Winning the tournament with practically a broken leg and then not accepting the money? He had no business barging in and rearranging policy to suit his needs, and then showing off by tearing up the check—

"Fantastic party, Tori!" Allen greeted her with laughter. "That Steed is something else, isn't he? Well, I have to run. It's past my bedtime." He dropped his usual peck on her cheek.

Tori looked up to see Erik Steed standing before them.

Allen held out his hand. "Erik! I certainly appreciated your generosity. I've thought for years the amount of that prize money wasn't necessary. Well, good night!" He walked off, still chuckling.

Chin lifted, Tori met Erik's gaze. His deep-set eyes were shadowed, but she saw the hint of a smile about his mouth. She tried to concentrate on what she needed to say to him and not to think about how even more handsome he looked with his wavy brown hair brushed back off his forehead. A sixties-style beach tune wafted through the open doorways. Two couples walked past and called good night to her.

"You should always wear red, Mrs. Jeffers." He paused. "It's the perfect complement for flared nostrils."

"Oh!" The audacious comment obliterated any threads of coherent thought. "Oh!" Tori spun around, clicking her heels across the flagstones.

His laughter followed closely behind as his hand touched her elbow. She yanked away her arm but faced him again.

"I'm only teasing." He chuckled. "You look especially lovely in red." His face grew sober. "Regardless of the position of your nose."

"Are you finished, Mr. Steed?" Tori crossed her arms.

He grinned. "Not quite. I want to get something straight with you. Was that money mine or not?"

"Who kept your game score?"

Eyebrows raised, he cocked his head to one side.

"All right, yes, it was your money, but—"

"To use however I pleased, correct?"

"Yes, but this has never been done."

"So?" he countered.

"So what gives you the right to single-handedly change policy when the board voted against it?"

"Because I'm an excellent golfer who doesn't care about money?"

"No, it must be your humility."

Erik laughed. "My mother says I do tend to show off."

"If you'll excuse me—"

"I was curious, Mrs. Jeffers . . . You've organized this impressive party, and . . . Well, I would have guessed you to be more innovative, more spontaneously creative. A consistent breaker of rules. And yet you appear frightened of change."

"I'm not frightened of change, Mr. Steed. It's just that some things need to be done properly. Like the details of Little League policies that affect hundreds of kids."

"No place for extravagance when you're dealing with the masses, eh?"

"Excuse me."

Tori quickly found her way to the ladies' lounge and sank onto an overstuffed chair, grateful the room was empty. Her stomach flip-flopped. Who did he think he was making accusations like that? She wasn't afraid of change; she just liked to keep things orderly.

She of all people knew how to handle change. Her life had been a continual series of the proverbial rug being pulled out from under her. Growing up in a military family, she had faced constant change in cities, homes, schools, friends. Five years ago she had faced an insurmountable change and lived through it.

Well, God had given her the strength to live through it. She had learned to accept the changes He passed along to her. But no one else had any business saying she needed to just go along with change.

Taking a deep breath, she shook her head and stood, determined to enjoy the party. Her party.

Like a tidal wave of sound, the rock-and-roll beat of drums, electric guitars, and keyboards washed over her. She smiled at the scene. Strobe lights flashed across the room, illuminating dancers who loudly sang the familiar words along with the band. She laughed. The carefree music was the perfect antidote for the uncomfortable feelings attached to being around one Erik Steed.

Fond memories accompanied the music. She thought of her three older siblings, twin sisters and a brother, and their favorite dance shows that often blared from the television as she was growing up. They spent hours singing and dancing to those little forty-five records. The music always went with them, diminishing the concern of a new city or house or school. When the four of them were together with the music, she felt secure.

Tori walked the perimeter of the dance floor, stopping to chat with those sitting at the tables. She heard laudatory comments about the evening and felt satisfied. When something disagreeable was noted, she laughed with a shrug and put her hands to her ears as if the loud music prevented her from hearing.

Turning to find herself an empty seat, she discovered a white ruffled shirt just inches in front of her face. She looked up at the lopsided grin.

"May I have this dance?"

Slow, soft music played. Tori shook her head. "I only dance to the fast ones."

"Then perhaps the next one?"

"No, thank you."

He leaned toward her. "May we talk?" he asked in a lower voice. "About the team?"

His cologne smelled nice. Masculine, not sweetly overpowering. She only caught whiffs of it. It wasn't like the one kind Allen wore. "Can it wait?"

He shook his head.

Better now than making an appointment to meet him some other time, she thought. Through the open doors she spotted a small, deserted table on the patio and walked to it.

"You're limping," she accused as they sat down.

His grin was sheepish. "I know. My therapist is going to chew me out tomorrow."

"Your mother's right. You are a show-off. Why in heaven's name would you golf in a tournament when—"

"I rode in a cart every step of the way!"

Tori shifted her gaze to the dance floor, drumming her fingers on the tabletop.

"Is that what you hold against me, Mrs. Jeffers? That you see me as a show-off, not to be taken seriously?"

"I don't hold anything against you." Inwardly she cringed. Now that was an out and out lie.

"I disagree. Whenever we speak, I sense you're mad about something. So whatever the problem is, let's get it out in the open. You and I have to work together for this team. If we can't communicate, we'll be a weak link, and I don't like weak links in my team."

Tori looked at him. Only a few inches separated them as he leaned forward, his arms resting on the table. In the soft lighting his face appeared relaxed and open, and yet there was almost a stern determination about it.

Gathering her own determined wits, she decided to accept his invitation to be open. She folded her hands on the linen tablecloth and smiled tightly. "Let's just say that your philosophy of life and mine are diametrically opposed."

He didn't bat an eye. "Pray tell, in that delightful 'Tinnissee' accent of yours, what do you know about my philosophy of life?"

"What is it people have against a southern accent?"

He held up his hands in protest. "I think it's charming. Really."

Tori pursed her lips, wondering how she could rephrase her opinion of Erik Steed so she wouldn't have to use the word *jerk* to his face. "I would guess, Mr. Steed, that you were a star athlete in high school? In baseball?"

He nodded slightly.

"And class president in high school and college?"

He nodded again. "Well, treasurer in college."

"And homecoming king who dated the queen?"

His silence conveyed the affirmative.

"You breezed through life in an unrealistic world of wealth."

"Well, I like to think my parents tossed in some realism here and there."

"But generally speaking, there haven't been an overabundance of pits in your life's bowl of cherries?"

"How did you figure all this out?"

"From the way you drove your Jaguar around the gas station."

He raised an eyebrow.

"Like you own the place," she concluded.

"And that's my philosophy of life? That I own the place?"

"Well, basically, yes."

Erik Steed threw back his head and laughed. She stood.

"Unfair." He touched her arm. All trace of laughter vanished from his face. "It's my turn, Mrs. Jeffers. Please, sit down, just for a moment longer."

Wary of his narrowed eyes and resolute tone of voice, she sat down again.

"I would guess you wear a gold necklace, bracelets, and large earrings at the beach. The last time you stepped anywhere near the water was approximately seven years ago when Danny toddled in too far."

"Who says it's mandatory to resemble a drowned rat at the beach?" She placed her elbow on the table, cupping chin in hand.

The corners of his mouth lifted while his eyes studied her face. "Shopping and lunches are priorities, but serving on numerous committees ranks a close second."

She clenched her jaw, consciously dropping a veil between

them, ensuring he would read nothing in her face, no matter how falsely he accused. "This is fascinating, Mr. Steed. Please, go on."

"Your boys are great, so I assume you give them the emotional stability they need. But in your preoccupation with keeping the status quo, it's apparent that you ignore the fact that in six years they'll more or less be gone from the nest."

She bit her tongue.

"You regularly take your ex-husband to court to raise the amount of your child support."

Never breaking eye contact, she lowered her hand. "I suppose you figured all this out from the way I drive on the freeway?"

"Right. And from your no-nonsense hairdo. And from the way your red lipstick is always perfectly in place. And from this here." His finger traced a feathery line near one corner of her mouth, then the other. "And here. Proof of your determination to keep every one of life's little niches packaged neatly and under control."

"And that's my philosophy?"

"Yes." His eyes held hers. "You were correct. It is opposed to mine."

Tori stood. "Well, I'm certainly glad we've had this little chat."

"Yes. Perhaps now we can make allowances and manage to tolerate each other." He stood, blocking her path.

She looked into his serious face, wavering for just a moment. "You really are the rudest man I've ever met, Mr. Steed."

He stepped aside. "That's just the nature of show-offs."

Tori walked quickly into the crowded banquet room, melding with shadowed bodies and loud music. She and Erik Steed would never agree on anything. Not that it mattered. As she had suspected, he was a pompous snob, incapable of understanding worlds outside his own. What did the boys see in him?

Two weeks after the golf tournament, Erik sat in his Blazer on the street outside Tori Jeffers's house and drummed his fingertips

on the steering wheel. The curse forming on his tongue gave way
to an accelerated thumping in his ears. His hands clenched into
fists, and he took a deep breath.

Okay, Doc. He began the familiar, mental dialogue with his
physician. *I'm breathing deeply.*

He imagined the doctor's calm voice. *Good. Now, what
seems to be the problem?*

This woman. I—

It's a situation you can't control. Give it up.

But she has managed to ruin today's schedule. Not just mine but—

Oh, stop your whining and relax.

He leaned back in the seat and forced himself to take
another deep breath while focusing on the view. He noted it was
a pleasant neighborhood with a sidewalk along the short street
that ended in the cul-de-sac where he'd parked. Acacia, palm,
eucalyptus, and pine trees stretched above small front yards
packed full of cacti, bird of paradise, tall, feathery pampas, red
bougainvillea, and brightly colored azalea. Most of the houses
were stucco with wooden frame fronts. Tori's was like that,
painted a light tan with a darker brown on the trim and garage
door. A bright, multicolored wreath hung on the front door.

Her yard contained more grass and less plants than the neighbors'. A white picket fence would have been appropriate. He had
felt it the night of the parents' meeting—a warm, old-fashioned
sort of *Leave It to Beaver* ambience in her home. Which was why
he hadn't hesitated to leave his nephew Nick in her care.

She had certainly hesitated, though. Remembering her con-
sternation, he thought that he probably caused her more grief
than she did him. Yesterday, after a late-afternoon baseball practice, Dan and Dave had asked if Nick could spend the night with
them. When he saw the look of pure joy on his nephew's face,
not even the threat of his sister's disapproval kept him from saying yes. The boy needed the friendship that the twins offered.

They were special kids. Almost the tallest boys on the team,
they were strong and solidly built. Their outgoing, encouraging
natures made them the spirit of the team. They listened respect-

fully to him when he spoke and followed his directions. In the past three weeks of practice, he forgot they were related to Tori Jeffers.

Their athletic ability impressed him. He had asked once if their dad taught them baseball. They nonchalantly answered that they remembered playing catch with him when they were little, but that he had been gone for about five years. They said that when Matt's dad was in town, he played with them.

So he welcomed their invitation for Nick, who was quiet and somber, usually without a friend after school, slight of build, and unacquainted with baseball.

They had walked together to the parking lot—he, the twins, Nick, and Matt. All wore baseball caps and dirt-covered white baseball pants and assorted T-shirts. Tori was sitting in her car, reading a newspaper. He hadn't seen her since the fund-raising banquet the previous week.

"Mom, can Nick spend the night?" Dan had asked through the open window. "And Matt?"

She lowered the newspaper. Erik stood behind the boys, watching her reaction. Dark sunglasses covered her eyes, but the straight line of her mouth said it all. "Danny, you know you're not supposed to invite anyone without asking me first."

"But you never come to the diamond, and Coach has to get going, so we couldn't wait!"

"Mom," Dave interrupted, putting his arm around Nick's shoulders and pushing him closer to the window, "this is Nick McHenry. Nick, this is our mom."

She smiled then at his nephew and shook his hand. "Nice to meet you, Nick."

"So can he stay, Mom?"

"Well, honey, we have some things to do—"

"What are we doing? You said we were just staying home tonight and eating lasagna and playing games!"

"Danny, lower your voice. You both need shoes, and this is our only time—"

"Nick can go with."

As their pointless discussion continued, Erik suspected his

relationship with this mother had something to do with her reluctance. "Boys," he interrupted, "go wait over there and let us adults resolve this." They shuffled toward the club entrance gate. He leaned toward the window, resting his hands on the car door. "I should have talked to you first."

"Yes, you should have."

"Look, I know you have a problem with me, but my nephew's a nice kid, and he'd really like to spend some time with the twins."

She didn't say anything.

"As a matter of fact, I'd like him to spend some time with them. They're a good influence on him."

"We have to go to the mall."

"He won't mind."

"And we're probably going to church in the morning."

"That's fine. I'll bring some clothes over for him."

"No, I'm sure we can find something for him. We'll call you when we get home tomorrow. It should be about noon."

"We have afternoon plans. I'll be there at noon."

Noon had passed forty minutes ago. The white station wagon cruised by him, then screeched to a halt in the driveway. Four doors burst open.

"Uncle Erik!" Nick ran toward Erik as he climbed from his car, then leaped at him. Erik caught him in midair and received a bear hug from the usually undemonstrative boy. "Can I stay longer? Please? Their mom said she'd bring me home."

Two other pairs of arms encircled his waist from either side. "Please, Coach."

He looked down at the twins and swallowed a lump in his throat. Nick's arms tightened around his neck.

"Guess I should have talked to you first." Tori was grinning up at him.

"Yes." He cleared his throat. "It would have prevented some disappointment." He turned his attention back to Nick, lowering him to the street. "Grandma Steed planned to take you to the zoo this afternoon, remember? She's leaving tomorrow."

"Oh, yeah, I forgot. Well, we don't want to disappoint her."

"Why don't you run inside and get your baseball clothes," Tori urged. "They're on David's bed." The boys ran to the house. "Come on inside, Coach. They might get sidetracked and then you'll be *incredibly* late."

"Forty minutes isn't *incredibly* late?" He mimicked her emphasis on the superlative.

"No. Ninety minutes is incredibly late. Is your Jag in the shop?"

"My Jag?" He opened the front door for her. "I don't have a Jag."

"Yes, you do."

"No, I don't."

"But at the gas station—"

"That was my sister's."

She stopped inside the living room and turned toward him. The confused expression on her face dissolved when she burst into laughter. "Does that mean," she paused to catch her breath, "that everything I've said about you is wrong?"

Her laugh seemed to bubble up from inside her and spill over onto anyone within range. In spite of himself he chuckled. He noticed how her face softened, how her eyes shone. They were uncommon eyes, a deep violet, like amethysts. "Totally."

"Oh, dear." She bit her lower lip. "Guess I'd better call a truce. How about a cookie as a peace offering?"

"Sure." He followed her into the kitchen. She wore a crisp, white, long-sleeved shirt tucked into blue jeans that accented an attractive shape. Her dark hair hung in a straight line above the collar. She looked like a teenager. He slid onto a stool at the counter while she walked around it.

"Well, I have no preconceived notions about drivers of four-by-sixes, so you've got a clean slate."

"A four-by-six is an index card. What I drive is called a four-by-four."

"Oh." She giggled and set a plate of peanut butter cookies in front of him. "I'm sorry we're late. Did you know Nicky has never been to the T-bird Diner?"

"What's that?" he mumbled through a mouthful of cookie, watching her pull a gallon milk jug from the refrigerator.

"It's a fifties-type restaurant. It has a real Thunderbird car inside. Well, the front end of the car anyway." She poured milk into a glass and set it next to the cookies. "The old music they play is deafening, and the waitresses wear poodle skirts and yell and smack bubble gum and make obnoxious comments to the customers."

"Sounds delightful."

"Yeah, I know, but the kids think it's great." She leaned her elbows on the counter. "They talked me into it. We left church immediately, but the place was packed already. You're raising your eyebrows. Don't you believe me? The freeway was a little crowded, and I didn't want to go eighty miles an hour, but—"

"You just don't look as if you went to a restaurant directly from church."

"What?" She glanced down. "Oh, you mean the jeans? We're pretty casual. I guess our church is a southern California interpretation of the New Testament. Have another cookie."

"Thanks." He took one.

"I'm curious. Nicky tells me that you broke your leg skiing in Tahoe while on vacation."

"Right." He bit into the cookie.

"And that the doctor said to take another vacation."

"Umhmm."

"And that's why you're here for the entire baseball season."

"Umhmm."

"That doesn't add up."

"What are you, a detective or a reporter?" He took a drink of milk.

"A reporter."

He raised his eyebrows. "You work?"

"I'm crushed. Don't you read the bylines in the *Gazette*?"

"What's the *Gazette?*"

"The community weekly. You've never read it?" Her tone was incredulous. "It's delivered to everyone, free of charge."

"Newspapers would clutter Susanne's house. She doesn't allow them."

"Why did you look so surprised when you asked if I work?"

He paused, considering his words. He had just assumed from her attractive-but-cold appearance and sassy attitude that she was like his sister—occupied with spending money and dictating to a man how much she wanted. "You, umm, don't seem the type."

"Oh, that's right, if I work, then shopping and lunches must not be my priorities. Or serving on numerous committees. Isn't that how you put it?"

For some reason he felt relieved to see a smile in her eyes. "Something like that. I think we're even, Mrs. Jeffers."

"Then you can call me by my first name. Now, to get back to my question—"

"Is this off the record?"

"If you insist."

"I insist." He bit into another cookie.

"I guess I'm curious that you would leave your company for such a length of time. From what Allen says, you're involved in a demanding business. A three-month baseball season seems an awfully long vacation."

"It is, but I broke my leg."

"Now you sound like Nicky. The cast is off."

Erik gulped the remainder of the milk. "Well, let me back up. The skiing vacation was forced upon me because my years of working sixteen-hour days had resulted in a temperament that my father and uncle refused to tolerate any longer. My time out lasted two days. I woke up in the hospital, immediately phoned my secretary, and basically just got back to work, long-distance, leg in traction, looking at the ceiling." He folded his hands and made eye contact with her. "After two weeks in the office, I collapsed. The doctor said if I didn't take an extended leave of absence, away from San Francisco, I'd be forced into a permanent leave of absence from everything fairly soon."

"Oh." She paused. "That sounds serious."

"About as serious as you can get."

"I'm sorry."

He saw genuine concern in her face. "We'd better go."

They walked to the living room, and Tori called down the hallway, "Time for Nicky to leave, guys." A moment later the three appeared. She knelt before his nephew and gave him a hug. "Come back anytime, okay?"

"Okay. Thanks, Tori."

"You're welcome." She stood and smiled up at him. "Thanks for letting him stay, Erik."

"Thank you, Tori. See you at practice tomorrow, guys."

"Bye, Coach. See ya, Nick."

"See ya, Nick."

"See ya." The boys all slapped hands.

As he followed Nick through the front door, Erik felt a vague discomfort, like a yearning for something he'd lost. What was it? He didn't have a clue.

— *Three* —

"LET'S GET JUST ONE THING STRAIGHT." Tori stood near first base, legs apart, hands on hips. "I won't tell you how to coach, and you won't tell me how to be team mom. Agreed?"

A few feet away, Erik's stance and glare matched hers. "Agreed." He pulled his black baseball cap down over his eyes. The crooked grin spread across his face. "But only because you've got great-looking legs." He turned on his heel and sauntered out to the field.

"Oh!" Tori fumed, berating herself for suddenly feeling conspicuous. Her shorts were modestly styled. And besides, everyone wore shorts today. The hot, dry Santa Ana desert winds were blowing, and the noonday sun beat from a cloudless sky. The only available shade was under the cover at the scorekeepers' bench. "Hey, Coach!" she yelled.

He turned.

"You have to give your lineup to the scorekeeper. Now!"

"Is that the coach's duty or yours?" he shouted.

Tori clenched her jaw and marched through the opening in the high, chain-link fence into the dugout. He was by far the most unpleasant coach she'd ever encountered. The two of them had just wasted ten minutes discussing where she would sit during today's first game. She had won, not, it seemed, because of any merit in what she'd said, but because of the way she looked in shorts. Of all the nerve!

She plopped down on the aluminum bench. Obviously her

first impression of him had been on target. In spite of their truce, in spite of the fact that he did not own a Jaguar, he was rude and obnoxious. A pompous snob. That gentleness she had glimpsed in his demeanor with Nicky at her house last Sunday was definitely a personality glitch.

She put on the black team cap she'd ordered for herself. It matched the boys' with a white O above the bill for Orioles. She watched the boys out on the field warming up for the game, thinking how cute they looked in their professional-type white pants, black belts, and bright orange jerseys. They wore black baseball shoes and white socks with orange stirrup-like stripes tucked into the elastic hems of the shin-length pants.

Tori felt someone poke her back through the fence. She turned.

Linda grinned. "Need some help?" she asked.

"No, thanks. They've all got water bottles, so I really don't need to do anything yet. Besides, I think I used up all our coach's good graces just getting permission to sit in here." She placed the cap on her head.

"Tori, you know team moms for this older division don't sit on the bench."

"Well, I always have. They're not too old for me to encourage one on one, and to make sure they drink enough water."

"You'll probably encourage Erik too . . . with your great-looking legs."

Tori's mouth dropped. "You heard that?"

"The bleachers are right behind you, hon," she whispered. "You might want to tone it down. Or give us parents something to talk about besides baseball!" Overcome with giggles, she walked away.

During the game Tori was ignored by the coach, his two assistants, and the boys. She remembered this being the norm and took no offense. In her opinion, adult males remained far too sober and intense at these affairs. For not much going on, they always had plenty of instructions to shout.

Although everyone's attention remained on the game, her response was more personally enthusiastic to the boys' smiles after making a run as well as sympathetic to their teary eyes after a strikeout. And she never forgot to remind the boys between innings to drink water or eat orange slices.

The Orioles won their first game. Erik graciously transferred the parents' congratulations to the boys, while Tori distributed cookies and boxes of juice.

She ignored the dirt and sweat as she hugged Danny and David. "You guys played great together!"

Erik stood nearby. "They tell me it's their first season on the same team." His orange *Coach* T-shirt was covered with dirt from hugging all the boys.

"Yes." She picked up her plastic containers that had held orange slices and cookies and stuffed them into the now-empty cooler.

"I'm fortunate to have both of them. The way they communicate, with Dave pitching to Dan's catching," he shook his head in amazement, "they're a natural duo."

"Great," she replied. "Well, let's go, guys."

"Coach invited us over to swim at Nick's house." Danny bent to finish unbuckling his catcher's gear.

"Can we go, Mom?" David asked.

"I'll bring them home, Tori, say around 5? Some of the other boys are coming too."

"Well, I do need to do some shopping," she said, emphasizing the last word.

The boys groaned. "Go without us!"

Tori laughed. "Okay, okay. Come home and change, and then I'll drop you off. What's your sister's address?"

He gave her directions.

"I don't know how you drafted both of them, Erik. I don't think I want to know. But they are enjoying being on the same team. It certainly improves my schedule, too, with only one game to attend." She lifted the cooler.

"It probably lessens your wardrobe needs, too, with only one matching blouse to buy." His crooked grin returned, and incredulity colored his next words. "Did you actually do this team mom thing for both of them? Sit on the bench and pass out goodies to two teams every week?"

Tori pulled down her cap. "Ever since they played T-ball in kindergarten." She turned and marched across the field. The man really was insufferable.

The weeks of April fell into a pattern. Daily work and school, Tuesday night baseball practice, Wednesday one committee meeting or another, Thursday night game, sometimes dinner with Allen on Friday night, Saturday game and errands, Sunday church and time with friends or a visit to the zoo. Coach Steed often invited the team to swim after a game or to the batting cages after school on Fridays.

David and Danny so obviously enjoyed these times that Tori appreciated Erik's male companionship for them. Although she did her best to provide it with family friends or with Allen since they'd started dating a few months ago, she knew the boys sorely lacked individual masculine attention.

Still, Erik's coaching methods grated against her sense of nurturing. None of the boys complained about his demanding nature, however, and the fathers agreed with his strictness. Tori coated her disapproval in sarcasm, which was never lost on the coach who retaliated in like manner.

Although she was aware that the Orioles were undefeated after eight games, Tori seldom paid attention to the score during a game. She watched only for sullen faces to encourage and grins to congratulate. On the first Saturday of May, however, dismal countenances pervaded the entire team. Even she realized their winning streak must be in jeopardy.

The boys trudged into the dugout. A few threw their mitts on the ground. All remained uncharacteristically silent, including Coach Steed and the two dads assisting him.

Tori pursed her lips. What an unbelievable display of sulking! She pulled on a white sweater, glad she'd worn jeans to this late-afternoon game. The sun was nearing the tops of the western hills, and the air had grown chilly. No desert wind today.

"Put on your jackets, guys," she advised.

From the other end of the bench, Erik glowered at her over the heads of the boys. She crossed her arms and leaned back against the fence.

Their first batter struck out.

"Have an orange slice, hon." Tori held the plastic container out to him as he slumped down near her. "You'll hit it next time."

"No, thanks, Mrs. Jeffers."

"Oh, go on. It'll give you extra energy."

"Mom . . ." David peered around a few boys to explain. "We're losing seven zip. We're not hungry."

Erik scowled at her again, then turned his attention back to the field.

Tori wrinkled her nose at him. Why didn't he and his assistants do something besides frown? Honestly, it was just a game. She studied the row of dejected faces. "Come on, Orioles! You can't quit yet. You've got three innings left!" She jumped up. "Danny's at bat. Let's show some team spirit. Go, Danny!" she yelled. "You can do it!"

A few meager cheers joined her until the third strike was called.

Danny plopped down beside her. "Aww, Mom, that umpire stinks!" His scrunched-up face predicted tears.

Tori put an arm around his shoulders. "I know, sweetie. He's not very good, but—"

"Dan!" Coach Steed stood over them, his voice low and threatening, his finger pointing. "You knew that pitch was good. Don't ever, ever watch that third strike go by. Do you understand?"

The boy stared up at him and nodded.

"Ball players don't whine to their mothers. Go sit down there." He gestured to the other end of the bench.

Danny scooted, and Tori flew to her feet. "Don't you ever talk to my son that way!" she hissed through clenched teeth, glaring up at him.

He leaned down until only inches remained between their faces. "Team mothers are no longer allowed on this bench."

Tori squeezed her hands into tight fists and held them stiffly at her sides. "Where did you find that rule in the handbook, Coach?" She spat the words.

"It isn't in there—yet."

"Right. Well, I'm sure you can coerce the board and have that changed in no time at all!" Rage pounded in her chest.

His eyes were narrowed slits, his mouth a grim line. "Get out of my dugout before I pick you up and throw you out," he growled quietly, then stood aside.

Fragmented retorts flew around her mind but refused to cohere in her fury. She stomped past the team and through the dugout opening. Of all the nerve! The board would hear about this. The man couldn't be allowed to—

Without warning, a sharp pain exploded around her right eye. She felt a sensation of racing down a blackened corridor tinged in red.

"Tori!"

She moaned.

"Mom!"

Pain shot across her forehead. Something soft pressed above her right eye.

"Mom!"

Faces blurred, dancing, throbbing behind her eyes, escaping focus. She felt the hard ground beneath her. Her hands at her sides groped through dirt. "What happened?" The words stuck in her throat.

"She's okay."

"Wow, she was knocked out!"

"Just for a few seconds." Erik's voice. "Dave, get some ice."

"I'm sorry, Mrs. Jeffers!"

"John, this isn't your fault." Erik again. "Do you understand? It was an accident."

"Hey, John, straighten it out next time. That coulda been a double!"

"Yeah!"

So many voices. Why didn't they answer her? She closed her eyes again.

"Tori."

"Mom!" A small hand squeezed hers.

She recognized the panicked edge to Danny's voice and moved to sit up. "I'm okay, hon. What happened?" A hand held her shoulder.

"Lie still," Erik ordered. "You got hit by a foul ball. Right here." The pressure increased above her eye.

"Wow, there's blood all over!"

"Ooh, is that your hankie, Coach?"

"I bet she's gonna have a black eye."

"Sit down! All of you!" Erik roared.

She winced.

"Tori," he lowered his voice, "what were you doing? You stomped right out toward third base."

The pain throbbed to the back of her head now. Faces and voices floated as if in a fog.

"Tori!" It was Linda. "Erik, let me see it."

The soft cloth lifted from her head. Danny's hand tightened over hers.

Linda groaned. "Oh, dear. Tori, you need stitches! And your eye's almost swollen shut. What on earth were you doing?"

"Here's the ice pack, Coach."

"Thanks, Dave."

Cold pierced her skin. She gasped. "Let me up!"

"Lie still," Erik commanded again, now pressing the ice to her head.

"David, run get your mom's purse from the bench," Linda directed. "I'll take her to the emergency room."

"No, I will."

"I'll do it." Linda's voice had risen an octave. "I can't believe you two! Arguing like little kids! Tori, just what is your problem?"

"Linda, calm down." She pushed aside Erik's hand and sat up. "We've been through worse than this. I'm all right. I'll drive myself."

As Erik helped her to her feet, she heard applause and groaned.

"Just like in the real Majors, Mom!" Danny explained.

David met them at the gate. "Mom, are you okay?"

She forced a smile. "I'm fine. But I guess it's my turn to get stitches."

Danny squeezed her hand. "It's not much fun."

"Do you want us to come with?" David asked, handing her the shoulder bag.

"I'm going with her, guys." Erik knelt before them, holding an arm of each. "It's my fault she got hurt. I'm sorry. I promise to take good care of her. Ride home with Matt's mom, okay?" He stood. "Now get out there and play ball!"

Why did they never hesitate when Erik spoke? "All right, Coach! See ya, Mom!" They ran back toward the dugout.

Tori gripped the fence, supporting her trembling legs. "I'm not going with you." She stared defiantly at him, trying to focus her left eye on his face. She could only see his mouth clamped shut below the baseball cap. "I wouldn't want you to miss your precious ball game."

"Tori, please!" Linda implored.

Her whole body trembled now. She touched her forehead. The pounding had increased. Erik's hand came around her elbow, urging her away from the fence. Linda took her other arm, and they walked silently through the grass to the parking lot.

"Don't worry about the boys, Tor," Linda hiccuped. "I'll make sure they take showers and eat—"

"Linda, stop crying. I'm all right!" She peered into her friend's tear-streaked face.

"I can't stand to see you hurt." They hugged each other.

"Let's go." Erik helped Tori climb into his Blazer. "Here, hold this ice pack on your head."

She took it from him. "I don't want you going with me."

"Shut up and hold the ice."

"It's dripping."

"You have to keep the swelling down." He hooked the safety belt around her, then slammed the door.

She leaned back against the seat, closing her eyes, fighting the desire to cry. Waves of nausea washed over her.

"I'm sorry, Tori."

"Just drop me off at the hospital."

"Can I have an aspirin or something?" Tori was slumped in a hard chair at the admissions counter, rummaging through her large purse. Where was that insurance card? The throbbing pain disoriented her. "Do you really need this? The kids are here all the time. They always get sick or hurt at night, when the doctor's office is closed, so we always come here. I've been here three times in the last six months!" Tori recognized the shrill edge to her voice despite a magnanimous effort to be polite. "I mean, can't you just find this information in the computer or something?"

She squinted at the woman across the counter. The harsh lights and thick, antiseptic stench bombarded her senses, intensifying her discomfort. It was the presence of Erik Steed, however, that threatened to topple her composure. He sat close beside her in the cubbyhole, and he was being so—so nice.

The woman behind the computer exuded warm efficiency. "Sorry, honey, I need to see it." Her fingers paused in their flight across the keyboard. "Address?"

Without a word, Erik lifted the purse from her lap.

"One, one . . ." Tori frowned.

"Two, five, eight," Erik finished for her. "Caliente Court, Rancho Lucido."

From beneath her swollen eyelid, she watched him open her
wallet and begin flipping through cards.

"Phone?"

She bit her lip as Erik supplied the answer and handed the
insurance card to the woman.

She accepted it, then began typing again. "Thank you."

"Tori?" He leaned toward her, placing his arm across the
back of her chair.

She looked up. Dark splotches stained the front of his
orange T-shirt. Indentations through his wavy hair marked
where the cap had creased it. She had never seen his face so
sober, not even during that wretched baseball game.

Tears welled up in her eyes. "Oh, why don't you just go
home?"

"What, and miss this fall of the iron curtain from the infa-
mous Tori Jeffers's image?" His soft voice removed the caustic
sting of his words. "Anyway, I'm responsible for all this." His eyes
studied her injured brow.

"You're right about that, but I'm the one who walked out on
the field!"

"More like flew out to the field. I know your real name isn't
Victoria, is it?"

She frowned at his face leaning close to hers.

"It's Tornado. Tori is short for Tornado." He chuckled.
"Torinado."

"Very funny."

"Marital status?"

"What?" Tori transferred her attention back to the woman.
"Oh. Widow."

She felt Erik stiffen, heard his intake of breath.

"Place of employment?"

"*Rancho Gazette.*"

"And what do you do there?"

The questions droned endlessly. At last they were ushered
into a large room adjacent to the lobby. A row of white curtained
areas ranged along the left side. To the right was the nurses' sta-

tion. Stainless steel trays and instruments gleamed everywhere, reflecting the bright lights.

A nurse positioned Tori, then pointed to a lettered eye chart on the opposite wall. "Cover your left eye and read this."

Tori attempted the task. "I can't! Everything's blurry. My head is pounding."

Erik slipped his arm around her waist. "Can't we skip this part for now?" he asked.

"That's all right. Just follow me over here." She pulled aside a curtain. Climb right up here, Mrs. Jeffers, and lie down." The nurse patted a high, narrow bed. "The doctor will be with you shortly."

Erik helped her do as the nurse instructed, then stood over her, holding up his hand. "How many fingers can you see?"

"What fingers?" She folded her arms across her waist.

"Tori!" He muttered something under his breath. "Why can't we ever talk to each other like normal people?"

"Go home." She closed her eyes. "You're just being nice because you feel guilty."

"Victoria Jeffers, what in the world happened to you?"

She looked up into a familiar face. "Dr. Thomas! Oh, I'm glad you're here."

The short, balding man reached across Tori to shake Erik's hand. "Hi. Ted Thomas."

"Erik Steed."

The doctor leaned over to study her eye. "Whoa! I think you'll beat Danny for number of sutures in one sitting."

"Swell. Now he'll think we're in a contest."

He smiled. "Let's see. It's below the eyebrow. That's good. You won't have a permanently crooked one. You'll still be able to effectively arch it. How many fingers am I holding up?"

"Thirty-two."

"Cute." He sat down on a stool behind her head. "What happened?"

Erik answered, "It's my fault—"

"Stop saying that!" Tori grimaced as the doctor squirted water over the cut.

"We were in the dugout at her sons' game, and I ordered her off the bench. She walked out and got hit with a foul ball."

"Tsk, tsk, tsk. What were you doing in the dugout, Mother?"

Tori pressed her mouth closed. Erik cleared his throat. "She's team mom."

"Hmm. I thought team moms made phone calls. This is going to sting a little. Baked cookies, that sort of thing. I didn't know they coached."

The needle pricked. She bit her lower lip.

"Sorry. Have to do it one more time. We want to make sure it's numb. So, how old are Danny and David now? Nine?"

She felt Erik's hand cover one of her tightened fists. He answered, "They turned ten in February."

"Hmm. And once more."

Tori concentrated on the gentleness of Erik's thumb stroking the back of her hand.

"Done. Victoria, trust me." Lowering his face, he patted her shoulder and whispered, "God created little boys to grow up and play baseball without their mother hovering. Now relax. I'll be back."

Tori closed her eyes. Erik's thumb traced a pattern around her knuckles.

"Why didn't you tell me?"

From his hushed tone, she knew he referred to what apparently was news to him, that she was a widow. Seldom did she have to tell anyone. It was a given that that sort of knowledge was shared within her circle of acquaintances. And Erik was in that circle now. "Don't you talk to anyone?"

"About your personal life? No. Why didn't you tell me?"

"What difference would it have made?" she countered.

He didn't answer.

She refused to look at him, refused to see his handsome features distorted with pity.

After a few moments he spoke, his tone hesitant. "I, uhh . . . umm . . . when the boys mention their dad, it's in the past tense. Like he used to play catch, or he used to fly. But I understood . . .

I assumed it was just something . . . just something he doesn't do anymore because you're divorced and he's chosen . . ."

She heard his release of breath. "Erik, I know how they talk." She lifted her eyelids far enough to watch his thumb stroking the back of her hand. "How I talk. As if he has moved away, which is truly what I believe, until it's time for us to follow him. We just don't broadcast the fact that their father is dead."

"When . . . ?"

"Five years ago. Please stop asking questions."

In an odd way, Tori drew comfort from the repetitious movement of Erik's thumb. It was like a birthing labor technique she had learned years ago, choosing a focal point outside of her internal uncomfortableness, disengaging her mind from the pain.

To remember Joe did not cause uneasiness. Layers of years had soothed the early, raw grief. She related to the boys what they'd done as toddlers with their dad, how they resembled him in behavior or looks. His mother visited regularly, overflowing with stories of his childhood. They all knew the comfort of God's promise that Joe, the most devoted follower of Christ she'd ever met, was with Him now, and they would all be reunited someday.

In that belief, Tori wove together Joe's absence and presence into one reality, a natural, private entity in their lives, one that didn't require attention from outsiders.

Was that it? Was she avoiding Erik Steed's attention? Of course. The thought of exposing herself to his pity irritated her. It would be an obvious disadvantage to her in their relationship of mutual contempt.

"Excuse me, are you Mr. Steed? There's a telephone call for you."

Tori watched him leave with the nurse.

Dr. Thomas took his place. "Well, are you ready, Mom?"

"You're grinning like a Cheshire cat, Doctor. You don't think I can do it."

He laughed and walked around behind her head. "Not true, not true! I know how tough you are." He gently placed a paper sheet over her face. "It's your friend. He looks a little green around the gills."

"You're joking."

"I told the nurse to keep a close eye on him. She said she was anyway. Nice-looking chap."

"Umm." Unable to see the doctor, she sensed him preparing behind her, listened to his off-key humming.

"Doctor?" Erik had returned "Are you sure it's numb?"

"I'll do my job, son. You do yours."

She felt Erik's fingers come around her left hand, prying loose its grip from her right arm.

Tori murmured, "Thank you, Dr. Lamaze."

Misunderstanding, Dr. Thomas said, "You're welcome, Victoria. This won't hurt, but you will feel a slight pulling."

Erik held her hand between his two. "That was Dan and Dave on the phone. They wanted to know how you're doing." He paused.

"And?"

"And they won. Nine to eight."

Tori giggled. "They just needed us out of the way."

"Hold still, Victoria."

Erik squeezed her hand. "Maybe neither one of us belongs in that dugout."

Some time later, his job finished, Dr. Thomas helped her sit up. "That's it. I know you're a veteran at this, but the nurse will go over the procedures anyway." He paused. "Victoria, you can't be alone tonight."

"I'm fine—"

"I mean it. You sustained a head injury, you were momentarily unconscious—"

"I don't think I was completely—"

"Victoria! Someone will have to wake you up during the night."

"David will do it."

"Listen, young lady, he can play baseball without you, but you can't lay this responsibility on him."

"Okay, okay. I'll call my neighbor."

"Sir," the nurse asked Erik, "would you like to sit down?" She pushed the stool toward him.

"Yeah, I think I will." He dropped onto it.

"Put your head between your knees."

Tori chuckled. "This is great, Erik," she teased, dangling her legs over the side of the bed. "I told you to go home. Now I have to call someone to come get both of us."

"This has never happened to me before." His voice was huskier than usual. The nurse placed a wet cloth on the back of his neck. "I've been around sports and injuries and emergency rooms my entire life."

"Sure." Tori couldn't suppress her laughter.

"You'll be fine in a few minutes, son," Dr. Thomas assured. "I don't mean to sound suggestive, but make sure our little friend here doesn't spend the night alone. Good-bye, Victoria. Avoid the dugout."

"Good-bye, Doc. Thank you."

"Thanks, Doctor," Erik mumbled.

Tori's entire head felt numb. She only partially heard the nurse's instructions. "Well, you two are free to go whenever you feel up to it. Good-bye."

Tori grinned down at Erik. At least he could lift his head now. He was leaning against the wall, combing his fingers through his hair.

"All set?" he rasped.

"I'm hungry. Let's get a pizza!"

He moaned.

"You really are green," she laughed. "Boy, have I got one on you, Coach!"

For a moment he stared at her. "I've got a better one on you." He stood, his mouth curving into that lopsided grin as he sauntered toward her and lowered his face. "I'm not letting you out of my sight for the next twenty-four hours."

— Four —

"I TOLD YOU NOT to come back here!" Tori stood inside her front door and wrapped a large, white fuzzy afghan around herself. Although she wore stretch pants and a heavy, oversized sweatshirt, she felt chilled.

"And I told you I'm spending the night here." Erik brushed past her. Black sweats had replaced his jeans and bloodstained shirt.

"And I said that's ridiculous." She continued holding the door open. "Linda and the kids will come over. I hardly know you, and what I do know I don't even like."

Erik reached above her, shoving the door closed. "We had this discussion in the car. Linda has enough to do, and you don't need all that commotion here. This is my responsibility. If I hadn't lost my temper in the dugout, you wouldn't be in this situation. I understand you dislike me—you can spend the remainder of the evening telling me to what extent—but it really doesn't matter. I'm here, and I'm staying."

His authoritative tone echoed through her head, drawing her attention to the fact that the pain reliever hadn't quite numbed everything. She turned on her heel. "Fine. Do whatever you need to do to relieve your guilt, Mr. Steed."

In the kitchen Tori resumed tea preparations.

"Let me do that."

She slammed the tea bag box on the countertop. "Stop being so—so solicitous! You're making things even worse!"

"I know." Placing an arm around her shoulders, he guided her to the family room. "Given our history, it's difficult for you to accept me in this light. Just think of it as a show-off's effort to work out the guilt. We can go back to being politely tolerant of each other tomorrow. And who knows? You may even like me by then."

"I seriously doubt that possibility."

"You are a challenge, Tori Jeffers. Put your feet up on the couch here." He plumped pillows behind her. "Shall I turn down this lamp? Do you like Cary Grant and Audrey Hepburn? *Charade* is on television tonight. Is this the remote? Shall I turn it on for you?"

She grabbed the remote from him. "I'm not an invalid!"

"Did you call the boys yet?"

"You haven't been gone but ten minutes! I only had time to clean up." She paused. "It looks awful, doesn't it?"

His smile faded. "Does it hurt?"

She raised a shoulder.

"Tori, you can drop the stiff upper lip with me. You've just been through a traumatic experience."

"Don't you have a date tonight?"

"Of course, but I'm such a sincere, responsible guy I canceled it when I realized you needed me more."

She grimaced.

"I should have asked earlier—would you rather have Miller over tonight?"

"He's visiting his son at college. And besides, he doesn't spend the night here."

"Well, I guess that almost answers my question."

"I really would like that tea."

Erik lightly brushed bangs from her forehead. "First I'll get some ice and the telephone. The boys need to talk to you." He held up a hand. "How many fingers?"

"Twenty-two."

"You are impossible."

From her position on the couch, Tori watched Erik move about the kitchen while she talked on the phone. It was like before—her house shrank in his presence and yet . . . and yet he fit somehow. She sensed the in-control businessman again in his movements that were neither clumsy nor hesitant.

"Are you comfortable?" He handed her one of the cups he carried, then sat on the floor and leaned against the couch. Directly across from them pictures flickered quietly from the television, but his eyes were on her face. "Are you sure you're not hungry?"

"You're hovering. Can I take this ice off now?"

"For a while. I'll take it." He got up and carried the ice pack to the sink, then returned to his sitting position. "Are the boys all right? Not worried?"

"They're ecstatic over the win and over spending the night with Matt." She smiled. "Danny is impressed with my suture record. Other than that, the injury is no big deal."

"Good. How about Linda?"

"She's calmed down." Tori didn't bother mentioning Linda's ecstatic response to the idea of Erik spending this time with her.

"I gather you two are old friends."

She sipped the tea. "We've known each other since we were fourteen. Our daddies were stationed here in San Diego with the Navy, and we were both trying to graduate from high school before we all got shipped out again."

"I take it you moved often?"

"All the time. Linda and I knew there was a good chance we'd spend our senior year in some foreign port with a bunch of strangers, so we worked double time and beat the Navy."

"What did you do after graduation?"

"I guess you could say the Navy beat us then."

"Huh?"

Tori grinned. "We had made this solemn pact to never, ever date military guys because we abhorred the lifestyle so much."

"And?"

"Well, after graduation we went over to Pensacola to visit my sister who lived real close to the Navy base. Linda met Tim, and I met Joe." She looked down into the steaming tea. Memories tumbled over one another.

"And you both fell head over heels in love and tossed the pact?"

She met his blue eyes. "Wild and crazy in love. Do you remember what it's like being seventeen?"

His eyes crinkled in silent mirth. "Well, it was longer ago for me than you, but I have a vague recollection."

"Anyway, Joe and Tim were different from any guys we'd ever met. They were older, more mature. They took us to Bible studies, of all things, and talked about Jesus like He bunked next to them. Goodness, everything happened so fast. I decided God was for real, I'd rather do things His way than mine, and became a wife, all within about four months. The babies were born a year later. We moved around some, then got transferred to San Diego right before Joe's last cruise. He spent only about two months in this house."

"Do you blame God for your loss?"

"I did at first, but death doesn't come from Him. I don't know why, but I know He allowed it for some reason, for what was best for us. When Joe left, I had to depend on the fact that God didn't leave. I know I'm not alone."

Erik was thoughtful for a moment. "And Linda married Tim at the same time?"

She nodded. "We had a double ceremony. And she was a mom before I was, because Tim had been married, and his wife left him with Kelsey who was three by then. The Navy transferred them here about four years ago, and we've been working together at the newspaper since then."

"And what about Allen?"

"He's not in the Navy."

"I know that. I mean, is he a good friend of yours?"

"Yes, we're quite compatible. We've been dating for a few months now. He's a widower, with kids in college, a solid, secure kind of man. You know, not prone to transferring around the world or trying to make it a better place for the billions."

"Joe was like that? Trying to make the world a better place?"

She nodded with a smile.

"Tori, why didn't you tell me?"

Her eyes locked with his. "What difference does it make except that the government signs the child-support checks instead of an ex-husband?"

Erik sprang to his feet and began pacing the room. "You're so young . . . I had no idea . . . I wouldn't have been so harsh on you." In a gesture of exasperation he combed his fingers through his hair. "I never would have made that wisecrack about you taking your husband to court."

"You're feeling guilty again. I knew where you were coming from when we talked at the dinner. You figured I was just like other wealthy divorcées you've probably met here. The point is, Erik, I am. The result is the same in me. My pixie face might crack if I smile too much."

He winced.

"We single moms have to be tough and determined. We can't let anything control us because we are more or less solely responsible for the day-to-day upbringing of our children. And that is a very, very difficult job."

He sat beside her, his brow furrowed, his voice intense. "But your circumstances are different. You didn't choose to move all the time as a child. If there are unpleasant memories in that, of course you're going to choose to keep as much of life as possible under control. You fell in love—like my sister and her friends did, supposedly—and married, but you didn't choose to have your husband die. You have a right to be overly determined. You are alone. Those women, my sister included, haven't a clue to—"

"Erik!" Tori placed her hand over his mouth. "That's too harsh. You can't understand."

He stared at her.

She lowered her hand.

"You are the most exasperating woman I have ever met," he professed in a matter-of-fact tone.

"Why? Does every other female simply agree with whatever you say?"

He frowned. "See? There you go." He stood and resumed his

pacing. "You possess an innate ability to get under my skin. I think the doctor must have prescribed you as part of my therapy. I mean, I was doing fine, learning how to relax, readjusting my perspective. Then I met you." He shook his head. "If I learn how to cope with you, in or out of the dugout, I will undoubtedly acquire a clean bill of health. I can't believe my behavior at that ball game."

"If you're going to apologize again, I'll scream."

His laughter filled the house.

"Erik, you have to admit it was just as much my fault. I think I attacked first."

"After you thought I hurt Dan. You do have a mother-bear temper about you."

"I'm getting hungry as a mother bear too."

"Your wish is my command. What can I get for you?"

"Soup. You don't look quite as green. Are you hungry?"

"No. Sit back down."

"I'll just get things out for you."

He walked into the kitchen. "No need. I'm quite familiar with kitchens, soups . . . and microwaves."

He served her dinner on a tray, then sat in the wooden rocker near the foot of the couch.

"Thank you, *garcon*. This looks wonderful. I'm beginning to feel like an absolute queen."

"Good. That's the intention. After what happened, I owe you—"

"Erik."

"Well, if I can't win you over with good deeds, I'm out of luck." He paused. "Perhaps you could tell me outright what it is you dislike about me. Why is it we can't talk like normal people? Do you have something against out-of-town uncles who coach Little League?"

"Hmm." Tori swallowed a spoonful of tomato soup, feigning deep consideration of his question when in reality she knew she was beginning to enjoy his company. *It must be the extra-strength pain reliever,* she mused. "Exactly how wealthy are you?"

Erik laughed and began rocking. "I can't believe you asked that."

"Ooh," she teased, "that much?"

"I have a sufficient income." He looked at her. "Is that what it is?"

"Hmm, no, not really." She took another bite.

"Well?"

"You're too tall. I don't like tall men."

He stopped the rocking motion and leaned forward. "Are you having fun?" She giggled. "Tori, I'm serious!"

"Okay." In mock sobriety, she drew down the corners of her mouth. "Your sister snubbed me once."

"Just once?"

"Umhmm. We've only spoken—or not spoken—that one time in the five and a half years I've lived in this town."

He narrowed his eyes. "And you hold that against me?"

"Of course. Siblings are cut from the same mold."

"I see. Do you have any siblings?"

"Twin sisters and one brother, all older than I. We're all lovely, delightful people."

Erik burst into laughter. "I give up! You know, of course, that my sister is threatened by you."

"Oh, right."

"Seriously. You're much too confident."

"Well, now you can tell her it's all show. I've just been at this longer than she has. One of these days she'll even be able to buy her own gas."

He pointed a finger at her. "That's when this all started, young lady! At the gas station. You disliked me from the first moment. Why?"

"It's not relevant now."

"I think it is. After all, you deciphered my philosophy of life from that one incident." His tone was relentless.

She glanced at him. "All right. I had just returned from

interviewing the school district's superintendent. Attempting to interview him, I should say. In reality he had given me a well-rehearsed runaround. I was tired, late for Little League, out of gas, angry at people in general who behave as if the world revolves around them."

"So I entered the ring with, let's see, one, two, three, four counts against me?"

"I may have overreacted a little, but you must admit you certainly gave the impression that you owned the place, that you didn't need to wait in line. You had to have been blind not to see me there!"

Erik stood and reached for her soup bowl. "Finished?"

"Yes, thank you." She puzzled at his sudden quietness as he walked to the kitchen. "Oh, my goodness, you probably do own that place."

From the sink he turned and smiled at her. "No." He moved to the refrigerator. "You need to put ice on your eye again."

She groaned.

Erik returned and sat on the edge of the couch, gently holding the ice pack against her head. "I don't like to make excuses. I admit I was driving too fast, but I really didn't see you that day because I couldn't."

She stared at him.

"I only have partial vision in my left eye."

"Why didn't you tell me?"

"A familiar question." He grinned. "Well, at the gas station it really didn't matter. You were a stranger. Then at the dinner . . ." He shrugged. "It still didn't matter because you were pretty much on target. I am driven and impatient and figure either the world should keep up with me or get out of my way. And I think I just answered my own question. I wouldn't be a likable character in your book, if you wrote one, would I?"

Tori smiled softly. "What happened to your eye?"

"I was pitching for our college team my senior year and just didn't react fast enough. They called it a smoking line drive."

"Was baseball important to you?"

A corner of his mouth lifted. "The contract with the Pirates became null and void."

"You were that good?"

He lowered the ice pack. His eyes, focused on her brow, were as unrevealing of emotion as was his voice. "Oh, some said I could have been. It's ten o'clock. Shall we watch the movie?"

"Sure."

"Hold this ice." He stood. "Where are the TV listings?"

"On that table." While he perused the magazine, she studied the back of his broad shoulders draped in the black sweatshirt. She sensed that the image she carried of him was false. "Erik?"

"Hmm?"

"That sounds like a fairly large pit in your bowl of cherries."

He turned and slowly grinned. "Well, yeah, it was." He walked back to the couch, leaned over, and took the ice from her. "Don't tease me now. Cover your left eye and tell me how many fingers you see."

She did as he requested. "Twelve."

He stared at her, his mouth a grim line.

"We'll just stick together, Mr. Steed. You stay on my right side, and I'll stay on your left."

"Tori!"

She laughed. "Okay, okay! I saw three."

His face crumpled, and he dropped to his knees beside her. Covering his eyes with a hand, he said in a low voice, "I held up two."

She stopped laughing, then saw him peeking at her between his fingers. "Oh!" Leaping to her feet, Tori yanked a pillow and smacked him with it. "That was mean!"

"Ow!" From his kneeling position, Erik grabbed her arm before she could swing it again. Their quick movements threw them both off balance. She tumbled with him to the floor, and they burst into laughter.

His arms came around her back. "Are you all right, Torinado?"

Their eyes met. The pounding of her heart beat away the laughter. She pushed her hands against his chest and slid from him. They stood.

"Can I make you some more tea?"

"Yes, thank you." She sat back on the couch. Her voice sounded breathy. She wasn't all right. Erik Steed had held her like only one other man had in her life. Suddenly chilled, she pulled the afghan around herself.

The movie served to divert her attention from the man sitting in the rocker. By the third commercial she was amused by the characters and concluded that any flying sparks had originated in her imagination. Erik Steed, handsome as he was, would not be her choice for romance. The heavy-duty pain reliever must be causing these odd feelings.

"Tori?"

"Hmm?"

"Can I get anything for you?"

"No, thanks." Growing tired of her sitting position, she snuggled down onto the couch and closed her eyes. "Isn't this a fun movie? It's one of my favorite oldies."

"Mine, too." He chuckled. "Now that must be the first thing we've agreed on. Does your head hurt?"

"It's just a dull ache."

"Do you mind if I ask you something about your husband?"

She looked at him, recognizing in his hesitant tone a desire to ask details of his death. "Joe was a fighter pilot. He flew F14s and was assigned to an aircraft carrier in the Pacific. He and his radio intercept officer were flying maneuvers in a storm in the South China Sea. Monsoon season." Her monotone voice never wavered. "He miscalculated while landing. The bodies weren't recovered."

"You said it happened five years ago?"

"Five years ago this July 30th, we celebrated his thirtieth birthday. The next day he left on cruise. The accident was

September 18th. The boys were five. They had just started kindergarten the week before." She made a wry face. "I can't remember their first semester of school."

He stared at her in silence.

"Erik, I don't mind telling you about it, but you have to promise not to hold it against me."

"What?"

She closed her eyes again. "You can't feel sorry for me and let it get in the way of our polite tolerance of each other."

He didn't reply. She peeked at him. Elbow propped on the chair arm, he rubbed his forehead. Hadn't she told him straightforwardly enough, without room for misinterpretation, without begging for explanations? There were no answers. It was just a fact of life.

"Erik, it's all right. Really."

He lowered his hand, glancing about the room. "I'm—" he rasped. "I'm so sorry."

"I know." She noted his confusion and turned away. "The movie's back on. I forget how these two ever get together. Oh, yeah, once she figures out who he really is. But who is he?" She stole a glance at him. He sat very still. Though he faced the television, she sensed his mind was focused elsewhere.

The storm had been on the twentieth. She had the date wrong. With the dateline, it would be easy to confuse today with yesterday, or yesterday with tomorrow—

"Erik, you don't have to spend the entire night, you know. It's after midnight now." Tori's voice interrupted his spinning thoughts.

"I will." He noticed the television was off, and he turned toward her. She looked so small, so vulnerable wrapped in the afghan on the couch. "Unless you're uncomfortable with that."

She nodded slightly. "Just call me in the morning, and if I don't answer—"

He stood. "No. I have to call before that. Do you have a phone by the bed?"

"Yes."

"And give me the front door key just in case you don't answer."

"Is this necessary?" The afghan trailed behind her into the kitchen where she opened a cupboard and pulled out a key.

"Doctor's orders. Now, where do you sleep?"

"You're not tucking me in, Mr. Steed!"

"I have to know where you are in case it's necessary to wake you up." He pocketed the key and followed her through the living room and down the hallway.

"This is really strange. In here. Now go home."

His eyes were on the dresser.

"That's Joe."

Erik went to the framed photo and picked it up. The man appeared to be an older version of the twins, but his hair was more blond, almost a golden color. His right arm was raised, holding a helmet above his head. His smile was radiant. He wore a jumpsuit. Something was stitched above the breast pocket. "Golden Boy," he whispered.

"That was his call name. They all have one. Sometimes they called him Goldie."

He cleared his throat and replaced the photo. "Seems appropriate."

"Oh, it was more than his hair. He had the Midas touch—not with money, but with people." A tender smile rested on her lips.

"Tori, remember the statice?"

She didn't reply.

"I was wrong about that, too. It's not prickly. Just delicate around the edges. I'll call you at three o'clock."

Erik couldn't remember the forty-minute drive. He only knew his breath would not come until salt air filled his lungs and the roaring surf pummeled it from him. When it was released, the accompanying cry echoed off the cliffs, flinging it through the blackness, down the deserted beach.

He ran now, near the water's edge where the packed sand held firm. *Cody's been hit. Cody's been hit.* The words beat in cadence with his footfalls.

At last he sank to his knees, covering his lowered head with his arms. The name was Cody. Loud static had muffled the voices, but that's what he heard. Cody. He wasn't even supposed to hear. The intercom was on by mistake. It was all a coincidence. She probably had the date wrong. Or the government did. Yes, the government would do that. Wouldn't tell her the date of her husband's death. Or the time. Or the place.

"Oh, God!"

The memories hit him like a sledgehammer blow to his stomach. The pain was inescapable, and he cried. After a time the images receded, the heaving sobs lessened. He crawled a few feet away from the lapping water and curled into a fetal position, letting exhaustion cover him like a thin sheet.

Damp coldness stirred him.

Call Tori. He sat up and peered at his watch. It was too dark.

Numbness permeated him. The only thought that filtered through was that he had to call her.

He headed back down the beach to the steep stairway leading up to the parking lot. Under a lamp he looked at his watch. 2:45. Inside the car he reached for his cellular phone, then swore. It was one of the things he had forfeited for this time of recuperation.

A familiar knot began to form in his stomach. He drove to the main road. Everything was dark. He headed inland until the lights of an all-night gas station caught his eye in the distance. It was 2:58.

"Please deposit seventy-five cents."

He slammed down the phone. What was his access code? His mind blanked. He didn't even have the card with him. He headed inside the station.

"I need change." He slid a twenty-dollar bill across the counter to the cashier.

"Gotta wait your turn, buddy."

Two other people glared at him. Three o'clock in the morning and he had to stand in line. "Keep the change. I need seventy-five cents."

After the eighth ring he heard a thump, as if she had dropped the phone. "Tori?" The knot twisted now. "Tori?"

"Umhmm."

"Are you okay?"

"Umhmm."

"Can you say something besides 'umhmm'?"

"Will you let me sit on the bench?"

The knot loosened. "No. Go back to sleep. I'll call you at 5."

I will take care of her. I promise I will take care of her.

— *Five* —

"TORI."

The masculine voice penetrated her consciousness. Dream fragments scattered; brightness glowed inside her eyelids. "Go away. I'm fine." She pulled the soft comforter over her head. "Turn off the light and let me sleep."

"That's the sunshine. It's nine o'clock."

"Hi, Mom!"

"Hi, Mom!"

Tori peeked out at three grinning faces. Erik held a tray. "What is this?" She sat up.

The boys talked at once. "Breakfast! We made pancakes, and Coach saved some for you . . . Wow, your eye looks gross . . . Awesome! . . . It's purple! . . . Just like the other one . . ." They punched each other and howled. "Let me count the stitches . . . Five! . . . Cool! . . . How many inside? . . . She beats you, Dan . . ."

"Hey, guys, back off a minute." Erik pushed between them and set the tray across her lap. "They said pancakes are your favorite. With an egg, black coffee, and orange juice."

She surveyed the tray. "And one red rose in the crystal vase. You boys are so sweet—"

"That part was Coach's idea," David expounded.

"Oh." Tori kept her eyes on the twins.

"Well, I would have thought of it, but he already picked it," Danny defended.

Erik cleared his throat. "I'll leave you three alone and go clean up the kitchen. Do you need anything else?"

She shook her head. The boys chattered nonstop until Erik returned. He turned the desk chair to face the bed and sat down. "Let me talk to your mother alone . . ." He winked in an exaggerated manner. ". . . about you know what. Take the tray with you, please."

"I'll keep the flower." Tori set the vase on the nightstand as the boys scurried from the room.

Their eyes met in the silence. Erik's rumpled black sweats and disheveled hair made her wonder if he had slept at all. Shadows underlined his deep-set eyes, blending with the dark brows and lashes to mask their blueness. Stubbly growth, unrelieved by a smile, covered the lower portion of his face.

The fuzzy memory of him phoning her in the night sharpened to a crystal clarity. How many times had he called and tenderly asked her if she was all right? A sudden awareness of Erik Steed's masculinity pervading her bedroom rushed through her. She looked down at the white comforter on her lap.

"This is, umm," her fingers twisted the soft fabric, "awkward. I usually don't entertain guests in here."

"Not usually, hmm?" His teasing tone drew her eyes back to his. A grin spread slowly across his face. "I apologize for making you uncomfortable, but I'm relieved to see how you're doing. How do you feel this morning?"

"Better than you look, I think."

"Have you glanced in a mirror yet, Mrs. Jeffers?"

"We do look as if we had a rough night." She chuckled. His smile faded, and she guessed that he had indeed endured a rough night. "How many times did you call?"

"Three times. And I confess, before your neighbors do, that I came in for a look-see at 7. The swelling is down. Does your head hurt?"

"No. When did the boys come home?"

"About 8. We're making plans." He rubbed his jaw. "Remember my promise to take them to a Padres game?"

"That was a bribe, not a promise." What had he been doing alone in her house from 7 to 8 A.M.?

"Well, anyway, there's a game at 1 this afternoon, and we'd like to go."

"They'll love it."

"We want you to go with us."

Tori grimaced. "I never go to those things."

"So I heard." He paused. "Let me rephrase the issue. You're going with us to the Padres game this afternoon because I'm not leaving you alone."

Her jaw dropped. "Don't start that again—"

"I'm continuing it. Someone still needs to keep an eye on you. Besides, it's time you understood a little more about your sons and their important world of baseball." In one stride he moved from the chair to sit on the edge of the bed. "If your chin falls any further," he quipped, lifting her jaw with a finger, "you'll trip over it."

She hugged her knees to her chest, breaking eye contact with him to stare through the window's parted white curtains near the foot of the bed.

What he had dared to assume rang true, and that realization only added fuel to her discomfort. While the boys accumulated baseball cards, filling their minds with facts and figures beyond her understanding, she focused on what she thought she did best. She increased allowances to buy those cards, permitted them to attend professional games with friends, involved herself with the Little League board, and cut innumerable orange slices.

Erik spoke softly. "I wasn't accusing you of negligence. The boys just mentioned you've never been and said that's probably why you don't know anything about baseball. So I suggested we take you with us, and they thought that was a great idea but said it wouldn't work because you can be real stubborn sometimes."

Tori frowned at him. "You're doing it again."

He raised his eyebrows.

"Barging in where you've never been before and changing things!"

"Like I own the place?"

"Yes!" she shouted.

"Does that mean you'll go?"

"No!"

"Mom!" The boys burst into the room, ran to her bed, and climbed around Erik to hug her from either side. "Say yes! Say yes!"

"Oh, what if I ask a lot of dumb questions?"

"You always tell us there's no such thing," David shot back. "Come on, Mom."

"They've got the best hot dogs!" Danny added.

Tori looked from one little face to the other, blue eyes pleading from each. "You really want me to tag along?" Their heads nodded vigorously. "Oh, all right."

They whooped and squeezed their arms around her even more tightly. Tori laughed, hugging their waists, relishing in their delight and in the sheer, unadulterated fact that they were her sons.

From the corner of her eye she glimpsed Erik's sober face. He stood. "I'll be back in an hour," he uttered in a gruff tone and strode from the room.

What was his problem? The boys left her no time to ponder the question as their hugging quickly turned into a giggly wrestling match.

"As your attorney, Erik, I have to question the wisdom of this plan."

"And as my friend, Jack, you're just going to have to accept that this is crucial for my peace of mind." Erik propped the phone between his chin and shoulder while he pulled on socks. "If I don't take care of this immediately, I might lose it again."

"You sound exhausted. Are you sure—"

"Yes!" He yanked on a tennis shoe and took a deep breath. "Sorry. Look, it's not as if I'll ever need the money."

"But we're talking hundreds of thousands of dollars for someone you've just met! Bear with me a moment. This is what you pay me for. It just isn't like you to give away so much. I mean, you're generous to a fault, but it's usually tax-deductible. What in the world does this woman have on you?"

Erik massaged his forehead. "I can't talk about it. Don't worry, it's not illegal."

The lawyer fired back an expletive.

"That was professional, Jack. So, can you have the papers ready for me to sign by noon tomorrow? I'll be stopping by the office on my way to New York."

"I think all that sunshine has gone to your head. Yes, I'll get it done. Victoria, Daniel, and David Jeffers, correct?"

"Right. And you'll make absolutely sure that she will not find out?"

"No problem."

"Jack?"

"Yes?"

"Promise me, if something should happen before I sign, you'll see to it that my wishes are carried out."

His friend was silent for a moment. "Of course I will, Erik. Take care."

Danny jumped from his seat in the baseball stadium. "We'll be right back, Mom. Coach is buying us hot dogs." He scooted toward the aisle.

"All right. I'll save your seats."

David leaned to whisper, "You don't have to. They're reserved. And they cost a lot cuz we're in the first row right behind first base." He followed his brother.

"Oh."

Erik slid into Danny's vacated seat on her left. "Can we bring you something? Hot dog, pizza, nachos, ice cream?"

"They serve all that here?"

"That's only a partial list. What would you like?"

Tori studied his face just inches from hers and realized she missed his crooked smile. The crow's-feet around his eyes were more pronounced today. He must not have slept. "You're being solicitous again, Mr. Steed."

A trace of a smile brushed his lips. "I promise to stop tomorrow. But while I'm at it, I must say you look especially lovely this afternoon."

"Thank you." Tori straightened the floppy white straw hat and smoothed the white folds of her cotton, short-sleeved dress. "The boys acted as if it were a bit much until I reminded them of *The Natural*."

Erik raised an eyebrow.

"The baseball movie. My favorite part is when the hero's at bat, and the heroine stands up in this filmy white dress and captures his attention, and then he hits this magnificent home run."

"Hmm. You know more about baseball than I thought. But I think you've attracted enough attention at ball games. Promise me you won't stand up, Torinado."

She wrinkled her nose.

"Humor me." Gently he pulled off her sunglasses, then covered her left eye with his hand. "Read that board behind center field."

She sighed. "That flashing one? It says, 'Erik Steed is driving me up the wall.'"

"Wrong. It says, 'Tori Jeffers is an exasperating tease.'"

"Shouldn't you go with the boys?"

"Not until you read that."

"Okay." She read it correctly. "Satisfied?"

He stood. "Yes. Do you want to come?"

"No, thanks. I'll just sit here and soak up this unique ambience."

Tori sensed excitement in the sun-warmed air. Upbeat organ music blared. Thousands of people roamed throughout the huge, multilevel stadium. Across the field, moving about the various tiers, the fans appeared toy-doll size. Players dotted the grassy area and ball diamond, throwing the ball back and forth over tremendous distances. Even the crunch of peanut shells under her sandals contributed to the anticipatory flavor.

"We got a hot dog for you, Mom," Danny announced as they returned. "I knew you'd want one."

The boys sat between her and Erik. Often he leaned over to explain things to them. Often, it seemed, his eyes were on her.

"Coach, we know that!" Danny squawked after two innings. "Sit next to Mom. She's the one who doesn't know anything." He jumped from his seat, persuading Erik to take it.

"I apologize for my son's rudeness," Tori offered.

"He's right. I'm talking too much. They can't watch the game."

"Well, you can tell me about it. Why is that man doing that?"

Tori questioned, Erik patiently explained, and a very pleasant afternoon passed.

The boys chattered excitedly from the backseat of Erik's Blazer as they drove north on the freeway after the game.

He interrupted, saying, "Would you like to go out for dinner?"

The twins whispered before answering.

Tori and Erik exchanged amused glances.

Danny began, "Our mom makes really good lasagna."

"Yeah," David continued, "and she made it yesterday, but we didn't get to eat it last night."

"And we probably should eat it, huh, Mom?"

Tori looked over her shoulder. What were they plotting?

"And we always have leftovers, so there'd probably be enough for Coach." David smiled.

"Maybe he has other plans," she countered evenly. "He's been with us all weekend." Goodness, this was resembling marriage. Her eyes widened, then narrowed at her tow-headed angels.

"No, I don't have any plans," Erik maintained.

Tori studied his handsome profile. Exactly where had this plan originated?

"Mom!" Danny remonstrated.

She cleared her throat. "Well, would you like to come for dinner?"

He glanced at her with a grin. "I'd love to. If you're sure it's not too much trouble?"

"Not at all. Besides," she rationalized as much to herself as to him, "I owe you. I don't think I've thanked you for last night. I still don't believe it was necessary, but I appreciate what you did."

"Anything for my favorite team mom." He flashed that crooked grin.

"Right," she scoffed.

"Hey, look, Coach! That's what our dad used to fly."

They were driving past Miramar Naval Air Station where the thunderous jets were a common sight. The nearby runway lay perpendicular to the freeway, allowing closeup views of the powerful machines.

"What are they?" Erik leaned over the steering wheel for a better sight of the underside of a jet roaring overhead.

David explained, "F14 Tomcats. Look, there's another one. They have a pilot and a RIO."

"A what?"

"Radio intercept officer. He sits in the second seat and does other things. Our dad was always the pilot. That's what I'm gonna be."

"Hey, Coach, we can take you to the Blue Angels show this summer. Everybody gets to go on base and see all kinds of jets up close."

"He'll have to take us, Dan, cuz Mom never goes."

Tori looked out the side window at the green, chaparral-covered hills, ignoring the cloudless blue sky and its noisy intruders. "Sweetie, I'll go when you're a Navy pilot."

"Your dad must have really liked flying," Erik said, prompting the boys to talk more about their father and the jets.

Tori's mind followed a different thread. Liked it? It was his passion. A living, breathing entity with which she chose not to compete because she knew she would've lost. Anyway, she had only needed him part-time. Long-distance. It had been enough. Hadn't it?

She pushed aside that train of thought. It never led anywhere. Instead, she remembered what attracted her to him.

Her memory did not exaggerate the man. Energy flowed from him, affecting everyone in his path, like Midas's golden touch. He gave from deep within himself, giving God the credit for his strength. His goal was to make the world a better place, whether that meant to turn it upside-down for a nervous, backward seventeen-year-old girl blind to her own potential, or to fix a broken tricycle for his son, or to protect the country he loved. He declared that as long as he had her love and his F14, he could change the world. Day in and day out, his actions proved that he truly believed it.

Tori blinked. Like Erik Steed. Is that why she didn't like him? Because, as Linda had discerned from the beginning, he really did resemble Joe in this way? No. There was a missing ingredient in this man. His faith was in himself. His motive to change the world sprouted from an unreal life, from a selfish desire to rearrange what didn't fit into his mold. That's what she saw in his attitude. That's why she didn't like him, didn't trust him. No matter his lost dream of baseball, no matter his kindness toward her this weekend.

Too bad Allen wasn't coming over tonight instead of Mr. Steed. She could use some quiet, orderly male companionship.

"Yippee! We're home!"

She sighed. Everything was a major event in Danny's life. Erik opened her door. Ignoring his outstretched hand, she slid her feet to the driveway. "Dinner will be at 6:30. Do you want to come in now?"

"Thanks, Coach! Give us the keys, Mom!"

She fumbled in her purse. "Here."

They raced off.

"I'll leave you alone for a couple of hours. May I bring anything?"

"How about your unpleasant, just barely tolerable personality complete with a show-off grin?"

He stared down at her, then lifted off her hat. Brushing aside bangs from her eyebrow, he inspected the injury yet again. "I'll see what I can do, Mrs. Jeffers," he whispered.

She sensed a weariness settle inside her at that moment, as if she'd been struggling for years for something she could never quite attain.

"We're not using those tonight!" Tori snapped at Danny who clutched a pair of brass candlesticks to his chest. Standing between the open, tall doors of the kitchen's pantry cupboard, mother and son conducted their face-off.

"We always use them for special dinners," he challenged in a stage whisper.

"This isn't that special!"

"How come it is when Allen eats here?"

Tori gritted her teeth. She recognized defiance written all over the boy's face, but with Erik Steed sitting just a few feet away, this was not the time to assert her authority nor to expound her opinions of the two men.

"All right! Put them on the table!"

Her head throbbed. Last night's interrupted sleep coupled with the tension now caused by Erik's unwelcome presence chipped away at her equilibrium. Raw emotions bubbled underneath a thin layer of composure.

"May I help?" Erik's voice was just behind her.

Tori continued staring into the pantry. "I can't remember . . . Oh, this is what I want." She pulled a bottle of salad dressing from the shelf and turned. "You can put this on the table."

He took it from her, his eyes intent on her face. "Does your head hurt again?"

With a shooing wave of her hand, she stepped to the refrigerator and yanked it open.

Like a shadow, he followed. "When did you last take something for it?"

She grabbed another bottle and handed it to him over her shoulder. "This morning." Next she picked up a plastic gallon container of milk.

He took it from her. "You're allowed more."

Nudging the refrigerator door shut with her hips, she shoved a large salad bowl at him, then spun back around toward the counter. "I know."

"Tori," he spoke quietly in her ear, "how bad is it?"

"David?" she called out, sliding open a drawer and reaching for a knife. "What's the name of that jet that just hovers and hangs around and makes lots of noise?" She slammed the drawer shut.

"You mean the Harrier?"

"Yeah, that's it." She tilted her head up at Erik. "I'm going to start calling you Harry."

"Ha, ha. How bad is it?"

Tori sliced through the lasagna's thick, steaming noodles and cheese. "It just started. It's not a 'watch-for-these-symptoms' kind of headache. I'm hungry and tired and really anxious for you to stop hovering. Here, Harry." She lifted the casserole and turned.

With bottles of dressing in one hand, the milk carton under an arm, and the salad bowl under the other, he opened his free hand to receive the dish. "Stick a match between my teeth," he winked, "and I'll light those special candles for you too, Mrs. Jeffers."

Tori swept past him. "Time to eat, guys!"

He followed. "That oven must be hot. Your face is bright red."

After David said grace, he and Danny noisily dominated the conversation, recounting the day's game in detail and strategizing for their own upcoming baseball activities.

Tori ate silently, now and then glancing at the man across the table. Candlelight sparkled in his blue eyes and softly outlined his square jaw. Interacting with the boys, he smiled more often. A few short, brown locks grazed his forehead. The apricot shade of his short-sleeved cotton shirt emphasized the darkness of his hair.

"Your mom does make the best lasagna."

She blinked.

"Thanks, Tori. That was great." He smiled at her.

"I'm glad you liked it."

"Can we get it now, Coach?" Danny asked.

Erik nodded. The boys raced from the room yelling, "Close your eyes, Mom!"

"What's going on?"

"Just close your eyes," Erik replied. "You'll find out."

Tori did as she was told, muttering, "This three against one business is getting tiresome."

"Open 'em!" The twins stood on either side of her.

On the tablecloth before her sat a small, black, satin-covered box tied with a lavender ribbon. Puzzled, she stared at it. "It's not my birthday."

"It's cuz you got stitches, Mom," Danny explained.

David continued, "Everybody who goes to the hospital should get a present."

Erik chimed in, "Like a glad-you're-feeling-better-I'm-sorry-it-happened kind of gift."

"Coach thought of it."

"He paid for it too."

"But it's from all of us. Right, guys?"

"Right. Open it, Mom!"

Tori bit her lower lip. She knew it was a jeweler's box. She knew something exquisite lay inside. She knew her impression of Erik Steed was growing more complicated by the hour. She looked up at him.

He stared back at her, his face expressionless. "Don't say I shouldn't have. It's just a token for our team mom injured in the line of duty."

"Gosh, you're slow, Mom. Open it!"

Tori slid the ribbon from the box, no easy task with shaky hands. At last she lifted the lid. She gasped. From within folds of creamy satin twinkled a pair of amethyst earrings. Teardrop in shape, they were set in antiqued gold filigree, joined at the tip by a small diamond.

"Wow, they really do match your eyes!"

"Put 'em on, Mom!"

The pounding of her heart echoed in her ears.

"Do you like them?" Erik's voice tunneled through the great noise in her head. She looked up. "I know they're not as large as you usually wear, but I thought they were, umm, appropriate."

She swallowed and whispered, "They're absolutely beautiful. Why . . . ? I can't—"

"Yes, you can."

Confused, she looked away. No one had ever given her anything even approaching such extravagance. Why had he? Because he still felt guilty about her injury? Or did he pity her because she was a widow? Drop a few morsels to the less fortunate and thereby ease the conscience?

"You're acting really weird, Mom."

Candlelight darted before her eyes, creating a surrealistic glow. The throbbing within her head intensified, rapidly building to migraine proportions.

"Tori, did you take more aspirin yet?"

She felt tears welling. "No, I—"

"Where is it?"

"I'll get it, Coach."

"Tori, go to bed." Erik was behind her, pulling out her chair.

"The kitchen—"

"We'll clean up."

"I'll do it tomorrow." She stood.

"Be quiet and take these." He placed capsules in one hand and a glass of water in the other.

"The boys have to be in bed by 9." She swallowed the pills. "Their bikes have to go in the garage." Her voice was barely audible. "Put the lasagna in the . . . I'm sorry . . . I—"

He cupped her face in his hands and lowered his head. "I said be quiet. I'll take care of everything."

She peered into his eyes. If he were Allen, she would quit. She would give in this very moment to that temptation of letting him take control. Didn't she need that? Didn't she deserve that? But he was Erik Steed, and he had no right to do that for her. "I don't want you—"

"Shh. Don't cry, Tori. Go to bed."

The blinding pain left her no choice.

They raced with the billowy white clouds under an azure sky. Hillsides painted the deep green of late spring rolled beneath them in quick succession.

Her laughter sang out with Joe's in the small cockpit, rising above the deafening engine roar. He turned to her. Golden sunlight radiated from his hair, his face. He pulled her to himself, his mouth descending to hers—

And then he was gone. "Joe!" The engine chugged, the propellers stopped, the plane dipped.

Where were the boys? She had to find them! "Don't go! I can't do this alone!"

Everything quieted. Then the low hum, the sensation of plummeting.

The sound of her own scream woke her.

Tori huddled in the bed on her knees, perspiration soaking the neck of her flannel nightgown. She gulped deep breaths, fighting down the choking terror.

"Mom!" The lamp snapped on.

"It's okay." Still gasping, she pushed damp hair from her forehead.

"Tori."

What was he doing here? "Go away!" His arms came around her trembling body. "Leave me alone!" She pushed at him.

"He's a good hugger, Mom." Small hands patted her back. Erik's arms tightened until her head rested against his chest.

"It's just a dream," she gasped.

"I think it's a nightmare, Mom."

"Was it that same one?"

"Daddy's there . . . And then—"

Erik's hand pressed her head closer to himself, muffling her cries.

"And then," a small voice explained, "he disappears, and she has to fly the plane by herself."

Why wouldn't it stop this time? It was just a stupid dream! Why couldn't she tell them it was all right? She clutched a fistful of Erik's shirt.

"Your mom and I are going to talk for a while, guys. Go on back to bed. Tori, let's go sit in the family room."

As they made their way through the house, Tori continued to battle intense fear. It was as if she'd plummeted again with the plane, as if the intensity of the sensation had cracked something within her, wrenching loose deep sobs.

In the family room, Erik guided her to the couch. He sat beside her, his voice soothing; his hand caressing her back. At last her breathing slowed, and the tremors lessened. Still he held her, absorbing fragments of panic. She fell asleep.

Tori drifted between midnight blackness and predawn gray shadows. Joe lay in the morning haze, his arms encircling her, his chin resting on her forehead. She kissed his neck, kissed away the darkness of sleep. How . . . ? When . . . ?

It didn't matter. She would wake him, and he would fill the ache. Snuggling closer to him, she again kissed his neck.

Chuckling softly, he tightened his arms around her, kissed her forehead, then her temple.

Joe.

Shivers danced along her spine.

I knew you'd come back . . .

His fingers stroked her neck.

Joe's gone . . .

He kissed her ear.

God, let him be real this time, please.

His stubbly cheek brushed hair from her forehead, and then, with great tenderness, he kissed her right eyebrow.

Like an icy ocean wave, total consciousness poured over her. *Erik Steed!*

The predawn hush splintered in her cry. "No!" She pushed him away. Through gray shadows, she stumbled through the house to the bathroom and slammed the door shut.

"Tori?"

She leaned against the door. "Go away!"

"Tori, I didn't mean—"

"Get out of my house!"

Muffled footsteps reached her ears, and a few moments later, the opening and closing of the front door. An odd mixture of relief and disappointment flooded her. She slid to the floor, too confused to know whether to laugh or cry.

Concentrating at the weekly Monday morning staff meeting was beyond Tori's capabilities. She doodled on the pad, thankful for Linda's absence and for the fact that the editor, Helen Anderson, was busy talking with the owner of the newspaper about matters that did not concern Tori. The two other women and the one man on the staff had not questioned why both of her eyes were red and puffy after being hit by a baseball above the right one two days ago. Linda would pry loose the entire story, but Tori wasn't ready for that because she herself did not yet understand it.

The nightmare had been so violent this time, so terrifying. Her reaction seemed totally beyond her control, unlike in the past. Always she would awake crying, snap herself to a standing position, then turn on all the lights and walk the house for hours, praying away the fears that hung about like shadows. If the boys' sleep was disturbed, she quickly tucked them back into bed. This time—what happened this time? There was no split second of awareness when she could grasp the Lord's hand. It was as if those shadows had swallowed her, pulling her down into emptiness until she felt the soft folds of Erik's shirt beneath her fingers, his arms around her like protective armor. A human shield. What would have happened if he hadn't been there to comfort her as he had? Would she have become hysterical? What would the boys have done?

But what was he doing there? What audacity to give himself permission to remain in her house through the night! He was so arrogant, so absolutely rude. And how in the world could she have fallen asleep with him still in the room? And then that dream, that sense that Joe was home, the unchecked yearning to have him beside her . . .

So her mind rambled. The man had absolutely no business giving her amethyst earrings and taking the boys to the ball game and talking about Joe and buying her gas and changing rules.

"Excuse me," the receptionist interrupted from the doorway. "There's a man here to see Tori." She emphasized the word *man*. Everyone around the table looked up. With a flourish, she whipped a bouquet of flowers from behind her back.

Tori stared at the purple blossoms wrapped in deep violet tissue paper. "Tell him I'm in a meeting and cannot possibly be disturbed."

"I did. He said if you don't come out, he's coming in."

All eyes turned toward her. "Excuse me."

Trepidation filled her as she walked down the hallway, the bouquet clutched at her side. Sooner or later they would have to meet, but she needed time to sort through the confusion. This was happening too quickly.

Erik stood in the lobby, leafing through a newspaper. Tori's anxiety increased at the sight of him dressed in a black suit, crisp white shirt, and mauve tie. A businesslike demeanor cloaked the tired but handsome face he lifted to her. She understood now why the receptionist could not convince him she was unavailable.

"May we talk?"

She turned back down the hallway and entered a small, unoccupied office. Not bothering to flip on the lights, she walked behind the desk to a window, keeping her back to Erik, toying with the flowers still in her hand. She heard the door click shut and said, "I don't have anything to say."

"Well, I do." His voice was as stern as his face had been.

She heard him take a deep breath.

"Tori, I didn't intend to . . . I didn't intend for that to happen. Please believe me, and accept my apology. I was asleep. I thought . . . I thought you were someone else."

A derisive laugh escaped her. "That's swell. You make a pass at me, only it's not me you're making a pass at. Not that my feelings are hurt, because you're the last person on earth I want making a pass at me."

"It wasn't a pass."

She twirled around. "Just what would you call it, Mr. Steed, in your high and mighty vocabulary?" Her voice rose. "Just what did you think you were doing?"

"You'll be glad to know that you're the last woman on earth I'd want to make a pass at."

"Fine! Then we're even. Let's just forget this."

He took another deep breath. "What I would call it is wanting to be with my wife."

Tori closed her eyes.

"I guess I was dreaming. I sensed . . . I thought you were my wife."

"That's a good line, Mr. Steed. It's original anyway."

"It *is* original," he replied in a quiet voice. "I've never thought it before. I've never even had a wife." He cleared his throat. "At any rate, I apologize for upsetting you. Again. I stayed in the family room with you because I fell asleep there, holding you so the boys wouldn't be frightened by your crying.

And I was in your house in the first place because I was concerned about your headache."

She turned around. "I appreciate that, but it wasn't necessary. Please stop feeling responsible for what happened."

His eyes closed briefly, his forehead creased. For a moment he didn't reply. "Do you have that nightmare often?"

She shook her head. "I did, at first." She fingered the flowers still clenched in her fist. "Joe took me flying once, just like in the dream." She smiled. "It was the most frightening, most exhilarating, awesome experience ever. He was such a—" Again she shook her head. "He was bigger than life. The dream, the nightmare, comes once in a great while now—when I'm feeling stressed out or anxious about being solely responsible for everything. But I . . . I never cry like that."

"Perhaps you could this time because someone was there to bear it with you."

"I've always depended on God for that middle-of-the-night comfort."

"He uses people to do His work, too, though."

She thought a moment. Would He use this man? "Yes, I suppose He does."

"Tori, nothing immoral happened. I was asleep on the couch in the family room when I heard you scream."

"You heard me from there?"

"That was about four o'clock. I was home before 6, so it's not like I spent the whole night next to you. You don't have to feel guilty. All right?"

She bit her lip, remembering the fact that she had kissed him first.

As if reading her mind he smiled and said, "God and I both know you didn't mean to kiss me."

In spite of her uncomfortableness, she laughed.

"You're not what you appear to be, Tori Jeffers. Your innocence is more exasperating than anything."

"Innocence?" she asked in a puzzled tone.

"Yes. Or naiveté. You're an intelligent, working, single parent, a part of contemporary society and yet . . . Well, I've never met another woman who would be in the least bit distraught over this incident."

Her face felt flushed. "And that exasperates you?"

"Well, yes. I guess I don't know how to respond. I was hoping flowers would help."

She threw him a brief smile.

"I wouldn't knowingly hurt you," he said in a hushed tone, then cleared his throat. "Listen, I think you should go home. When was the last time you took a day off?"

She shrugged. "I'm all right."

"No, you're not. You're exhausted. For the boys' sake, go home."

"Okay, okay."

"Good. I'm leaving for New York, but I'll be back in plenty of time for our campout."

"New York! Erik, do you think you're ready for that much?"

"I have to be. A Vietnamese delegation is coming. The first. It's what I've been working toward for years. I have things to do, things that can't be done from here."

"That sounds rather historic."

"It is." His smile eased the weary lines in his face. "For the time being, though, it's off the record. I wouldn't want UPI learning it from the *Rancho Gazette.*"

"I didn't hear a thing. What were you saying about a campout?"

"I invited the boys and Matt to go camping with me and Nick in the mountains. It's mid-season break, so we don't have any games this week. You don't remember agreeing to this last night? We'll leave Friday and come home Sunday afternoon. You'll have the entire weekend to yourself."

He was barging in again, but energy to argue did not exist at the moment. And the task of fighting the boys' disappointment loomed an insurmountable burden. Perhaps time without them, a rare occurrence, would refresh her. She nodded.

"Then it's settled. I'll pick them up at 4." He stared at her a moment, his eyebrows furrowed, then turned. "Good-bye."

She followed him to the door. "Thank you for cleaning the kitchen and taking care of the boys last night."

He smiled down at her. "You're welcome."

"And . . ." She paused. His summer-blue eyes sparkled. "Thank you for the earrings."

"You will look lovely in them. Take care, Torinado."

She closed the door behind him and plopped onto a chair.

For a moment in that never-never land just before dawn, she hadn't been able to cope with the loneliness. Erik's almost con-stant physical nearness since their argument in the dugout, his kind attentiveness, the gift, that awful nightmare, his comfort in the night had all spiraled together, forcing her into an extremely vulnerable position.

Perhaps it was more than that, though. Perhaps the boys were right—they all needed someone in the flesh to help take care of their practical, human needs.

Dear Father, is this your answer to the boys' prayer? If it is, then I'm serious this time. I need a husband, and I think Allen would be perfect . . .

—*Six*—

"THAT WAS WONDERFUL, TORI. WHAT'S IT CALLED?" Allen smiled across the table. Candlelight reflected from his glasses.

"It's just some French chicken concoction I whipped together," she answered, trivializing her Saturday hours spent shopping and cooking. "Would you like more?"

"No, thank you. I'd sleep through the ten o'clock news."

"Why don't we skip that? Let's have coffee in the front room. There's wood in the fireplace. I think it's cool enough tonight for a fire, don't you?"

"I'll just watch until the sports comes on, give you time to clean up." He stood. "Then we'll light the fire."

"All right." Tori cleared the table while Allen meandered to an easy chair near the television. With more important things on her mind tonight, she chose not to draw attention to this chauvinistic tendency. She determined to let nothing ruffle the atmosphere she had so carefully designed. He was going to notice her femininity, and if that meant biting her sharp tongue, so be it.

"Where are the matches?" Allen walked into the kitchen area.

"On top of the fridge." Tori dried her hands on a towel. "The coffee's almost done."

"Is that chocolate ambrosia pie?" He peeked over her shoulder.

"Umhmm." She turned, smiling at him.

"What's the special occasion? A fantastic dinner, my favorite dessert, and you looking really pretty in that outfit." He eyed her deep purple, silk jumpsuit.

Tori slid her arms around his waist. "I thought it was about time we enjoyed an evening alone, in private. Without kids. Allen, I want you to know how much I appreciate your friendship."

He straightened his glasses. "Well, thank you. I, umm, I think you're one very special lady." Placing his hands on her shoulders, he smiled. "And I appreciate your friendship, too. Speaking of friendship, it sure was great of Erik to take the boys camping. I never was much of an outdoorsman myself."

Tori blinked. "You could always learn."

He laughed. "At forty-three, I'm too set in my ways. Pitching a tent and sleeping on the ground?" He shuddered. "Sounds like nasty business! Coffee's ready. I'll go light the fire."

Tori sighed as he left the room. Was she coming on too strong? Or not strong enough?

They cared deeply for each other. She loved him as a very dear friend. Their minds were compatible, their personalities harmonized. Their faith was an integral part of their lives. They were comfortable with each other. How could he resist her? She just wanted to share her life with him. To be Mrs. Miller and ask his opinion of countless decisions that lurked on the horizon. *Lord, is that asking too much?*

Stifling another sigh, she turned up the volume on the stereo. A romantic Mozart concerto accompanied her into the other room, where she set the tray on the coffee table between the hearth and couch. The fire crackled, filling the room with a warm glow.

"So, do you miss the boys?"

"Not yet." Tori dimmed the lamp, then sat next to Allen on the couch, handing him a plate and folding her legs underneath herself. "But I will by tomorrow. Two nights without them is enough."

"Thanks."

"Allen, do you ever get tired of being alone?"

"Umm. This is delicious. Well, between work, my kids, and church activities, I'm really not alone much."

"I mean at night. And first thing in the morning." She stared at the flames.

Not answering immediately, he sat very still. "I have my moments."

She handed him a cup of coffee.

"Thanks. Do I detect a lonesome note in your voice?"

She kissed his cheek.

Setting his cup on the table, Allen removed his glasses. In his tired mannerism, he rubbed his eyes. "Are you thinking maybe you don't want to make a lifetime career as a swinging single?"

Tori's chance to decipher his question escaped at that moment due to a loud banging on the front door.

"Mom!" a voice cried. "Mom!"

She rushed to unlock the door and flung it open. "What's wrong?"

David entered. "Danny barfed all over the tent!"

Erik followed, carrying Danny in his arms.

"What did he eat?" Tori felt her sleeping son's forehead.

"Name it and he probably ate it in the last twenty-four hours," Erik replied with a sheepish smile.

"How could you let him do that?" she demanded.

The smile faded as his eyes focused somewhere behind her shoulder. His voice deepened. "Inexperience. I'm new at this. Shall I put him to bed?"

"Please. The bottom bunk. David, go to bed. Where are Matt and Nick?"

Erik brushed past her. "At Matt's."

"There is some type of flu going around," Allen suggested.

She glanced at him. "He doesn't have a fever. I'll be right back. Don't go away."

In the bedroom, Erik was pulling off Danny's shoes. Together they tucked him under the covers. He continued to sleep as his mother, hands on hips, vented her dismay in loud whispers.

"I can't believe this! You drive all the way home at eleven o'clock at night! Couldn't you handle this until morning? Little boys throw up when they eat whatever they want, and then they're fine, and then they sleep!"

Erik's narrowed eyes locked with hers. Gripping the top bunk and leaning toward her, he expounded in like manner, "Excuse us for disrupting your intimate tête-à-tête. Dan was very ill and wanted to come home to be with his mother. I guess I was wrong in assuming anything could be more important than that!"

"Oh!" Tori fumed and spun on her heel. How dare he insinuate that Allen meant more to her than her son! She marched into David's room.

"How are you, sweetie?" She breathed a calm note into her voice.

Mumbling sleepily from his bed, he launched into a detailed account of their camping adventures. When Tori heard the closing of the front door, she cut him short and bade him good night.

As she entered the living room, Erik greeted her. "Your friend said it was getting late."

"It is." She spoke through clenched teeth. Without looking at him she noisily gathered plates, coffee cups, and saucers onto the tray, then left the room. "Good night."

He followed her into the kitchen. "Miller left so quickly, I take it our interruption wasn't that devastating to your plans?"

Tori's whirling motion flung china crashing to the tile floor. "That is none of your business!"

"Don't move!" Erik commanded. "You're barefoot."

"Just who do you think you are—barging in here unannounced, chasing away my guest!"

"Where's the broom?" He knelt to pick up the shards lying between them.

Ignoring him, she turned, tossed the silver tray onto the counter, and yanked open the cupboard door beneath the sink, fuming all the while. "You take my kids for the weekend but obviously don't have any business doing so since you're totally incapable of handling even the most common type of ailment known to little boys!"

She grabbed the wastebasket from the cupboard, then slammed it down beside him, her voice rising in pitch. "I can't believe I even allowed them to go with you! After the way you reacted at the hospital . . . ! What if one of them had been hurt?"

"Where's the broom?" He asked again, standing up.

"I think I've had just about enough of you, Mr. Steed! Demand your way through gas stations and board meetings and fund-raisers and baseball teams all you want, but stay out of my life!"

"Where's the broom?" he roared.

She blinked, swallowing the hysterical stream of accusations.

"Where's the broom?" he repeated in a quiet voice.

"I'll—"

"Stand still! Just tell me where it is."

"In that closet behind you."

He worked silently, sweeping the entire kitchen area.

A feeling of defeat washed over Tori. Her throat ached. What had Erik said to Allen? Probably nothing. He'd left because he believed their discussion unworthy of further attention. He was set in his ways and didn't feel the need for a wife. *Oh, Lord, I'm sorry for trying to orchestrate things.*

She watched the interloper dump fragments of special china into the trash. "Your finger's bleeding."

"It's nothing," he mumbled as he replaced the wastebasket.

She reached up into a cupboard for the Band-Aids. "Wash it off."

They stood next to each other at the sink while he held his hand under the running faucet. "Tonight was that important, huh?" he inquired quietly.

With a sigh she handed him a towel and ripped open a Band-Aid. "Well, I thought it was. I swear, to get that man's attention I'm going to have to smack him over the head with my iron skillet. And even then it'll probably be up to me to propose! Hold still." She wrapped the bandage around his finger.

"Your hands are so small." He placed one in the palm of his. "Why do you want to marry him?"

Tori pulled her hand away from his. Not daring to look at him, she gazed at their shadowed reflections in the dark window. "I don't think you have the right to ask such a thing," she whispered.

"You're all alone, Tori—"

"That's not your fault! This is my life, and it's none of your business!"

She heard his sharp intake of breath.

"He's not the man for you."

"How would you know? He's good and kind and—" Her voice wavered. "And safe!"

"Yes, I imagine you've got him wrapped around your little finger. He doesn't get in your way, doesn't challenge you on any point. He allows you to do just exactly as you please."

She turned, glaring up at him. "And maybe that's what makes him the perfect man for me! I don't want anything more than a friendly companion, a sounding board, a—"

Erik's hands encircled her face, tilting it to meet his. The flow of words caught in her throat. She stood rooted to the floor.

"It's almost midnight, and your lipstick is still perfectly in place," he whispered. "Your mouth, dear girl, was not created for displaying lipstick."

His lips brushed hers, and it was as if a lightning bolt shot through her. She felt the tensing of his fingers around her face as his eyes searched hers. In that moment she understood that he was letting her decide. She did not move, did not utter a word. He lowered his head again and began kissing away time and memory and coherent thought. She knew only that the lips of handsome Erik Steed met hers. She knew only the electrifying awareness of her response, her heart racing, her legs trembling.

He pulled her to himself, holding her tightly against his chest. She felt his heart beating in rhythm with hers. "If you were going to marry me, Mrs. Jeffers, I would certainly hope you couldn't kiss another man like that."

She pushed away from him. "Just stay out of my life."

"I will. But think about it, Tori. He's not the right one. Just think about it." He strode from the room and out the front door.

A goosebump-raising, adrenaline-pumping, I-can't-remember-my-name kiss . . .

"You keep slicing like that, Steed, and I might give you a run for your money!" Allen chuckled as he drove off in the cart.

Erik hoisted his golf bag over his shoulder and sauntered toward the grove of eucalyptus trees that lined the sixth hole. *Yeah, well, you wouldn't be hitting straight either if you knew that last night I kissed the woman who intends to marry you.*

He wiped his brow with a handkerchief. From a brilliant, cloudless blue sky the early morning sun already warmed the landscape. It was unusual for May, everyone said. *Everything about San Diego is unusual, from coaching little boys to negotiating Susanne's divorce instead of a trade agreement to meeting Tori Jeffers who—*

He threw the golf bag toward the base of a tree to stop the thought from forming and yanked at his glove. The Band-Aid caught. With a muttered curse he ripped off both, then, kneeling, shoved them into a side pouch of the bag and pulled a ball from it. He tossed the ball and reached for his three iron.

The sudden thumping in his ears halted his movements. He took a deep breath and leaned back on his knees. *I had no right!*

He squeezed his eyes shut.

Don't go, Phil. You weren't drafted!

Gotta go, kid. You'll understand someday.

Erik concentrated on taking deep breaths, forcing the past back where it belonged. In a few minutes the thumping subsided.

Allen would wonder what had happened to him. He stood, determined to complete the game. His body automatically went through the motions of golfing, while his mind tried for the hundredth time to sort it all out. The outburst seemed to have helped. He detached himself from the emotions of last night and coolly reviewed his thought processes.

It wasn't that he thought Allen unworthy of Tori's affection. He seemed a genuinely decent man who could adequately care for her needs. He would be the friendly companion, the sounding board she said she wanted.

But she was too full of life to settle for a stodgy marriage of convenience. That's what had angered him so, what had goaded him to stop her foolishness with such a drastic measure as to kiss her.

Well, in all frankness, that had backfired. The moment his lips touched hers, all anger drained from him. When he searched her eyes, with Mozart crescendoing all around them, it was as if he was almost home. And when he kissed her, he knew he had arrived.

The anger had returned immediately. That sense of home was not for him. He had the least right of all men to interfere with her decisions. He could at least take care of her needs, though. The trust funds were in place. He had set up one for each of the boys when they turned eighteen and one for her, available upon his death or whenever he learned of a need. Dan and Dave would not have to think of paying for college; Tori would never have a financial concern in her life.

He had taken care of her, as he'd promised himself.

"Did you get lost?" Allen called out from the cart where he lounged next to the green.

Man, you don't know how lost. Erik waved his nine iron, then chipped onto the green, putted, and walked over to the cart. "Couldn't find that ball."

"No problem. We're not holding anyone up. Hop in." They drove toward the next tee. "Sure is unusual not to have this place crowded on such a beautiful Sunday morning. I forgot to ask—how was David when you left last night?"

"David—oh, Dan was the sick one. He was sleeping well. Probably just something he ate."

"Tori can overreact at times. She's something else, isn't she?"

"She did a proper job of chewing me out."

He chuckled. "The lady can hold her own."

"Allen, may I ask you a personal question? If you don't feel at liberty to answer, don't."

"Go ahead."

"What's your relationship with her?"

"Well, obviously we're friends. I suppose I think of her as a little sister. I offer her advice sometimes about financial matters. We did her taxes together this year. And we share dinner regularly, just to keep in touch." He parked the cart. "She's fourteen years younger and has a lot more vim and vinegar than I do! I enjoy her spunk."

"She does have that."

"So, if you want to ask her to dinner, Erik, go ahead. We're not—how do they say it?—seeing each other."

"That's not what I was asking." They climbed out.

"Well, if you were, I'd offer only one piece of advice. Want to hear it?" They slid their clubs from the bags and walked to the tee.

"Sure."

Allen glanced at him. "She won't get serious about a man who doesn't have faith in Christ. That conviction is like a steel rod in her spine. I think Joe spoiled her, so to speak, in that way." He placed his ball on the tee and drove it down the fairway.

"Well, I'm out of here right after the last Little League game."

Allen chuckled. "Bet she won't let you go until the end-of-the-season party. The point is, Erik, faith is a question to consider, whether or not you plan to get to know her better."

Erik teed his ball and swung.

"You must've lost your slice on that last hole."

They climbed into the cart together.

"Only an idiot would believe that the world exploded into being," Erik commented.

"God didn't quit after creation," Allen replied as he drove. "He's involved in the details of here and now."

"Yeah, I heard that once. I'd rather do it myself," he quipped in a bitter tone.

"Well, when things don't go the way we think they should, God's big enough to take our blame and our anger. Trusting Him doesn't mean we'll understand everything or that we'll not know pain."

Erik sensed he spoke from personal experience. "What did it mean when your wife passed away?"

"It meant I had a source outside of myself who gave me the strength to keep going. It meant there was a reason for it, even if I didn't know what it was. It meant that I didn't have to figure it all out. There's a tremendous sense of relief and release in that."

Their conversation continued in that vein. By the eighteenth hole Erik's respect for Allen had deepened. But the thought of Tori being married to him still didn't feel right.

"Hey, Allen, do you have any idea how Tori views your relationship?"

"The same as I do."

Erik shook his head.

Allen looked at the sky. "Oh, no! That's what she was getting at last night! She talked about our friendship and mentioned something about getting tired of being single. I thought she was hinting at my opinion of you!"

The two burst into laughter.

"I know her opinion of me, and it doesn't resemble favorable. But if I were you, I'd duck if she pulls out her iron skillet!"

Tori thought about Erik's parting shot, not because he'd said to, but because she could think of nothing else. All through the night she'd thought about it and now, sitting in the backyard, her face warming in the early morning sunshine, her bare toes wriggling in the dewy grass, she thought about it some more.

The questions circled through her mind in maddening repetition and never landed on a solution. Why had she let him kiss her? He had given her the clear opportunity to stop him, so why hadn't she taken it? And why in the world had she responded as if she enjoyed the kiss?

The tall, wooden gate creaked near the side of the house. She opened her eyes to see Linda emerge. A tattered blue robe hung on her; a mug dangled from her hand.

"Hi, Tor. Thought you might be back here if you were up." Sandals slapped against Linda's feet as she shuffled through the grass to plop in a chair beside her friend. "You look awful."

"How would you know? Your eyes are closed. Nice hairdo."

Linda patted her tangled mess. "Thanks. I worked on it all night. In between taking care of Matt who evidently picked up that flu bug. At least Nick slept through it all."

Tori groaned. "Do you want some coffee or did you just want to hold that empty mug?"

"Is there some? Let me get it." Linda stood, reaching for Tori's cup. "You really do look worse than I do. Was Danny up all night too? Is David okay?" She plodded toward the sliding screen door.

"Umm, yes. And yes." *Erik Steed kissed me.*

Peering over her shoulder, Linda pushed open the door and mumbled, "I bet this cut into last night's plans."

Tori closed her eyes. *Cut into them? How about hurled them light-years away? Exploded them into undefinable fragments?* Plans with Allen receded to a minor question, overshadowed by the puzzle of Erik Steed.

"Do tell all." Linda handed her a cup and sat down.

"Thanks. Does Matt have a fever, too?"

"I hate it when you change the subject. It's down. He's been sleeping now for two hours, so I thought it safe to slip away."

"Why don't these things strike in the daytime?"

"So, did you have time for anything before they came home?"

"Well, dinner was very nice. Then after the news we sat in front of the fire, and I led into things rather creatively, I thought,

116 SALLY JOHN

talking about loneliness. Allen caught on, but we didn't have a chance to discuss it further."

"The boys arrived?"

Tori nodded. "And Allen left."

"Hmm. Given more time, do you think he would have proposed?"

"Linda, he left! I'm sure I scared him away."

"Oh, you know Allen. He's a little set in his ways. He just needs some time to consider the consequences. He thinks you're terrific."

"Umhmm." Tori sipped her coffee. *But Erik Steed kissed me.*

"Who left first?"

"What?"

"Who left first? Allen or Erik?"

Tori stared at the brown liquid in her cup.

"What's wrong, Tor?"

Erik Steed kissed me, and I kissed him back. "I . . . I—"

Linda clutched her arm. "What is it?"

She met her friend's alarmed brown eyes. "Nothing. It's just that Erik . . ." The words refused to form.

"Erik what?"

Tori's shoulders heaved as she took a deep breath. "He kissed me."

"Oh, my. Well . . ." Linda cleared her throat. "Well . . ."

They drank their coffee in silence for a few moments. "Well," Linda repeated, "I take it Allen left first then?"

"Erik Steed isn't that rude!"

"Do you want to talk about it?"

Tori shrugged and looked away. Though the twins had told Linda about the amethyst earrings, Tori had never discussed with her what had occurred during that night. A dreamlike quality covered the incident, and she had succeeded in pushing it aside, but this . . . this was something else.

"Linda, could you really enjoy kissing someone you don't care about?"

"You mean, just get into the physical, lustful aspect of it all?"

"Yeah, I guess. Imagine you're not married."

"My first thought is, maybe. Even though I know it would be wrong, I imagine if I were out of touch and lonely and this good-looking guy was giving me attention, perhaps. But I wouldn't like myself later, so, no, on second thought I couldn't really, thoroughly enjoy kissing him."

"What if he surprised you with extravagant gifts and he spent lots of time with your kids and your kids liked him and he made you laugh and he was the most tender, most thoughtful, and even the most handsome man you'd ever met?"

Linda stared at her. "Well, since you're not out of touch and lonely and have only one guy noticing you, I suspect you do care somewhat for him."

"But I don't!"

"Well, was it like kissing Allen? You like him."

"Oh!" Tori jumped to her feet and strode into the kitchen, grabbed the coffeepot, and strode back outside. "It was nothing like kissing Allen because Allen has never kissed me like that!" She sloshed coffee into their cups, then set the carafe in the grass between their chairs.

"Be totally honest with yourself, Tor. Why is it you don't like Erik?"

She slumped onto the chair. "Because I don't want to."

"Tell me what happened."

Briefly, she related their argument, the broken china, the kiss. "So with that snide remark about not kissing someone besides the one you're marrying, I'd say he doesn't care a whit about me either and that he's just an experienced womanizer who caught me at a weak moment."

Linda was silent for a moment. "Perhaps. He *is* charming and good-looking, but he's also thoughtful and caring and wouldn't hurt you that way if he weren't terribly angry."

"Angry?"

"Maybe jealous."

"Jealous?"

"Of course. He was just reacting to your obvious choice of

Allen. He walked in on what appeared to be a seriously romantic moment."

Tori frowned, letting her friend's words sink into her heart.

"His snide remark was a cover-up. It was probably also the
truth. You're too mature and self-confident to love one guy and
carry on a purely physical relationship with another. I think we
need to ask some serious questions here, Tori, like," she lowered
her voice, "exactly how did you feel when he kissed you? Were
you seventeen again?"

"No." She bit her lip, then took a deep breath. "I was
twenty-nine with two feet firmly planted on the ground, both
eyes wide open, a responsible, sensible mother with a career, and
suddenly the earth stood still, and every thought and feeling I'd
ever had just disappeared. Nothing existed apart from him."

"That bad, huh?"

Tori dismissed the emotion with a shake of her head.
"Chemistry."

"Oh, honestly. You can be friends with the man, get to know
him, find out where he is spiritually. Why are you dismissing him?"

"Do you remember my first impression of him? Well, it
hasn't changed. He raced through that gas station like he owned
it, because that's his attitude toward everything. Then he shoved
his weight around at the board meeting. Throw in a little money
with all that sweet charm, and he can make any kind of change
he wants, just to suit his own whims. It goes against my grain."

"An incurable optimist to make the world a better place."
Linda's sober eyes met hers.

"I can't love another Joe. I can't do what you and Tim do.
Those months of separation. I want a husband who's home all
the time."

"Have you prayed about this?"

"Of course I have!" she snapped.

"I bet you said, 'Lord, Allen would be perfect for this position. Take care of it.'"

Tori stared into her coffee cup.

"You know better than I that when we think we've got it all

figured out, God surprises us with something different. And the sooner we adjust our attitude to accept whatever He brings our way, the sooner we can stop fretting."

"Erik has a full life outside of this place. He'll be gone next month after baseball season is over. I don't want to talk about him anymore. Ever."

"I have to say one more thing."

"Linda . . ." she pleaded.

"We'll just get all this unpleasantness over with at once." She paused. "I invited him to the fly-in."

Tori stared at her.

"And he's coming. Matt told him about it, and he expressed an interest in it. Tori, he's been a good influence as Matt's coach while Tim has been gone. I want them to meet." She smiled.

"I know," Tori replied in a small voice.

"There will be so many people at the fly-in, you won't need to talk to Erik if you don't want to. And besides, you'll have Allen with you. You won't change your mind, will you?"

Tori thought about the special event scheduled for next Sunday at Miramar Naval Air Station. Linda's husband, along with the other pilots and RIOs from his squadron, would fly in after six months' duty at sea aboard an aircraft carrier. Memories would descend without mercy on her in such a setting, but she had determined to be prepared for them. She owed it to the boys to experience a fly-in with them now that they were old enough to appreciate this part of their heritage.

"No, I'll go." She smiled crookedly. "Linda, I'm sorry to be so preoccupied. Are you ready for him?"

Linda squealed, "Ooh, yes, yes! I mean no! I have to buy a new dress. Come shopping with me today. Kelsey can stay with the boys for a few hours. And what's-his-name is picking Nick up about noon."

Tori studied her friend's expectant face. The encouragement Linda had offered through the years flashed through her mind. "Sure."

"You know, you haven't bought a new summer dress for ages.

No doubt there'll be some unattached males waiting for pilot friends to fly in, eyeing attractive, unattached females waiting for their friends . . ."

The soft rayon folds slid through Tori's fingers as she hung the new dress in her closet. She had succumbed to the inevitable consequence of two females shopping as an antidote to emotional distress, but the price hadn't been outrageous, and the dress was lovely. Pale lavender with an oversized white, embroidered lace collar. V-necked with buttons to the bottom of the flowing, mid-calf length skirt. She had even purchased anklets and flat slip-ons like those in the store's photo of a model wearing the dress. Perhaps she would keep it.

The doorbell rang. Tori's hand flew to her stomach, a reflex to soothe the tightening muscles.

"Hey, Mom!" David's voice echoed down the hallway. "Allen's here!"

The tense muscles relaxed. Tori met her son outside his bedroom door. "David, that was rude."

He glanced sideways at her and entered his room.

"David!"

He shut the door.

It would have to wait. She walked to the living room.

"Hello." Allen smiled at her. "Sorry to barge in on you, but I wanted to talk. Do you have a few minutes?"

"Of course." What was this? He never stopped in unannounced. "Have a seat. Can I get you something to drink?"

"No, thanks." He sat on the couch, patting the cushion next to him. "I think we were interrupted last night, right about here."

Tori blinked. "Umm, I need to check on Danny."

"How is he doing?"

"Much better. Excuse me." She bolted into the family room where the recovering Danny was watching television.

"Mom, can I have some more soup?"

"If you're sure you feel like eating." She took her time serving him, puzzling if she wanted to continue last night's direction with Allen. She didn't know. She really didn't know. "You need to go to bed at 8, all right?"

Allen smiled at her again as she entered. She sat next to him. "There's still some pie."

"No, thanks. I can't stay. Remember I mentioned the annual Palm Springs golf outing with my old college friends?"

"The one that's scheduled for three weeks from now?"

"Yes, well, we've had to rearrange our schedule. One of the wives just learned she needs surgery. If we don't go this coming week, we won't get it in. Then I plan to swing north to pick up my daughter. She's coming home for the summer—"

"Allen, the fly-in!"

"I know. I'll miss it, and I'm disappointed about that." He rested his arm on the couch behind her.

"I wanted you there for moral support."

"I know, Tori, and I'm sorry. But you're strong. You'll be fine. You always are at those sorts of things."

This isn't one of those sorts of things!

"Besides, you'll have Linda there."

He echoed Linda's words about him that morning, and in that instant Tori became aware of a separateness creeping between herself and her two best friends.

He removed his glasses and placed them on the coffee table. "Tori, I thought about what you said last night. I guess you caught me by surprise." His arm came around her shoulders. "You are important to me." He leaned toward her.

"I need help with my math." David stood directly behind them.

Allen jerked away.

"David!" Tori fumed.

"I don't get the fractions—"

"David, go to your room!"

His brows furrowed. He turned on his heel and stomped down the hall.

"Allen, I'm sorry—"

"It's all right." He replaced his glasses. "Life at your house is always like Grand Central Station. It's one of the, uhh, unique things about you. Do you understand fractions?"

"What? Oh, yes." Did he like that uniqueness about her?

"I could help."

"Thanks, that's all right." She smiled tightly.

"Well, I really should get going then." He stood. "I have lots of loose ends to tie up before I leave."

She followed him to the door. He kissed her cheek. "I'll call you when I get back, and we'll have dinner."

Tori sighed heavily, then made a beeline to David's door. When he didn't answer her pounding, she opened it. He was sitting at his desk.

"I figured it out," he muttered.

"What I want to figure out, young man, is your rudeness tonight!"

He shrugged, his back to her.

"That's not like you. Yelling down the hall that Allen's here. Interrupting my discussion with him like a two-year-old brat who doesn't know even how to say excuse me."

She heard him mumble.

"What did you say?"

"Nothing."

"Look at me and tell me, right now!" she ordered.

Slowly he scooted around in his chair, his eyes downcast. "I said it didn't look like a discussion."

Tori saw the telltale trails down his chubby cheeks, and it knocked the wind from her raging sails. Sighing again, she sat on his bed. "It was personal. You should have known better."

"Are you gonna marry him?"

"I don't know, honey. Is that what's bothering you?"

For a moment he didn't reply. He glanced up. "Why were you and Coach yelling last night?"

Now she studied the floor. "It was just a misunderstanding. I'm sorry you heard us."

"How come you don't like him?"

"I . . . I like him. We just don't see eye-to-eye on some things."

"Like what?"

Tori looked at her son. "A lot of grownup stuff I can't explain to you right now."

"You always explain everything."

"Well, this is different!" She bit her tongue.

"Danny really did have the flu, didn't he?"

"Yes, I was wrong. Do you feel okay?"

David nodded, but his sober face wasn't convincing.

"Why do you have homework on a Sunday night?"

"I don't. This isn't due until Wednesday."

"Oh, David, go to bed."

The week did not improve with time. Danny felt better on Monday, but by noon the school called Tori to pick up an ailing David. She spent that night and the next day nursing him. She accomplished newspaper duties in a haphazard manner. By Wednesday midnight she herself experienced the viral symptoms she knew so well.

The vague discomfort of attending the fly-in grew into a clearly defined fear. Her exhausted state dried up her usually strong mental resources for coping in difficult times. Linda was, understandably, occupied, and Tori missed her friend's optimism.

Through it all the question of Erik Steed hovered, intensifying every anxious moment. If he were jealous, why would he have promised last week to stay out of her way, right after the camping trip? A man did not pursue a woman with that kind of promise.

If he simply believed Allen wasn't compatible for her, what gave him the right to be so angry? It really wasn't his business. They hardly knew each other, and he wasn't the type to care much what happened to strangers. He was a hard-nosed, driven businessman, wealthy and accustomed to having his own way.

From his ungenerous attitude toward his sister and her friends, he appeared not to view women in a serious light.

Was it because Tori openly disagreed with him that he found her a challenge, unlike most females who fell at his feet? Was his tenderness when she'd been hurt just part of the game? Was his extravagance a means to make her indebted to him?

Oh, none of it mattered because developing a relationship with him was not an option.

Then why, when the phone or doorbell rang, did her stomach tie itself into knots? Why did she feel disappointment, then relief, then disappointment again when it wasn't him?

At last on Thursday, after the twins left for school, she fell into a deep, dreamless sleep. At 3 they woke her, unable to find their baseball uniforms for that afternoon's game.

Later in the kitchen she sat on a stool, slicing oranges. "I don't think I can go, guys. Linda will take you."

She glanced at Danny's crestfallen face as he whined, "You never miss our games."

"Daniel, I can't help it. I'm sorry. Fill up your water bottles." She threw a handful of slices into a plastic container, then attacked another orange.

"Mom," David asked, "what are you doing?"

"Typing. What do you mean what am I doing? I'm cutting oranges for your game. You can take them."

"Coach doesn't want 'em."

Tori stared at the narrowed eyes and grim mouth on the face of her little boy whose middle name had always been Cooperation. "But I think you should have them."

"Coach doesn't want 'em."

"I don't care."

"Coach says no food and no women in the dugout."

Danny interjected, "And he's the boss, Mom. In the dugout anyway."

Tori tossed the knife into the sink. "Fine!" she yelled, then stomped from the kitchen, knowing full well she was behaving childishly. "Go to Matt's house!" was her shout from the hall.

IN THE SHADOW OF LOVE

While they were gone, she soaked in a hot bathtub. Tears and steam flowed down her face, calming her after a time. She managed to fix dinner.

The boys returned, hungry and disgruntled.

"We lost!" they wailed in unison, then began accusing each other of bad plays.

"Hush! Wash your hands. We'll eat now. What was the score?"

"Four to nothin'!"

"What happened?"

"Coach was grumpy," Danny explained.

"He's always grumpy during a game," she offered.

"Mom, he just has his head in the game," David expounded. "Tonight he was grumpy like you are."

Danny added, "Yeah. He even left before we did, and we saw him driving Nick's mother's Jag about a hundred miles an hour in the parking lot!"

Tori laid down her fork, her small appetite squelched. "I bet he just needed some orange slices," she quipped.

The boys howled in reply, and she felt a sense of optimism, the first in a long time.

"Are you doing a commercial for some cleansing product?"

Before responding to Linda, Tori eyed her ragged blue jeans and oversized, faded yellow T-shirt. She tightened the scarf knotted around her hair. "What, are you embarrassed to sit with me? First I get kicked out of the dugout, and now you don't want me here in the bleachers. Just where am I supposed to sit?"

The two friends sat on the top row for the Saturday afternoon baseball game. Tori had chosen the spot farthest from the players' bench. It would be her first game since the accident and her first glimpse of Erik since the night in her kitchen. She'd spent this morning cleaning house in an attempt to soak up nervous energy, but she fidgeted now, trying not to look at the field.

One of the other mothers approached. "How's your eye, Tori?"

She slipped off her sunglasses. "Fine, thanks. Stitches are out."

"Looks like you might have a tiny scar, but nothing real noticeable."

"The game's starting." Tori smiled and replaced the glasses, cutting off further comment on her inane behavior.

"Sure hope we do better than Thursday."

Tori's peripheral vision watched Erik; her ear sensed his voice. "Linda, can I do anything to help you get ready for your big day tomorrow?"

"Tell me how to wait for it. I'm so excited, I can hardly stand it. Who's that?"

"Who?"

"Bottom row, to our left. Is that what you call Nordic? She's beautiful. Those have got to be the shortest shorts I've ever seen, but on her they look good."

Tori spotted a long-legged blonde. "Umhmm. I don't think she belongs to our team."

At that moment Erik turned around to face the bleachers. He smiled in the direction of the unknown woman.

"Hi, Coach." The deep feminine voice carried to the top bleachers.

"Uh-oh," Linda moaned.

Tori looked at the field. "Guess she does belong to our team. Told you I wasn't his type."

"Maybe they're cousins."

The game progressed like a slow-motion, silent movie before Tori's eyes. She watched, but her mind was engaged in the agonizing process of swallowing the lump in her throat and ignoring the hollowness in the pit of her stomach.

"We won," Linda unnecessarily announced an hour and a half later.

"And without orange slices or treats." Her voice sounded high, forced.

"But only by one run."

The blonde strutted toward the gate.

"Linda, the boys rode their bikes. I'm going to vamoose. Call if you need anything. Tonight I'll be at that Little League board party, though."

Erik greeted the woman with a smile, placing his arm around her shoulders.

"Oh, that's right. Have fun. Too bad Allen's out of town. What are you wearing?"

The woman's arm slid around the back of his waist.

"Bye, Linda. See you tomorrow, one o'clock."

"Tori!"

She hurried across the grassy area toward the parking lot. There was a lot of heavy-duty cleaning left to be done at home. She had to be sure no flu germs survived!

What was wrong with her? If the baby-sitter wasn't already in the family room with the boys, she'd probably skip this gathering. Victoria Life-of-the-Party Jeffers would just as soon stay home. She bent at the waist and fiercely brushed her hair.

Maybe *he'd* stay home. With his tall friend. Attending the Little League party wasn't mandatory for board members, and he was only temporary anyway. Maybe he wouldn't care about a silly local party.

But why should it concern her whether or not he was there? All right, so she was a little disappointed that he had a tall friend. That it proved he wasn't interested in her. All right, so maybe she'd been a little interested in him and would have enjoyed challenging his viewpoints. She never would have been serious.

Tori looked in the mirror while she applied lipstick. The lines about her mouth were distinct, drawn.

She spoke aloud to her reflection. "It's okay to be disappointed. You'll get over it. Smile. Go talk to people."

"I heard Linda Peterson's husband comes home tomorrow. Gracious, I just can't imagine having your husband gone for six months at a time like that! I mean, how would you survive?" The speaker drained her glass of wine.

Tori clenched her teeth, stretching her lips into some semblance of a smile.

Another woman in the small group poked the one who had spoken.

Tori backed away. "Excuse me."

She meandered toward another cluster, composed of men discussing the league.

"Tori, what do you think about . . . Oh, there's Steed! About time he got here."

"Looks like he has a new friend. Where'd she come from?"

Tori didn't turn around to welcome the newcomers but instead sauntered toward another group. They eventually moved toward the buffet table.

A hand from across the table reached simultaneously for the same plate. "Sorry, go ahead." She met the tall blonde's eyes.

"No, you go ahead."

Erik stood beside the beauty, talking to someone on his other side, his back turned slightly.

"Hi, I'm Tori Jeffers. I don't believe we've met."

The woman shook her hand. "Hi. I'm with Erik. I got to see his little boys' game today. It's all so in-ter-resting!" She giggled and slipped her arm through Erik's.

Good grief, Tori thought. *She's an airhead.*

Erik turned toward his tall friend, smiling.

Tori offered, "Nice game, Coach."

Until that moment she had never really understood the phrase of being looked through. Erik's eyes blankly passed over her as he spoke again to the man at his side.

The blonde replied, "Oh, were you there with the other team? Guess we beat you!"

Tori smiled tightly and concentrated on spooning food onto her plate.

"Hey, Steed," the man beside her said, "are you still undefeated?"

"No, we lost our first one the other night. The kids just weren't able to get it together."

Tori couldn't resist. "I heard the coach was grumpy."

Erik piled a handful of chips onto his plate. "They've really progressed as a team and can usually hit and field well, but not that night."

She turned on her heel.

"Tori," the man behind her called, "you missed the—"

Passing a coffee table, she set down her half-filled plate and, without a word or a glance toward anyone, walked out the front door.

— Seven —

THE EARLY AFTERNOON breeze rippled Tori's new dress about her legs as she stood inside an enormous hangar at Miramar Naval Air Station. One side of the narrow, rectangular building was open all the way to the lofty roof, affording a view of clear blue sky and steel gray Tarmac. A thin, yellow rope politely requested that guests stay within the hangar. Some distance to her left was an opening where a bright red carpet had been rolled out.

The quiet sky and vacant airstrip would soon roar with a squadron of F14s flying overhead in formation before descending like rolling thunder. One at a time would taxi toward the hangar while a family waited at the end of the red carpet for their flier to disembark. The reunions would be highly emotional. Tori anticipated them with what she felt an adequate degree of composure.

That composure had settled within her sometime during the night, after hours of tossing and turning during which she alternately regretted what she hadn't said to Erik and rehearsed what she would say when she saw him. Sleep eluded her until at last she sat up in bed and said aloud, "I quit, Lord! I quit! I can't control what happens at the fly-in, and I can't control my feelings for Erik. For the boys' sake, don't let me be afraid tomorrow, and don't let me love the wrong man. And don't let me be angry with the right one." She plopped back down, whispering a quick "Amen" just as sleep overtook her.

She awoke with a sense of quiet determination. Today wouldn't be easy, but everything would be all right. As for

Erik—well, if he didn't care for her, that was nothing to be concerned about. It was in God's hands.

Children's playful shouts echoed now in the hangar. Tori
looked around, making sure the twins weren't disturbing anyone
as they dodged adults in a game of hide-and-seek with the other
kids. About 100 people milled about, waiting.

She smiled. Only a group of Navy wives and girlfriends with
immeasurable anticipation could transform a dull, barren hangar
into a festive party room. Scattered tables draped in colorful
cloths displayed fresh flowers, coffee urns, and platters of sand-
wiches and cookies. Champagne and soda chilled in nearby
coolers. None of it was to be touched until the men arrived.

Linda emerged from a group of women, easily recognizable
as waiting girlfriends and wives because they wore the biggest
smiles and the most eye-catching outfits. Their heavy perfume
ensemble almost obliterated the ever-present fuel pungency.

"You look sensational, Linda."

"You already told me that," she giggled.

"I have to emphasize it. It's not just that gauzy white dress
and your tan and your hair. You're glowing. Tim is so fortunate
to be married to you."

Linda's smiled broadened, though her eyes sobered. "Are
you doing okay?"

Tori nodded.

Her friend hugged her. "Thanks for coming. The twins seem
absolutely thrilled. How was the party last night?"

"Oh, fine. Have you seen any of our illustrious co-workers
yet?"

Successfully skirting the issue of the previous evening, she
chatted for a few moments, then excused herself to powder her
nose. Linda was too highly charged. Talking with her added too
much stress to Tori's own on-the-edge emotions.

The outside entrance was located in a stairwell that led to
the upstairs restroom. As Tori neared the steps, Erik Steed sauntered through the doorway. Neither broke their stride. They
passed each other in silence. For a split second his eyes met hers,

and she thought that to have him look through her as he'd done last night was better than to meet such coldness. She raced up the stairs.

Was he alone? The printed invitation granting him access to the naval base could include any guests in his car, any tall friend. Knowing that Nicky was with his dad, she hadn't expected to see Erik without the Nordic beauty.

In the restroom Tori diverted her attention by eavesdropping on other conversations as she surveyed herself in the mirror. Women compared notes on whom they were meeting. She busied herself for a time, but during her third reapplication of lipstick, she began to feel conspicuous.

Downstairs again, Tori's eyes were drawn to Erik. His height made him difficult not to notice. She watched from a distance as Linda handed him her camera, pointing out its features. Tori recognized it as the complex one with a telephoto lens. She must have asked him to take pictures for her.

Her eyes lingered for a moment. His mahogany hair was damp and combed back. He wore a pair of casual black slacks and a robin-egg blue polo shirt. His face was sober. What had happened to his lopsided grin? He looked as if he had a headache. Was he working too much again?

She turned away, searching for a familiar face that didn't bear the name Linda Peterson or Erik Steed.

"Mom, you need earplugs!" Danny shoved a tiny packet into her hand. "Aren't they rad? They're little sponges. Do you know how to put 'em in? Coach is here!" Not waiting for answers, he raced off again.

Tori joined some friends from work and forced herself to enthusiastically participate in the small talk. It worked until Linda approached with Erik in tow, introducing him and instructing everyone to line up for a picture. If Linda hadn't grabbed her elbow, Tori wouldn't have faced the camera held by Erik. Unable to escape, she gritted her teeth into a smile.

"Fifteen minutes! They'll be here in fifteen minutes!" The word rolled like a wave through the crowd. Wanting to share the moment only with her sons, Tori excused herself to find them, no easy task in the busy hangar. She roamed toward the center, peering between adults for midget hide-and-seekers.

"Nine minutes!"

Tori's heart pounded in her throat. The crowd blurred. She bit her lower lip, fighting down the queasiness in her stomach.

What was she doing here? Those pilots were going to land, and she would remember Joe landing, climbing from his jet, racing to catch her in his arms. And she would remember Joe not coming home five years ago.

She gulped a deep breath, swallowing the panic.

David came into view. "Mom, it's time! Come on, we've been waiting for you." He tugged at her arm.

"I was looking for you."

"You told us to meet you by that section of the rope when it was time."

"Oh." She'd forgotten. They maneuvered their way through spectators to reach Danny near the rope.

"Coach took our picture. He took lots of you."

"What?"

"He took lots of pictures of you, with Linda's telephoto. He told me I better come get you cuz you looked like you were lost."

Two pairs of summer-sky blue eyes framed in dark lashes stared up at her. Tori stepped between her sons, slipping her arms across their shoulders, pulling them tightly to her sides. "I think I was, but I'm not now. Look up, guys. They're coming."

"Awesome!" exclaimed Danny.

Cheers erupted from the crowd as the eight jets roared overhead in formation.

David hugged Tori's waist. "Thanks for bringing us, Mom."

"Yeah, thanks, Mom!"

"You're welcome. Watch," she said pointing. "One of them will land. You might need those earplugs now. Can you get them to fit?"

"Coach is taking our picture again."

"Where is he?"

"By the red carpet."

Tori unwrapped the yellow, spongy plugs, glancing at Erik in the distance. He turned his back to them.

Danny complained, "How come he gets to be out there? I thought everybody had to stay behind the rope."

"I suppose he has permission in order to take photos of Matt and his family. See, there are some others with cameras. That one looks like he's from a television news station." She pursed her lips. Even the military bowed to Erik Steed!

The first jet thundered down the airstrip, then made its way toward the hangar. A family stood at the end of the red carpet, watching the F14's canopy rise and the pilot climb out.

The wait wasn't over yet. Removing his helmet, he greeted waiting Navy personnel and began the process of shedding his heavy vest and G-suit. Tori thought it an agonizingly slow procedure that added unbearable time to these last moments of a six-month separation. She held her breath.

A muffled voice announced the man's name through a loudspeaker. One of the greeters handed him a yellow rose for his wife, and at long last the pilot started his brisk walk to the red carpet as the RIO unfastened his vest.

Tori exhaled as the pilot's family embraced. One down and fifteen to go. Another jet rolled into view. She wiped a tear from the corner of her eye, then knelt between her sons. "You don't remember any of this, do you?"

They shook their heads.

Memories flooded her. The boys had been three years old the last time Joe returned. They were unable to remember because this was a detail she'd never reinforced. They hadn't heard the story of welcoming their father home from an overseas cruise. Now, speaking closely in their ears as jets landed and people cheered, she shared it with them.

Relating the past was her gift to them, and in the act of telling, she sensed a release. Her fear diminished, overshadowed by the delight in their eyes and the empathetic happiness she felt for the families reuniting today.

"There's Tim!"

In silence they watched. Linda, Matt, and Kelsey waited on the red carpet.

"Can we go see him now?"

"How come you're crying, Mom?"

Tori smiled. "I'm just happy for them. You go, but don't interrupt them, understand?"

"Aren't you coming?"

"In a few minutes."

As the boys made their way through the crowd behind them, Tori pulled a handkerchief from her pocket. She counted five jets on the ground. She'd wait here just a bit, let the memories recede, comforted by the knowledge that she need no longer fear them.

Erik watched the tender reunion through the camera lens, snapping countless photos of the event, slicing it into moments for the Petersons to savor in the future.

Tim, like the other members of his squadron, wore a royal blue flight suit. His appearance was that of the consummate young naval officer. His erect, slender five-foot-ten frame, light brown crew cut, and fresh, all-American face exuded discipline. He seldom let go of Linda's hand as he greeted their friends with a grin. Matt and Kelsey moved from their father's side only when the twins rushed at him.

"Erik," Linda called then, "come over here."

Dan and Dave, arms still wrapped around Tim, introduced Erik. He received the pilot's firm handshake and said, "Welcome home."

"It's good to meet you, Coach. I want to thank you for all you've done for my son."

"Where's Tori?" Linda's voice had an anxious note in it.

"I'll find her," Erik offered.

"Lin, let him take the rose." Tim looked at Erik as he spoke. His eyes seemed to convey more than his words, as if he sensed that Erik was the one who should give this flower to the widow of his friend.

"Yes," Linda agreed. "Here, I'll trade you the camera for this." She handed him one of the bouquets she held, a yellow rose surrounded by white baby's breath and green ferns tied with a royal blue ribbon.

He knew where she was. From the moment he had arrived, he knew where she was. His determination to keep his distance from her weakened with each glimpse of her pale lavender dress moving with a feminine dignity through the crowd. Each time the soft curve of her cheek graced the camera lens, his resolve diminished. With each deepening of her furrowed brow, as if the ache now pierced her soul, he renewed his promise to take care of her.

He found her still standing near the yellow rope, facing the Tarmac, her back still straight as a ramrod. He waited quietly, some distance behind her. Her shoulders lifted slightly.

She had sacrificed so much in loving Joe. It wasn't necessary for her to know the full extent. He would protect her from that. He would not hurt her again.

She swung around, spotted him, then turned back toward the airstrip.

He went to her side. "Tori."

"I really don't want to talk to you. That was your prerogative last night. Now it's mine."

He held the rose before her. "Tim and Linda sent this over for you."

She took it from him. "These are only for wives and daughters and girlfriends." Her voice was barely audible.

"I'm sorry Joe can't give it to you." He watched her profile, saw her still the quivering lower lip between her teeth. *How many tears must this woman cry?* "I think it's customary to receive a hug with this bouquet." Before she could respond, he pulled her to himself and enveloped her in his arms.

"This isn't fair." Her voice was muffled in his shirt. "This has

got to be the single most vulnerable moment in my entire life."
She slid her arms around his waist.

He rested his chin atop her soft hair. The clean scent of a
rain-washed summer day filled his nostrils. "Tori, you are the
most beautiful woman I've ever met."

She took a step backward and looked up at him. "Okay, vulnerable moment over. I'm fine now. I need to greet Tim." He saw
anger flicker in her eyes before she walked away.

He had glimpsed her strength today, the stuff of which she
was made, and knew it was not a given that she would respond
favorably to his apology. He would explain about last night, certainly, but her sense of righteous independence could easily nix
his attempts to promote a friendship.

His rehearsed explanation that the blonde was an acquaintance—what was her name?—whom he had invited as a favor
to his sister sounded hollow now in his mind. It was a half-truth.
In reality he had latched onto the first good-looking female to
walk through the door in an effort to divert his growing feelings
for Tori.

Ignoring her at the buffet table last night had been the most
flagrant act of disrespect he'd ever committed. Not being near
her this past week served only to heighten his awareness of her.
When confronted with her presence, the clear choice had been
to either wrap her in his arms for eternity or ignore her.

He wavered. The thought of admitting as much to her
seemed appropriate. When a man could think of only one
woman, preferred her company to anyone else's, got up in the
morning with the hope he would hear her laugh that day, didn't
he tell her so? And yet . . .

The old familiar chill settled again in his chest. Not feeling
was better. Emotional shutdown was—

"Oh, Erik, there you are! I've been looking for you."

He turned to see Helen Anderson, the white-haired editor
of the community newspaper where Tori and Linda worked. She
was an exuberant woman with a friendly but aggressive nature.

She now linked her arm with his and steered him toward another area of the hangar.

"Would you be willing to give us an interview? We like to do human interest articles about local people who are engaged in some unusual activity. I've never heard of anyone in our area who has taken a leave of absence from his international trade in order to coach Little League."

"Well, I'm not really a local."

"Oh, pshaw! Everyone is a local for a season in southern California. Vietnam is in the news again. Would you happen to know anything about that?"

"You're good at what you do, Helen." He smiled down at her.

She shrugged. "Simple deduction. What do you say? I'll assign my best writer—Tori. She's going to need a new project after today." She stopped, glanced around, then leaned toward him. "Say," she said in a low voice, "you could take her to dinner tonight, give the interview at a nice, quiet restaurant over on the coast. She likes that one in Del Mar with the patio right on the beach."

"Is that a matchmaker hat you're wearing?"

"No, son, just the efficient hat of a friend and editor. The girl needs a diversion, and I need an article."

"And I need . . . ?" he prompted.

Helen laughed. "As far as I can see, not a thing, not a thing. But a conversation with Tori Jeffers is always worth the price of admission. Come on, let's see if you can talk her into it."

"Me? That's your job!"

"You surprise me, Erik. I figured you were man enough for the challenge."

Her unabashed manipulation amused him. He was curious to see if she could convince Tori to do the interview. They found her in animated dialogue with Linda and Tim. Doubt slowed his steps. He wasn't in the same league as this naval officer. Had Joe been of the same caliber? Of course he had been.

Helen motioned to Tori. "I'm sorry to interrupt, dear, but I need to talk with you before I leave."

"What is it, Helen?"

At the sound of her voice, he knew there wasn't even a question about whether or not he would participate in the editor's plan.

"Erik and I have been chatting, and I've decided to run an article about his involvement with the Vietnam negotiations. Well, whatever he can tell us about it, that is. And, of course, about his coaching. I'd like you to do it."

Tori's face sobered. She appeared tired. "But—"

"We really could use it next week, so the sooner you get to it, the better."

"Helen, I—"

"Now, now, it's what you do best. I can't give it to anyone else." Helen clasped Tori's hands. "Honey, I know today has been horrendously difficult for you. The best antidote is to start something new."

She hesitated, still not looking toward him. "All right. I'll get to it Tuesday."

Erik cleared his throat. "Tuesday's not good for me. How about now? We could take a drive, then have dinner. I know a restaurant in Del Mar with a patio right on the beach."

She glanced at him, then looked toward Linda, who was hugging her husband. "The boys . . . It's too late to find a sitter. And I obviously can't ask my neighbors."

He sensed her defenses were worn down and that this was probably the true vulnerable moment. He threw up his last shot. "Susanne is home." *And she owes me,* he added to himself. "Nick will be there about 4. You know how glad he would be to have the boys there." He knew he'd hit a soft spot.

"Then it's settled," Helen announced. She kissed Tori's cheek. "Take tomorrow off, dear." Turning toward Erik, she gave him a covert thumbs-up sign while offering her other hand to shake, mouthed a "thank you," then flashed him a victory grin. "Good-bye, Erik. It has been a pleasure."

They rode in silence toward the coast. Erik didn't know how to begin and so just concentrated on the traffic, content with the fact that she sat in his car, grateful that they'd even made it to this point. After a time he noticed that she was asleep, her legs curled up, her face resting sideways toward him on the back of the seat.

He felt a warmth melting the edges of the chill.

Before Helen had left Miramar, she'd announced their plans to those present. Other arrangements were quickly made. Someone lived near Susanne, so they would drop off Dan and Dave. Co-workers who had car-pooled offered to drive Tori's car home so they wouldn't have to backtrack. Tori gave up her keys only after Erik retrieved the soft attaché bag she always carried that contained her notebook and tape recorder. Tim and Linda grinned as if in approval. But of course they hadn't stopped grinning all afternoon. On the telephone even Erik's sister, in a rare good mood, immediately agreed to cooperate and even gave him the name of the restaurant along with detailed directions and an offer to make reservations for him.

He chuckled now to himself. If Tori had had her wits about her, she would've accused them all of conspiracy. He parked the car. She didn't stir. He resisted the urge to brush hair from her cheek. That might break the spell. She was lovely, especially in sleep, without that facade of independence she usually kept in place before him, shutting him out. That's what made her so different from any woman he'd ever known. He didn't want to be shut out; he wanted to protect her from the world. But it was more than that. Wasn't it that she, in her innocence, offered him protection from the world? He would have to tell her somehow.

"Tori?"

She blinked, sat up, and squinted at the windshield, rubbing an eye with the back of her hand. "I need to walk." With swift movements she slipped off her shoes, then jumped from the car. He heard a whispered "Ouch!" when her bare feet hit the pavement.

He climbed out. "I'll tell them to hold a table for us on the patio."

As she walked gingerly across the parking lot toward the beach, she lifted an arm in silent reply.

"You can tell them to hold a table in Timbuktu," Tori muttered to herself. "Ouch!" A stone lodged itself under a toe. "It would make about as much sense. Oh, what on earth am I doing here?"

She stepped onto the beach. The grainy sand felt soft underfoot after the pebbly concrete. Trudging to the ocean's edge, she took a deep breath of the salty air and noticed the sun was not yet near the horizon. This was such a long day. Exhaling a deep sigh, she headed north.

That hug really wasn't fair, Lord. Why him? He doesn't care about me. Why not Allen? Why couldn't he have been there right then when I needed that? And why dinner? At this restaurant, my favorite of favorites?

Oh, why did You let him die? And why do I still ask You that?

When the why questions about Joe began to replay, she knew it was time to push the Off button. There were no answers this side of heaven, and to continue pounding on that closed door was a waste of energy. She walked briskly, arms swinging wide, wondering if she would have to march all the way to Camp Pendleton before her head cleared.

The sandpipers playing tag with the waves caught her eye. She heard the rhythmic rushing ocean and the seagulls' mournful song.

The day had been good. Exhausting, but that good sort of emotionally-stretching exhaustion that comes when something abstract but significant has been accomplished. Danny and David had thanked her again when they said good-bye. They didn't seem to need her as they merrily went on their way. It was like the closing of a chapter. She felt a twinge of regret and yet at the same time as if she possessed new freedom to . . . Well, to just move on.

To move on. I suppose that means accepting Allen as the good friend he is and not fabricate a role for him. And accepting the boys' growing-up stages. And, okay, even accepting Erik Steed as a friend

because he gives so much to Danny and David. Make that acquain-
tance. Temporary acquaintance. He'll be leaving soon.

As she neared the cliffs, she noticed the tide was in, blocking her route. This would have to be far enough. She turned
around with another sigh.

He does have an uncanny ability to show up at the right moment
with a solid hug, though. I guess that should promote him to semi-
friend. Temporary, semi-friend. I can live with that.

Speaking of friends, she reflected, Helen was right. A fresh
project would help. But they were ahead of schedule with
human interest features. Why this particular interview? And
why especially did it have to be done today of all days? Normally
her editor was an intelligent, caring woman who . . . who knew
exactly what she was doing.

Okay, Lord.

She spotted Erik sitting on the low concrete wall that divided
the beach from the parking lot. Walking toward him, she noticed
her attaché bag, purse, and shoes with the anklets tucked into
them arranged neatly beside him. The absence of his lopsided grin
tugged at her. Maybe this world-wise man needed a temporary
semi-friend too. She hoisted herself up onto the wall, crossed her
legs, and began brushing sand from one bare foot.

"Tori, are you all right? You're so quiet."

"I'm just trying to figure out how to conduct an interview
with a person who tends to ignore me when I speak to him." She
yanked on a sock.

"I can explain last night—"

"Oh, no need to!" She uncrossed, then re-crossed her legs to
dust off the other foot. "Pompous-natured men often have these
lapses in etiquette. Now, about this interview—"

"I didn't want to face you after the way I behaved that night
Allen left us."

She slipped on a shoe, uncrossed her legs, then sat quite still.

"When I saw you last night, I knew I had to make one of two
choices. Either pretend you weren't there or hide under the buffet table because I was too ashamed to face you and I didn't know

how to explain." He pushed himself from the wall and stood before her. "And pompous-natured men, no matter how large the lapse in etiquette, simply do not hide under buffet tables."

She raised her head to meet his gaze. "There's no buffet table here." A lump in her throat constricted her voice.

"Then you'll let me try to explain?"

She nodded.

He leaned forward, bracing his hands atop the wall on either side of her. "The thought of you marrying for convenience sake angered me. I reacted without thinking. I am sorry, so sorry, for kissing you in that underhanded way and saying those despicable things. I promise you it will never happen again."

In an instant she knew she could marry no one else as long as Erik Steed looked at her in that manner, his eyes full of hope and caring. "Why would what I do with my life anger you? You barely know me."

"What I know is that you are a special woman whom I admire very much."

"I forgive you."

"Are you sure, Tori? This is me, the pompous snob."

Her mouth twitched, and she nodded.

"Can we be friends?"

"Well, it depends, Mr. Steed. If Allen proposes, will you give me away at my wedding?"

"You drive a hard bargain, lady. I think there's a position for you in my company."

"That's my bottom line. What's your answer?"

"All right. Yes!" He smiled. "Yes, I will give you away at your wedding if Allen proposes."

"And what's your bottom line?"

He sobered. "Mine?" He focused his eyes somewhere beyond her shoulder. "When Linda gave me her camera, I looked through the telephoto lens and watched a beautiful woman work through one of the most difficult situations of her life with such dignity and character that it took my breath away. And I thought that if she never smiled at me again or welcomed me into her safe harbor of a home, my life would indeed be lacking."

When the pounding of her heart slowed, she had to clear her throat before the words became audible. "A smile and supper?"

He grinned down at her, the lopsided grin. "Is it too much?"

She laughed and slipped her arms around his neck. The world-wise man needed more than a temporary semi-friend.

"Umm, hugs are good too."

He wrapped his arms around her.

They sat across from each other at an outdoor table. Mounds of sand lay just on the other side of a low wall, level with the table-top, on which Tori set her recorder. The small dining patio, bordered on three sides by beach, was a popular place tonight, but she could hear the muted rhythmic pounding of waves.

The early evening air thickened like a canopy of damp salt and sand. In the distant northwest horizon, just beyond Erik's right shoulder, the sun's orange glow dimmed. Their waiter lit a small hurricane lamp before leaving with their order.

"Tori, are you sure you're up for this?"

She snapped a cassette into place and smiled at him. "Helen is a wise woman."

"I think you're a wise woman to have taken Dan and Dave to the fly-in."

"It's a part of their heritage, but I had to spend a lot of time praying about it. I really didn't want to do it." She shrugged a shoulder.

"You put a lot of stock in faith, don't you?"

"Well, in Christ I do. Losing my husband at the age of twenty-three still doesn't make sense. It still hurts, and I am still fearful of change and of not being in control. But the fact is, God is in control, He loves me, and He's always there."

Erik turned his head toward the ocean, his mouth a grim line.

"One time I stood with Joe under his F14. He explained all

about how the wings move, how their different positions were best for a particular maneuver. When he was flying, he'd think about me being under the shadow of those wings, protected. He said it's like trusting God. No matter where we are or what happens, God just moves His wings, keeping us in the shadow of His love, maneuvering everything into the best possible position."

"It sounds like you've got it all neatly figured out."

Tori noted his bitter tone. "It keeps me going. Hey, I'm supposed to do the interviewing." He looked at her then. On impulse she reached over and with her fingertips smoothed the wrinkles from his forehead. "It won't hurt much, I promise."

He smiled. "Sorry. I was somewhere else."

"Okay." She turned on the tape recorder, then poised her pen above a small notebook on the table. "So why wasn't Tuesday good for you?"

"Tuesday? Oh, I'll be in Washington."

"You seem to be picking up the pace rather quickly."

"We opened an office in Hanoi last month."

"I didn't realize the United States is back in Vietnam. What exactly do you do?"

"You mean besides coach Little League and take beautiful, violet-eyed mothers to dinner?"

Much better. She rolled her eyes.

"All right." He took a deep breath. "My grandfather, father, and uncle developed an international trading company about thirty-five years ago, back in the fifties. My cousin and I joined on after college. We're based in San Francisco and conduct business in the Far East."

"And that business is to . . . ?"

"To act as a liaison between countries."

"Which means?"

"Well, for example, when a foreign dealer wants to purchase an American-made tractor, he talks to us, and we talk to the U.S. manufacturers. We specialize in the details of foreign trade so they don't have to."

"Foreign trade sounds like federal government. Are you involved at that level?"

"Yes. We communicate with State Department officials and congressmen and lobbyists in order to remain current."

"And what about the foreign side of things?"

"My father attributes our success to personally knowing everyone on both sides of the world, in business as well as in government. He insists we be well-versed in foreign customs as well as American politics."

"So you travel overseas?" She looked up from her notepad. "And speak, what, Japanese?"

"Some. And French and Vietnamese."

"Oh, don't miss it!" She pointed behind him.

Erik's gaze followed her finger. "What?"

"The sunset. It's absolutely breathtaking. Every time." Tori watched in silence for the few moments it took the sun to slip into the ocean. When she turned back, his eyes were on her face. "No wonder you're stressed out, racing around the world speaking four languages and not watching sunsets."

A faint smile crossed his lips. "Guilty."

She studied his dark-lashed eyes. "Do you miss it?"

"To a certain extent. Though I must admit the three-month hiatus has been good." The waiter served their salads. "This will be interesting. I imagine you can take notes, ask questions, and eat at the same time?"

"And flip the cassette. Erik, how will you go back to it and not end up in the same condition?"

Studying the fork in his hand, he shrugged. "There's so much to be done." He spoke as if to himself.

"I can't understand why men insist on pushing themselves into the grave in the name of business."

Erik looked at her, then quietly explained, "We offer a service that provides equipment that raises the standard of living for millions of people."

"I'm sorry. I just can't comprehend the millions when I see

one close-up sacrificing himself. Can't you spread the work around?"

"Thanks for the concern. I have learned to delegate more of the responsibilities since I've been here, out of commission. What I've delegated out, I don't plan to take back immediately." He paused. "But there are some things, peripheral to the company, that no one cares enough about to put in the necessary time or effort to achieve."

"Why you?"

"Let's just say I've maneuvered myself into a unique position that no one else is interested in joining."

"Can you be more specific? Or does this have to do with what Helen mentioned? Something secret about Vietnam?"

He pushed aside his unfinished salad plate. "It's public knowledge that unofficial negotiations pave the way for official negotiations."

"So you're involved with that and I can print it?"

"Yes. I won't tell you anything you can't use, but it'll be up to you to judge what's necessary to include."

His cryptic words made her hesitate. "Well, the purpose of this article is to entertain and inform. Our readers enjoy learning about an unusual member of the community. So just the fact that you're involved in these negotiations is interesting. But how is that connected with your family business?"

"It's complex. Within the company we play different roles. Grandfather groomed me as the expert on international law and political connections. During the past few years most of my energies have been spent lobbying for the removal of the Vietnamese trade embargo."

Tori stared at her white knuckles around the pen. "Why Vietnam?"

"We had traded there for years. In 1961 President Kennedy created the Agency for International Development, which allowed us to provide farm and industrial equipment during the war. The equipment is still there, in need of repair, worthless because we can't get replacement parts into the country."

"So if you move back in, your company will make a bundle?"

"You know, for a journalist you do have a bad habit of interrupting and jumping to opinionated conclusions."

She scrunched her nose and looked up at him. "I know. When Linda does photos for me, she's always trying to keep me on track." The waiter arrived with their entrees. "She'll walk by and poke me with her elbow or test her flash right in my face."

Erik laughed.

"Umm." Tori leaned over her plate and inhaled the fragrant steam of seafood pasta. "This looks wonderful. Okay, let me back up. Vietnam is an emotional issue for me. When Daddy was there, I was between five and seven, so I didn't comprehend it. It just seemed that Mom cried all the time. After he came home, my sisters said he didn't laugh like he used to. My brother argued with him and refused to join the military when his draft lottery number came up 225. I equate it with a bad memory to be forgotten."

"I understand, but not all of us can simply forget it. A stipulation of lifting the embargo is that MIA information will be released. Over 2,000 guys didn't come home, Tori, dead or alive."

She watched his handsome features tense. "Who didn't come home for you?"

"My brother."

"Oh, Erik, I'm so sorry."

He squeezed her arm. "I know. It was almost twenty years ago. I was only fifteen, but Phil meant everything to me. That's why I won't stop until it's finished. No matter what."

"So the office in Hanoi isn't business-related?"

He shook his head.

The interview continued informally after dinner as they strolled the beach under a clear, starlit sky. Though Erik's face was shadowed, Tori knew from the inflection of his deep voice when his eyes crinkled and when they sobered. She'd watched him closely as he answered her questions at the table.

What she had labeled as haughtiness she now saw as confidence in what he was doing and why he did it. When he talked of his work, his face brightened. His heart was in it. She wondered if that was all he loved.

"Erik, shall I include that you're an eligible bachelor?"

He chuckled. "Does 'eligible' mean one is looking to lose his bachelor status? If so, then no."

"Have you ever?"

"No. I had a close call once but haven't found the time to invest in that type of relationship."

"What's a close call?"

"In college, after I quit baseball, my fiancée decided that Major League relations was more her style than international relations. She signed on with some other guy who went pro."

"How did you get started in baseball? Did you play Little League like Danny and David?"

"Sure. Phil taught me, though, from the moment I could walk. He was five years older and loved the game. When he was listed missing, I freaked out. Spent most of my sophomore year of high school stoned. His varsity coach, who was retired by then, got ahold of me, helped me through it, and got me back into the game."

"So Phil played too?"

"Yeah. He went to the University of Arizona on a baseball scholarship for one year, dated the sweetest girl on campus, drew a 360 in the draft lottery—and enlisted with the Marines."

"Why?"

"He said he sensed . . . sensed that he belonged there, as if God had something for him to do there."

Lord, he's blaming You. Please soften his heart.

"He said I'd understand someday." He drew a deep breath. "But I don't."

She walked quietly beside him, wanting to touch him, to absorb some of his pain.

"Thank you, Tori."

"For what?"

"For letting me talk. I haven't talked like this in a long time, especially with such an empathetic ear listening." He took her hand, squeezed, then dropped it. "It feels good."

"Just part of the therapy we offer here in Rancho Lucido for stressed-out businessmen who break a leg while skiing to relax. But next time you gotta watch the sunset!"

Tori stood outside the house of Erik's sister where the boys had spent the night, listening to the cavernous echo of door chimes, and looked around the neighborhood. She noted that the yards were more spacious here than on her street. Tall mansion-sized houses of whitewashed stucco and red-tiled roofs were situated at the far end of neatly manicured lawns and circular, mosaic rock drives. Everything was surrounded by an array of lush, tropical plants with a backdrop of rough, boulder-strewn, dry, brown hills.

She shivered in the misty, early-morning cool. Last night's sunset and Erik's smile seemed such a long time ago. This was his world, and she knew it was far removed from anything she'd ever experienced. It really was silly of her to imagine that he needed her for a friend. For a brief moment she considered dashing back into her car and tooting the horn for the boys. He would be gone, already halfway to Washington. There was no need to speak with his snobby sister—who was moving away soon—as if they had something in common like concern for Erik.

That was what intimidated her. It wasn't so much the wealth and power represented by these surroundings. In her heart of hearts she knew these were only material, temporal things and that her lack of them didn't mean she was less of a person. It was the realization that her experiences had not prepared her for fulfilling the needs and desires of a man from this background.

But what did fulfilling needs and desires have to do with their friendship? Their temporary, platonic friendship? Definitely platonic.

One of the tall double doors opened. "Hello." Susanne smiled at her and stepped aside. The resemblance to her brother was startling. Her hair, pulled into a ponytail, matched the deep mahogany color of the doors. She wore a knit, navy blue jump-suit. "Come in. I was out back with the children and thought I heard the doorbell. I hope you don't mind, they've been swim-ming. The pool is heated."

Her friendly manner eased Tori's discomfort. "No problem. Swimming in the morning is a treat for them." She followed the scent of Liz Claiborne across gleaming, white ceramic tiles of the spacious entry and down two steps onto cushy, white carpet. The opposite wall of the open living room was a bay of floor-to-ceil-ing windows.

"I don't like to leave them alone." Susanne stepped through an open French door onto a flagstone patio.

The view Tori had glimpsed through the windows and now saw clearly took her breath away. "Oh, this is magnificent," she breathed. Morning clouds were moving aside to reveal an end-less panorama of distant mountains. Groves of avocado trees dotted the low hills. Amazingly, no neighboring houses were in sight.

"Would you like to buy it?" Her tone was sarcastic. "The sale fell through yesterday. Boys, your mother is here."

The pool lay before them, on a terrace a few steps below the patio. Nicky, Danny, and David waved to her from where they sat on the diving board. "Ten more minutes, Mom? Please?"

Tori walked to the side of the pool. "Well—"

"Mom, can they?" Nicky interrupted.

Susanne smiled again. "Of course. Would you like a cup of coffee, Tori?"

"Sure. Thank you. All right, guys, ten minutes." They yahooed and splashed into the water as she followed Susanne to the end of the concrete terrace. They sat down in padded chairs next to a round, glass-topped table that seemed to hang sus-pended in space. Only a wooden railing separated it from a steep incline. Erik's sister was polite and friendly in a cool sort of way, but Tori sensed an edginess about her. "Are you sure we're not interfering with your schedule?"

Susanne poured coffee from a carafe into two mugs. "Here, try some. It's a wonderful mocha almond. Erik hates it. No, you're not interfering in the least. The only thing I have planned for today— since there's no school or baseball—is to sort through Nick's things with him. It has to be done. We have to decide which things to put into storage and which to take with us to my parents' home. We'll be living with them until I find a house." She sighed. "I can't believe I'm moving in with my parents at this stage of my life. But it's better than staying in this town."

"This must be a very painful time for you."

Susanne's face softened. "It is."

"I'm sorry."

"That's kind of you." She lifted a shoulder. "These things happen. By the way, Erik said the interview went well. He thought if you needed some details to fill in gaps, I might be of assistance."

"Well, that would be helpful." Tori's mind went blank. "Um, perhaps something along more personal lines that he wouldn't have told me."

Susanne sipped her coffee. "You know he's been interviewed by all kinds of newspapers and magazines, usually about international business."

"I didn't realize that." *Thank goodness*, she added to herself, grateful for the safe topic. "He's well-known in the business world?"

"Yes, and respected. I've always been very proud of him. He's a good man."

"The boys on the team think he's a great coach. Besides teaching them baseball, he knows how to make each of them feel special. Has he worked with children before?"

"No. He's always been close to Nick though. Closer than his father, actually. He once flew from Singapore to be at his birthday party."

"Hey, Mom!" Danny yelled. "We're getting out now. It's freezing!"

Tori waved. "Thank you for keeping the boys last night. Erik insisted it was not an inconvenience for you, but I apologize for not speaking directly to you."

"Oh, no problem. It was my pleasure. Nick talks about them all the time. It was nice to get to know them. They're so friendly and polite. I hope you don't mind if I smoke." She pulled a cigarette and lighter from a pocket. "It disturbs Nick, so I won't when he's around, but it helps my nerves."

"Are you and Erik twins? You look so much alike."

"Except he doesn't smoke." Susanne smiled. "The resemblance is remarkable, isn't it? He's two years younger and has none of my vices. We've been close, though, always good friends. He's been such a help to me here now." She turned her head slightly, but not before Tori noticed the tears shimmering in her blue eyes.

"Then he would've come even if he hadn't broken his leg?"

"That's a good question. I think so, for my sake, but not for such a length of time. He makes himself available for those he cares about, when needed, even though he works nonstop twenty-four hours a day, seven days a week. I should say, used to work. The accident definitely forced him to slow down." She inhaled on her cigarette.

"He seems to be getting back into the swing of things. New York two weeks ago. Now Washington."

"I imagine Vietnam is on the agenda too," she sighed. "He just hasn't told me yet. The real change, though, is his demeanor. It's calmer than it's been in years. And he smiles. Oh, he has his lapses. The night they lost a game, he was an absolute bear. Nick adores him, but not that evening. He always was too serious about baseball. Did he tell you about Chantal?"

"Uh, no." Tori was having a difficult time following Susanne's train of thought.

"That's the last time he smiled like this. They were an item for a while—three, no, four years ago. She was a journalist, tall and blonde, related to old money back east. She wrote several business and political articles about him. *Newsweek* published one. Another was for *San Francisco Focus*. She photographed him in his apartment and emphasized the fact that he was a wealthy, eligible bachelor."

"I asked him if I should include in this article that he's an eligible bachelor. I think he said he was an ineligible bachelor."

Susanne laughed. "I've tried matching him up with suitable women for years. I was thrilled when he took Britt out last week, but I just don't think he's interested. He never married, never even lived with a woman. The company and all that Vietnam business is his life." She leaned over and stubbed out the cigarette on a large, decorative rock, then flicked it over the railing. "Our parents have made it so far, but they're rooted in the tradition that no matter what, you stay married. Not that they've spent much time together with Dad living overseas more than at home. Erik has watched friends' marriages fall apart, and now mine. He has no reason to believe in it."

"Mom, we're ready."

Tori turned to see David walking toward her. She stood. "Well, thank you for the coffee, Susanne. We'd better go."

Danny joined them at the front door where they told Nick good-bye. In the car Tori noted, "Hey, guys, thanks for skipping the can't-we-stay-another-ten-minutes whine."

Danny, unusually subdued, didn't respond. David looked at her soberly. "I just wanted to go home."

"Yeah?" She gave him an understanding smile. "Me, too."

A short time later she sat at the desk in her bedroom, staring at the blank computer screen, replaying the interview tape over and over in an attempt to recapture the spirit of Erik that his sister had obliterated. At the bottom of the monitor she taped a photo of him, taken by Linda, with his baseball cap pushed back, grinning after a close game they'd won. They could print this photo of him with the article. His physical appearance would speak for itself. Even in black and white the blue eyes danced. The lopsided grin only emphasized the symmetry of his broad cheekbones and square jaw.

Tori imagined him on the beach, his face close to hers, talking about her safe harbor of a home and her smile. She prayed for insight. It took a while, but at last Susanne's cold eyes and heavy sadness diminished.

In recent months Erik had obviously been going through significant change, prompted by his accident. She reviewed what she knew of his life. He had played baseball well enough to become a professional. Forced to change athletic as well as marriage plans, he had immersed himself in the business and government arenas. The family's international trading company flourished as he gradually assumed his grandfather's role. His drivenness, energy, and ability to speak foreign languages were not only assets for business—they'd also enabled him to devote much time and effort to the MIA/POW cause.

It sounded as if he never stopped for recreation. His sister said he was well-known and respected, but did he have good friends, the kind that said, "You need time off, let's go skiing"? It was his father and uncle who more or less ordered him to do that, but he went alone. She shuddered at the thought of him crumpled in the cold snow, in pain, with only strangers to offer comfort and help.

Only after collapsing a short time later in the office did he recognize that he could do no more in his own strength. He remained in the hospital that time for a week of tests and then spent almost a month in his parents' home, where his mother treated him as she had when he was a stubborn four-year-old. He acknowledged that it was time to leave town; so he moved to San Diego to help his sister. The time off had served to calm him, but he felt it was the coaching that finally gave him a true sense of relaxation and pleasure.

Tori knew that was because of what he gave to the boys—baseball skills and unconditional love. In the giving of what he had been given, Erik had begun the process of giving himself away and receiving joy in return. The natural talent was innate, but the skills were learned, the love received. Who had—? Phil, of course. They must have been gifts from his brother.

She began to write about Erik Steed, a most unusual man.

—Eight—

AS SHE STEPPED from her front door, Tori saw Erik park his Blazer down the street and climb out. They walked toward each other, meeting on the sidewalk in front of Tim and Linda's house. For a moment only the chirrup of a bird's evensong interrupted the stillness.

"Hi." She smiled at him.

"Hi." He smiled back.

They stood looking at each other, as if unsure how to begin after parting in a friendly manner for the first time six nights ago.

"You're late, Mr. Steed."

"Then you must be early, Mrs. Jeffers."

"That should make us right on time for Linda's dinner schedule. Oh, I saw you in the *L.A. Times* this week, page 8."

He raised his eyebrows.

"They quoted 'an unnamed person' who attended some closed session in Washington, D.C. regarding MIAs."

His face remained expressionless.

"Was it you?"

The corner of his mouth lifted. "No comment."

"Well, how did things go for you in Washington?"

"Stressfully and nonproductively. Ah, I see you're bearing goodies as usual. Let me take that." He took the wicker basket from her, then lifted her left hand and examined it. "Whew."

"What do you mean, 'whew'?"

"Allen didn't propose."

She yanked her hand back and headed toward the house. "Oh, Allen is so horribly unromantic. He wants me to choose the ring. Just gave me his credit card. Imagine that!" She pushed open the front door and stepped inside, calling out, "We're here!"

"I guess that goes with the territory," he commented.

"What territory?"

"The marriage of convenience territory."

Tori saw the laughter shining in his eyes. "At least I get to choose exactly what I want."

"You're right. You can't do that with the romantic guys. Unless they're not paying very close attention. What exactly do you want?"

She laid a hand on his shoulder and leaned toward him, enunciating each word in an exaggerated way. "A huge, flashy diamond." They burst into laughter.

Tori noticed Linda standing in the kitchen doorway, an odd expression on her face, her eyes opened unnaturally wide. "Linda, we're here!"

"So I see. Come on in. Tim and the kids are out back. Well, except for Kelsey; she's on the phone. I'm sorry Nick couldn't come, but of course he'd want to go with his mother house-hunting in San Francisco." She was almost babbling. "What's in the basket?" Erik handed it to her. "Tor, I told you not to bring anything."

"Just some baked goodies for you all. Not for tonight. And they're from Erik, too, since he's," she narrowed her eyes at him, "empty-handed. I told Linda you're rude and shouldn't be invited. Allen would have brought flowers or—"

"Oh, I did bring flowers! I'll be right back."

She giggled at his retreating back. "All right, you passed the first test. We'll let you stay for hors d'oeurves." She followed Linda into the kitchen. "What's wrong, sweetie?"

Her friend set the basket on the counter and twisted her fingers around its handle. "For a minute in there—" Her hand flew to her mouth, her brown eyes welled. "Oh, Tor, I thought it was you and Joe. You were giggling and talking, and the way you yelled 'We're here' . . . I didn't know where I was, what year it was. It just struck me how alone you are and have been for so long, and I forget and I'm so sorry."

Tori put her arms around her.

Erik walked in. "Uhh, excuse me. Can I do anything?"

Tori shook her head. Words caught in her throat, so she simply waved him toward the sliding screen door. She watched him set a bouquet of flowers on the table and walk outside and across the patio to the small grassy area. A smiling Tim greeted him with a handshake. Danny, David, and Matt raced at him, almost tackling him with their exuberant hugging.

"Well, Miss Matchmaker, you're certainly doing all you can to change my situation. You got me here on this semi-date with my semi-friend."

"But you don't even like him!" Linda backed away and pulled a tissue from the pocket of her shorts. "Do you?"

"I'm wondering when to trust other people's judgment over my own. We have nothing in common, but you like him. The boys obviously like him. We'll see what Tim thinks. Allen likes him. Actually, Allen likes him a lot. He broke our engagement last night, by the way."

Linda giggled while blowing her nose. "Oh, Tor, are you devastated?"

"A little bit. He spent the entire evening expounding the virtues of Erik Steed! Not one word about our relationship. It was as if he were my big brother and I had asked him— which I hadn't—what he thought of some man I was interested in."

"Ooh, I hope you're interested in Coach Steed, Aunt Tor." Thirteen-year-old Kelsey breezed into the kitchen, stopping only long enough to plant a kiss on Tori's cheek on her way out to the backyard. "He's a hunk."

"Add Kelsey to the list. Can I help?"

"Yes. Will you take these plates to the picnic table?"

Tim slid open the door. "Hi, Tori." He gave her a quick hug. "He's a keeper. Honey, shall I take the hamburgers now?"

Linda handed him a platter and winked at her friend.

Tori dried her hands and surveyed the tidy kitchen. The men were still outside talking, the children playing hide-and-seek in the dark.

"Do you want some coffee?" Linda came from the hallway, carrying a small box that she set on the table.

"No, thanks. This has been fun, a relaxing evening. What's in there?"

Her friend removed the lid and pulled out a handful of 8 x 10 photos. "From the fly-in. These are the best." She spread them around the table. "Do you like the effect? I used black-and-white film before Tim landed, then color afterwards. Erik did most of these. He's very good."

"You must have been in your darkroom all week. Oh, my," she breathed. There were close-ups of her talking with friends, walking through the crowd, standing alone with an obviously anxious expression on her face.

"I can read your mind in these, Tor. Look, this is my favorite. Was that when they were landing?"

Unlike the others, it was in color. She knelt between the boys, hugging their waists, her mouth shaped around a word, her eyes bright.

"He loves you."

Tori shoved aside the photos.

"Why do you refuse to see it?"

Startled by Linda's vehemence, the harsh words tumbled out. "Because I will not live like you and Tim do. Never again. Erik travels all over the world, all the time." She bit her lip. "And most importantly, he doesn't have faith in Christ."

"We really don't know. He's hurting about something, Tor. And he's searching for the answer."

"How do you know that?"

"Tim just told me. We met in the bathroom. Don't dismiss him yet. Let him love you now. He could be gone tomorrow. He could be dead tomorrow!" She jumped up and rushed down the hall.

Tori's heart pounded in her throat. Why would Linda say that to her? Shadows tugged at the fringes of her mind. It was as if some dark, unnamed reality was searching for a way into her consciousness.

She found Linda in her bedroom, sitting on the bed, hugging her knees to her chest. "This isn't about Erik, is it?"

She shook her head. "Oh, Tori, I'm sorry." She took a deep breath. "We're moving!"

Tori stared at her. Now the dark reality had a name.

"The kids don't know yet . . . To Rhode Island . . . In four weeks."

"For certain?"

Linda nodded.

An expletive in reference to the Navy escaped Tori's lips. She immediately apologized.

"It's our decision, Tor. Tim asked for a position here, but there isn't one. He's going to teach, and we'll be together. No more six-month cruises."

Tori swallowed. "Then it's good. It's good." She hugged her friend. "Hey, are you okay?"

Linda blew her nose and wiped her eyes. "I will be. I don't want to leave you."

"I know, but your family comes first. You're not responsible for me." Tori stood. "Do you still want the boys to spend the night?"

"Tim wants them."

"Then I think I'll go. Now." She walked to the door.

"Tori—"

"I don't want to talk about it. I just need some time alone. Tell the boys to come home when they get up tomorrow."

"What about Erik?"

"Whatever. It doesn't matter." She hurried from the room, then out the front door.

The dark reality filled her now. It had a name, but no form, nothing to grab hold of so she could pull it away. Like ocean waves, it washed over her, a heaviness bearing her down, icy tendrils coiling around her chest and throat until at last she cried out, "Oh, God!"

In quick successive movements she yanked off one tennis shoe at a time, then flung them down the hall. As they hit her bedroom door, thuds punctuated anguished shouts of "Why, God? Why Linda?"

The silence of the empty house added weight to the dark reality.

Spinning on her heel, she hurried to flip on every lamp in the front room, then rushed to do the same in the kitchen. She switched on the stereo, turning the volume to high until rock and roll music reverberated off the walls.

"Everything will be all right," Tori comforted herself as she stomped to the hallway. "It's not like it's the first time. It's not like I didn't know it would happen again."

The monologue continued while she turned lights on in the bedrooms. In her room she halted, taking deep breaths. Still her heart raced.

There would be no respite from the dark reality tonight. The only option was to ride out the storm with . . . prayer? She was doing that. Food? Her stomach churned. A book? Impossible. Memories? Yes, but not in the abstract. She had to touch them. The photographs taken when they were together. The letters written when they were apart. The myriad of teenage trivia pressed between scrapbook pages.

With jerky movements, she dragged the desk chair from her room and down the hallway, then yanked open a linen closet door, talking aloud to herself all the while. "You've had her here for four years. That's a long time. That's centuries in military time." She climbed on the chair, reaching for the top shelf, shoving aside shoeboxes of letters. Fury coursed through her veins.

A box fell to the floor. She surveyed the spilled contents of bundled letters tied with yellow ribbons, then turned back to rummage among notebooks and file boxes.

The music stopped.

"Tori!" Erik's voice thundered through the house.

With an explosive "Oh!" and a sweep of her arm, she cleared the shelf. Everything landed at Erik's feet.

"What's going on?"

Turning back to the closet, she quickly surveyed the other shelf. The scrapbooks weren't here. They must be with the photo albums in the family room, in the built-in cabinet.

"Tori?"

"What!" she snapped as she jumped from the chair.

"What's wrong?"

She brushed past him. "It's none of your business."

Erik grabbed her arm. "Hey, I thought we were friends."

"I don't need you!" Tori yanked away from his grasp and brushed past him to the family room. Kneeling behind the table, she opened the cupboard door, pulled out a large, flat box, and threw off the lid. It was all here—memories of a friendship rooted fifteen years ago.

Her hand fell upon a photo album. From the first page Joe, Tim, a tot-sized Kelsey, and Linda and herself, both obviously pregnant, smiled up at her.

"I think we should talk about this."

Her head jerked up. Erik stood above her, holding a bundle of letters tied in a yellow ribbon.

"Don't touch those!" she screamed and flew to her feet.

He tossed them onto the table. "When are you going to bury him, Tori?"

The blow of his words knocked the breath from her. "You have no right to say that to me!"

"I think I do." He glared down at her. "I made the mistake

of going to Tim and Linda's tonight. You resent me for taking Joe's place."

"That's not true!"

"Of course it is. You leave without saying a word to anyone, not even your kids, then come home and dig up his letters and pictures. I apologize, Tori. I'm not trying to take his place."

"Ha! Don't flatter yourself."

His eyes narrowed. "Isn't it about time you stopped worshiping him?"

"I don't worship him!" The pounding of her heart echoed in her ears. She held clenched fists at her sides. Hysteria scraped her throat raw as she shrieked, "He left! I did everything by myself! I gave birth to those babies by myself! I moved us across the country by myself! I kept up houses and yards by myself! I didn't need him then, and I don't need him now. And I don't need Allen. And I certainly don't need you!" She rushed past him.

"You'll never find a man good enough for you, will you?" He followed her into the front room.

She spun on her heel. "For what purpose? So I can watch him walk away like Joe did? Like my family? Like Linda now? There are only so many disappointments I can take in one lifetime! Get out of here!"

"Gladly!" Erik opened the door. "I don't attend pity parties." Stepping outside, he threw over his shoulder, "Give me a call when you grow up."

Tori slammed the door as hard as she could.

The windows rattled, echoing through the empty house.

In one continuous swift motion Tori locked the door, raced to turn on the music again, then plopped on the floor and rummaged through the box.

She wasn't pitying herself. It was her way of coping. She had to get through the night. She couldn't let it just happen; she had to attack it with her own weapons. Instead of trying not to remember, she would inundate her mind with the memories.

She would allow the full weight of disappointment to hit now, so tomorrow she could hold it at arm's length.

After a time of reading old letters and lingering over teenage pictures, she felt tears begin to wash away the hot anger. The phone rang.

"Tori?" It was Tim. "Are you all right? Do you want us to come over?"

"Hunh-uh."

She sniffed through his words of explanation and comfort that ended with, "You're part of our family, you know. Do you want to move east with us?"

As she hung up, fresh waves of sobs engulfed her. All right, so it was a pity party. All right, so she was rehearsing every good-bye she'd ever said in her life. Who cared?

Chills shook her body. She quickly changed into a thick sweatshirt and pants. Box of tissues in hand, she climbed onto the bed and gave in to the hurting. The phone rang again. She counted ten rings. Why didn't the answering machine stop it?

Eleven . . . Twelve. *It's Linda.* Thirteen. *She'll be worried.* Fourteen . . . Fifteen.

At last she lifted the receiver.

"Tori?"

Erik. "I don't want to talk to you," she sniffled.

"Just answer one question. Are Tim and Linda being transferred?"

She only cried harder. How did he know?

"Why didn't you tell me? Why did you let me jump to wrong conclusions?"

"Stop yelling at me! This has nothing to do with you! You wouldn't understand."

"I'm coming over."

"No!"

"You don't have to be alone."

"I want to," she sobbed.

"Well, I don't want you to!"

"I'm fine!"

"I know." His voice softened. "But I'm coming now." The phone clicked.

Tori buried her face in a pillow until the persistent ringing of the doorbell reached her ears above the music. She stumbled to the front room and heard banging on the door.

"Tori! Open this door before I break it down!"

As she unlocked it, Erik pushed his way inside. He shut the door and muttered as he headed past her to the family room, "I'm turning off that noise."

"I need that noise!"

"What you need is to calm down!"

With what felt like physical force, the silence struck her. She tightly folded her arms across her waist in an effort to ease the aching there.

"Tori—"

She shrank from Erik's outstretched hand. "Just go! Leave me alone!"

"Let me hold you."

"No!" She wiped at her burning eyes. As his hand reached for hers, she stepped backwards, crying hoarsely, "Don't you remember? You don't attend pity parties, and that's all this is! I'm just feeling sorry for myself! I'm an immature fool who still believes people should never move away or die!"

"Stop it! I'm sorry for what I said earlier. I didn't know—"

"Who told you?"

"No one. You said 'like Linda now,' referring to people walking out of your life." He took a step closer. "I figured it out. Eventually. Sorry I'm so slow. Tori, it's only natural for you to hurt. There's no getting around that, but you don't have to do it alone."

"Yes, I do!"

"No, you don't. I'm here."

"But you'll walk out. In two weeks you'll walk out, too."

Erik touched her elbow and whispered, "Not tonight. I'm here tonight, sweetheart."

She stiffened as his arms came around her. "I can do it by myself!"

"I know you can. That's not the point."

At the sound of his husky voice muffled in her hair and the touch of his hand caressing her shoulders, something crumpled within her. She leaned into him.

"You're shaking." Erik held her close for several minutes. "You should be in bed. It's after midnight. The kids will be home before you—"

"The kids don't know yet. None of them do."

"I won't say anything. Believe me, Tor, it will be easier on them than on you. They'll all adjust. You need your rest, for them."

"I can't."

"You have to. How about some tea? Warm milk? Pizza?"

She shook her head.

"You're falling asleep on your feet. Sit down." He steered her toward the couch.

"I don't want to!" She pushed his hands away from her shoulders.

Gently but firmly, he took hold of her arms and, as if she were a child, pressed her to sit down.

A violent shudder tore through her. She knew it was fear now, gnawing at the dark reality. Would the nightmare come? Trying to ease the ache in her stomach, she curled up her legs and slid onto her side. "Please don't go," she whispered.

Erik positioned a small pillow under her head and pulled the afghan from the back of the couch to cover her. "I won't, sweetheart. Lie down. Just rest now." He sat on the edge of the coffee table and tenderly brushed hair from her forehead. "I'll be in the family room. I'm here. Just relax."

She laid her hand on his arm. Within moments she fell asleep to his soothing murmurs.

There had been no nightmare this time. No reason to hold her again. His arms almost ached from the weight of the emptiness.

Erik drained his coffee cup and set it on the round, glass-topped table next to the patio chair where he sat, the Sunday morning paper unread on his lap. He closed his eyes against the sun.

"Oh, you're here!" Tori stood next to him. Her small smile matched the note of surprise in her voice.

"I didn't hear you. I've already started the coffee."

"Thanks." She leaned over and quickly kissed his temple. "And thanks for staying."

The scent of summer and rain-washed flowers lingered as she stepped barefoot around the table to the opposite chair. She wore an ankle-length soft white dress, short-sleeved and loose-fitting. Her hair, longer than when they first met, was damp, tucked behind her ears where the amethyst earrings sparkled. Her eyes, those most uncommon violet eyes, were puffy.

"You're welcome."

"Maybe the neighbors will just think I've bought a four-by-six."

He smiled. "I parked my index card in the garage last night. You look particularly lovely this morning."

"It's the earrings." She touched one. Her voice was low, hesitant, as if speaking required more energy than she had available. "I have to go to church."

"Tori, whatever you've signed up to do can be taken care of by others."

"No, it's not that. I have to worship. With other people. With music."

It made no sense to him.

"It's the only way to deal with my anger toward God."

"I don't understand."

"I don't either. I just know from experience that it works. I asked Him all the questions last night. Now I have to accept the situation, even if no answers come."

He looked away, toward the private, grassy yard. White flowering oleander bushes grew along the grayish, worn wooden fence common in this neighborhood. Tall, fragrant eucalyptus trees towered from the steep hillside that led up to a house, unseen from this point. It all felt foreign to him, more foreign than Ho Chi Minh City. He wasn't needed here. She had every-thing in this senseless faith that made so much sense, that sounded so much like Phil's.

"Erik, will you go with me?"

He met the look in her vulnerable eyes.

"I . . . I shouldn't ask, after all you've done for me." She looked down at her hands. Her voice was hoarse. "I'm just so tired, I don't want to drive. Maybe Linda—"

"No, no. I'm glad you can ask me, that you can tell me what you need. That's why I'm here." *Yes*, he repeated to himself, *that's why I'm here*. "I'll go with you." He looked down at his rumpled clothes. He had dozed sitting up in a chair, but still they weren't exactly presentable.

"I told you it's a casual place. Chinos and cotton shirts are acceptable." She came around to him and slid the back of her hand along his cheek. "Stubbles, too. I'll get you a toothbrush."

There were no pews, no organ, no hymnals. Words to songs were projected by an overhead onto a screen. Windows ran the entire width of the front wall except in the center where a simple lectern stood, surrounded by potted ferns. From rows of folding chairs the congregation looked out at a panorama of blue sky and dry, rolling hills of bush-like avocado trees.

It was unlike any church he'd ever been in. By music Tori had meant keyboards, trumpet, flute, and thirty minutes of unin-terrupted singing. With peripheral vision he watched her. She stood close to him, on his right, the top of her head even with his shoulder. Her eyes were closed. Now and then a tear squeezed itself out through the corner. Her voice rose sweetly with the notes.

When they sat, she didn't look at him but touched his fore-arm, like last night, as if reassuring herself that he was still there.

". . . Vietnamese families to the zoo. We'll get the details in next week's bulletin."

Erik skimmed the two-page bulletin on his lap. There was an invitation to attend a potluck at a Vietnamese church with a downtown address.

The pastor began to speak. He was of medium height and had graying hair. His pleasant voice and natural manner caught Erik's attention. His subject matter kept it.

". . . and then David knowingly placed Bathsheba's husband in a situation where he would most likely be killed. That's an impossible event to relate to in today's world, but the point is that although he served God, he made this horrendous mistake. God waited for him to admit it, to ask for forgiveness. Until then David could have no peace."

Erik didn't hear the closing words or prayer or hymn.

"Erik . . ." Her hand slipped around his elbow, and she stretched to speak into his ear. "Do you mind if we skip the greetings and coffee and leave right now?"

Leave. Yes, that would be good. The tightness in his chest was increasing.

He followed her out, down a hall and through a side door that led to the parking lot. She held onto his arm as they walked to his car. He sensed she was exhausted and leaned on him for support. Shaken to the core, he called on every ounce of self-discipline to be the strength she needed, to squeeze her hand, to open doors, to fasten the seat belt when her fingers fumbled, to concentrate on freeway traffic. They drove the fifteen minutes to her house in silence. By the time he parked in her drive, his head was pounding.

"Erik . . ."

He turned to look at her, and a desire to kiss her almost overwhelmed him. He would draw the breath of life from her. The sweet softness of those lips would soothe the pain in his chest, his head.

"Do you remember when we first met, how much I disliked

you?" The corners of her mouth lifted slightly at the memory. "I was wrong. Please forgive me."

"For what, sweetheart?"

"For calling you a pompous snob." She winced.

Leaning over the space between the seats, he put his arm around her and pulled her close, her forehead against his neck. "Oh, but I am one, and worse."

"No, you're not. I couldn't have made it without you last night or this morning. Thank you for caring for me, Harry Harrier."

He chuckled. "You're welcome." Her hair felt like silk beneath his hand. "So now what?"

"Now," she took a deep breath, "now I have to be alone. Okay?"

"Okay."

He watched her walk into the house, taking with her all sense of beauty and purpose and hope. A yawning emptiness filled him.

Nine

TORI CLOSED HER EYES BRIEFLY in another attempt to focus on the grocery list lying on the counter. What else was it she needed for the team picnic tomorrow?

"Mom, why can't we take Matt with?"

"Danny!" she snapped, turning in the stool to see her son standing in the kitchen doorway still wearing a torn T-shirt. "Stop whining! I told you why. They have to visit with the Coopers tonight. We're not their only friends in town. Why haven't you changed yet? By the time we get pizza and groceries, the video store will be closed. This is your special Friday night you're wasting."

"Gee, you don't have to be so grumpy!" He stomped from the kitchen. "We can go to the video store first."

She pressed her lips together. The week had been one long series of conflicting emotions that left her nerves frayed. The initial shock of Linda and Tim's news gave way to a dull ache in her stomach. It greeted her each morning even before the thought shaped its ugly self. At least the children were dealing well with it, just as Erik had predicted.

She chewed on the end of her pen. Why did she think so often of him? She didn't want to, but he was always in the first morning thought and stayed put until late at night when sleep at last hushed her mind. The memory of him—and that's all he was this week, just a memory—softened the harsh reality of her friends leaving.

He had called early Monday morning when she was fixing breakfast for the boys.

"Hi."

"Hi."

"How are you doing? All right?" His tone expressed concern.

"Umhmm." She flipped a pancake. "I'm doing fine. Thank you."

"I'm glad to hear that." He cleared his throat. "Tori, something came up yesterday. I have to spend the week in San Francisco. It can't wait."

She swallowed. *Here we go.*

He'd continued, "I'll miss Thursday night's tournament game, but I know the guys are ready for it. They'll do fine with the other coaches. I plan to be back for Saturday's three o'clock game."

"And the team party?"

"And the team party."

"Oh, Erik, I forgot in all the commotion this weekend to give you the article. We're running it this week, and I really need your approval by tomorrow."

"Fax it to me. I'll get back to you by 9 tomorrow morning. Will that work? Here's the number."

He had faxed in return a note scrawled in bold letters. It was waiting for her when she arrived at the office at 8 on Tuesday morning. "Tori—Excellent writing! Technically accurate. One problem—who is this guy? I hope to meet him soon. ES." She mused to herself, *I guess it's the guy I see.*

That was all she'd heard from him. The twins' little fourth-grade promotion ceremony on the last day of school had come and gone without his presence. The baseball game had been won without his presence. Five days had passed without his presence.

She admitted to herself now that she missed him very much. She missed the husky voice that calmed her deepest fears, the sheer physicalness that was a strength she could touch with her hands. Anticipating his return tomorrow squelched her appetite. These were the most conflicting emotions of all. It meant that the next time he left, it would be worse. And if for any reason he should come back again . . . It was beginning—another long-distance relationship—and she didn't know what to do about it.

The doorbell interrupted her thoughts.

"Boys, are you almost ready?" she called down the hall as she passed it.

She opened the door. Erik stood there. She let out an involuntary, muted cry, and then he was kissing her. The confusion of the week dissipated. It didn't matter now. Like before, nothing mattered except that this man was kissing her.

"Coach is home!" David's voice erupted behind her.

"Yippee!" Danny added his reaction.

The boys thumped into them, one on each side. Erik laughed and seemed able to hug all three of them at once, his face still close to hers.

The boys launched into a play-by-play description of the game he'd missed the previous night. She thought she should quiet them, but her throat constricted, and the words wouldn't form. She watched Erik's eyes dancing through dark lashes as he looked from Danny to David and asked for more details. He wore a cream-colored suit and a hunter-green shirt. His tie, a swirl of colors, felt silky beneath her fingertips. He really was here. *Coach is home. Coach is home.*

"Mom, can Coach come with us?"

"What?" She cleared her throat.

"Coach says he'll help."

"Help what?"

"Get groceries."

"You want to go to the grocery store?"

His eyes rested on her face. "Sure."

"Right now?"

He smiled. "Yes."

"After pizza," Danny interjected.

"Right." After one more bear hug, Erik let them go, shrugged out of his coat, and draped it over a chair. "I'm starving. I didn't eat on the plane." He unbuttoned his collar and loosened the tie, then rolled up his sleeves. "Why don't we take your car? Mine's full of boxes and bags. Susanne insisted I move most of my things out of her house last week, and I didn't have anywhere else to store them."

He offered to drive. A warm sensation rushed through her as she handed him the keys. When was the last time anyone had shared these mundane responsibilities? Driving, choosing pizza, buying groceries, spending the evening fielding Danny's questions and asking David about his science experiments. She couldn't remember, but she relished the feeling of comfort as she sat with him in the front of her station wagon. He even reminded the twins before she could to buckle their seat belts.

With a wink but no comment, he stopped first at the gas station. The boys helped him fill the tank and wash the windows, then directed him to their favorite pizza parlor. The evening progressed as if it were quite natural for the four of them to eat together in a booth, laugh their way through the grocery store, argue over ice cream flavors until Erik threw four cartons into the basket, choose a family comedy video, and carry bags into the kitchen.

"I'll unload," Tori directed, "and you all start the video."

"Where's the ice cream?" Erik dug into a sack.

She pushed him around the counter. "Go! I'll bring it to you," she said with a laugh.

When she joined them with bowls of ice cream, he nudged the boys who sat on either side of him on the couch. "Make room for Mom, guys." They slid to the floor. After a time Erik put his arm across the back of the couch behind her. He smiled at her when she scooted closer to him.

When the movie ended, David asked, "Can Coach tuck us in?"

"Of course. Good night." Tori hugged her sons, carried the bowls to the counter, then sank into the easy chair, legs tucked under her, head leaned against the back. She knew it was only for the moment, but she basked in the glow of the most pleasant evening she had enjoyed in years. *Coach is home*.

Erik returned, subdued, and sat on the ottoman before her, elbows resting on his knees. "They're special kids, Tori. Thank you."

"For what?"

"For letting me tuck them in. For welcoming me tonight. For letting me be a part of your family."

"Thank you for joining. The boys were certainly more cooperative and content with you along."

He smiled. "They said the same thing about you." She looked down at her hands. Danny and David had probably gone into great detail about her short temper this past week. Would he surmise the truth, that it had been due to his absence?

"I've never met anyone like you, Torinado. I don't understand what's happening." He reached for one of her hands and held it between his, gently stroking it. "I get the feeling, listening to Dan pray, that it's out of my control. And I'm beginning to think I don't want control anymore. It's not like I have ultimate control anyway, so why do I think I know better than God?" His low voice was huskier than usual. "Dan said, 'Lord Jesus, thanks for bringing Coach home and for kissing Mom.' Like he was thanking someone for giving him exactly what he had asked for." Their eyes met. "Tori, a suitcase is my home, and I promised I'd never kiss you again."

"And I promised I would never give the time of day to any man who had the personality of a whirlwind."

"Does that mean I spend most of my time flying around?"

"Umhmm. Trying to change the world."

He studied her face. "So, did the boys ask God to bring me back and kiss you?"

She took a deep breath. "Well, three months ago they said we needed a dad and husband, and I said, 'How about Allen?' and they said no, so I said they knew what to do—ask God."

"I'm leaving for Hanoi on Sunday."

Tori's eyes stung. "I'm not going to count the hours until you go, nor the months until you come back. If you come back."

He reached for her, and she leaned forward until his hand was behind her head and his lips met hers.

After a time he rested his forehead against hers and whispered, "I'll come back, sweetheart. If you'll let me."

"Oh, Erik. I don't want you not to." That would be worse.

"All right." He took a deep breath. "I'd better go now."

Hand in hand, they walked through the house and out the front door. The thick sweetness of jasmine hung in the still night air. Under the stars, in shadows cast by the street lamp, they held each other for a few quiet moments. There was nothing more to be said.

Coach is home. Coach is home.

The following day, shortly after the final game of the season, the championship game, which they won, all the Oriole boys and their families met at the park for a team party and picnic. When the water balloon toss, three-legged races, and potluck meal were finished, everyone gathered in the shelter while Erik conducted the presentation of trophies to the boys and gave gifts to his assistants.

Tori sat atop a picnic table, fingering the gift bag she had placed inconspicuously behind a stack of paper plates. It was a photo album she and Linda had completed this week. Her friend had captured each of the boys individually at games or practices, as well as parents and siblings. Erik was in many of the pictures. Tori had organized them and placed funny sayings on each. On the cover was a brass plate engraved "To Coach Steed, with thanks, the Orioles 1991." She hoped he would enjoy it.

"Last but not least," he announced now, "our team mom, Tori Jeffers. Thank you for this great party, for the endless phone calls, for ordering trophies and collecting uniforms, and for generally teaching me how to coach."

At the sound of laughter, Tori's ears felt warm. Not looking at anyone, she remained seated, wishing he'd hurry up and finish.

Erik sauntered toward her, carrying a shoe-sized box wrapped in gold foil and tied with purple ribbon. "I considered giving you a knife especially made for slicing oranges and a lightweight cooler for carrying snacks."

The heat spread from her ears to her neck.

"But those seemed rather utilitarian." He stopped before her. "I thought about paying your hospital bill." He paused until the laughter quieted. "But I learned Little League insurance covers that. So . . ." He handed her the box with a smile.

Tori carefully pulled off the wrappings.

Erik described what she found inside. "All the boys autographed the baseball. The trophy is shaped like a glove to hold the ball, and the plaque beneath reads, 'World's Best Team Mom.'"

She stared at the trophy in her hand. He forgot to mention the delicate gold bracelet hooked around it. Tucking everything back into the box, she blinked rapidly and stood. "Don't go away. We have something for you, Coach. Boys . . ."

His team members grouped together, and David shyly handed him the bright orange bag.

"Aww, guys, you shouldn't have." He pulled out the photo album and leafed through the first few pages without a word. "I . . . This—"

It was the first time she'd seen him speechless, even awkward.

At last he looked up and smiled in her direction. "Thank you. Thank you all for a great season."

Everyone cheered, and the cleanup began.

A short time later, as the parking lot emptied, she lingered near her station wagon and watched the twins and Nicky making one last run through the twilight. She reopened the box.

"Need some help?"

"Erik, this is so beautiful. Thank you." He helped her hook the bracelet around her wrist. "I didn't know what to say. It's much too extravagant for a team mom gift." Impulsively she stretched on her toes and kissed his cheek.

"It's only a token compared to what you've given me."

"And what have I given you, Erik Steed, except a lot of grief and a few photographs?" she teased.

The corners of his mouth lifted briefly as he turned aside, gazing toward the tall, rocky hills sharply outlined by the setting sun now hidden behind them.

"Oh, I did give you lasagna once."

Hands in his pockets, Erik looked down at the pavement. "What you've given me . . ." She strained to hear his soft voice. "What you've given me is Tori Jeffers and a reason to believe in God."

She slipped her arms around his waist, and he held her tightly.

"I wish I weren't a whirlwind. We're just so close to the trade embargo lift. Perhaps three years. MIA information is trickling in. I can't stop working on it." An urgent tone rushed his words together. "I may have to remain in Hanoi for a long time."

"I understand. It's so important for so many people. And you need to learn about Phil." The tune was familiar. It was a different verse, but because she knew the notes, the words came easily.

"I talked with Tim about the schedule. I've worked it out to be back the day before they leave, in three weeks. I'll be here for you that day, I promise."

She bit her lip, but the sob still wrenched itself from her throat.

"The boys are coming." He kissed the top of her head. "The photo album is priceless, Tor. To think I didn't have a clue when I asked you to be team mom of what I was getting into. Or when I agreed to coach in the first place, just to fill up time more than anything. Did I tell you Nick's looking forward to staying with his grandparents?"

He continued chatting in a soothing tone until she had to face Nicky and say her first good-bye. She knelt and hugged the small boy. "Whenever you come to town, we expect you to call us, understand?"

"Okay. See ya, Dan. See ya, Dave."

"See ya, Nick." They solemnly shook his hand, promising to visit him in San Francisco.

At last Erik hugged the boys. "Take care of your mom." He quickly kissed her. "I'll call you."

Coach is gone. Coach is gone.

The story of David and Bathsheba and Uriah haunted him. The week following the visit to church with Tori, it had simmered on the back burner of his mind as he coordinated the logistics of his upcoming overseas trip, Susanne's move, what to do with the Blazer in San Diego until he had time to drive it north. He pondered it during the short flight with Nick to San Francisco, the brief visit with his parents where he left his nephew, and then the quick stops at his apartment and the office.

At last, settled in for the long flight to Vietnam, he opened the Bible Tim gave him, found the passage, and began reading it over and over, studying it.

Where was the forgiveness?

At nights in the hotel room in Hanoi, he discovered David's Psalms. Exhausted after a day of haggling—and it was haggling, not negotiating—over office space, rent, telephone service, and access to citizens and crash sites, Erik would fall onto the bed. A sense of dissatisfaction kept sleep from him until he read more. He anguished with the psalmist and wondered at the expressions of joy. Where was the joy?

"Oh, God," he would ask the walls, "what do You want from me? You took Phil. I give my money to help others. Tori is taken care of financially for life. I held Susanne's hand through that mess. I gave up my place in the company to do this for these people, to open trade, to find answers for families like ours. What more do You want?"

In the quiet that followed such outbursts, he would see Tori's lovely face, with its perky nose and shock of violet eyes, smiling up at him. He heard her voice, with its soft, southern lilt, redefining life in her caring words, in her description of living in the shadow of God's wings. He smelled freshly baked cookies and that scent of rain-washed flowers in her safe harbor of a home. Was his peace there with her?

After two weeks in Hanoi, he traveled south to Ho Chi Minh City to visit the grandson of a former dealer for a few days. The man, about his own age, was in the process of rebuilding his grandfather's business. He needed parts for U.S.-made farm and industrial equipment left after the war. The Steed company had been their American contact thirty years ago. With the economic embargo still in effect, it wasn't possible yet to trade.

Erik knew the importance of developing a rapport with Xuan, though. He had been granted special permission in recent years to travel here and had met with his friend on three occasions. This week, however, they were getting more specific about business details. With these preparations, they would be better able to step in when the governments reached agreement.

The words in the ledger ran together now before him. The neatly handwritten page he studied was a list of farm equipment. Erik blinked, but the words would not focus. He knew he was extremely tired. "Xuan, what are you humming?" He turned on the stool. "What is that song?"

Xuan's round face and deep brown eyes lit up. "You like it? Come to my house. We eat dinner and sing more songs."

A short time later they strolled along a wide, Parisian-like avenue. The late-afternoon sun still beat from the clear blue sky, but the city's proximity to the sea kept the temperature bearable. Erik thought the sidewalk cafes and markets appeared busier than on his previous visit. More foreigners were evident in the crowds. Xuan pointed out new shops along the route. Erik pondered the resiliency of the nationals.

Suddenly it hit him. "'Amazing Grace.' Xuan, that's what you were humming."

His friend just smiled.

He had visited Xuan's apartment before and met his lovely wife Tran, who now welcomed him again. The language and the food were familiar to Erik. The crowd of men, women, and children crammed into a small apartment was a typical gathering, but tonight their purpose was a surprise to him.

They sang about Jesus. He thought he recognized another tune from his visit to Tori's church. He hummed. When choruses were repeated, he was able to sing along. After a time the stifling heat became less noticeable, as did the closeness of those sweaty bodies seated beside him on the floor .

"Mr. Erik?" Xuan was at his elbow. "Will you read?"

"Read?"

"The Bible. It is in English, and it takes me long time to interpret. You do it tonight, when we find it. My wife hide it too good." He shrugged.

"Xuan, I have one." Erik stood and gingerly stepped between people. He noticed the eager look on their faces as his friend announced the book had been found. He reached into his briefcase tucked under the table, pulled out the Bible, and held it toward Xuan.

He just nodded with a smile. "Okay. Read."

Erik hesitated, then opened to where he had been reading in the Psalms. He completed just a few lines when he was interrupted.

"No, no. New Testament please."

New Testament? A Sunday school teacher's voice echoed in his memory. *First comes the Old Testament, then the New, beginning with Matthew.* He flipped through pages and looked up. "Matthew?"

"Please," his friend said.

He looked back down and began reading at the top of the page. "'Come to Me, all who are weary and heavy-laden, and I will give you rest. Take My yoke upon you, and learn from Me, for I am gentle and humble in heart; and you shall find rest for your souls.'"

Jesus.

At that high-destiny moment everything changed in the heart and soul of Erik Steed as he called out to the Savior he'd needed all along.

He slept soundly that night. He had left his Bible with Xuan, and his load at the cross. No matter what happened, everything would be all right now.

— Ten —

"IT'S FLOWN BY TOO QUICKLY, LINDA, these three weeks." Tori and her friend smoothed a sheet atop the pile of blankets spread on the family room floor. The furniture had been shoved aside.

"But they've been good, Tor. We've practically lived together." She giggled. "Well, more than usual, if that's possible."

"I know you've talked more than usual," Tim added. "I didn't think that was possible." They threw pillows at him as he hurried out the sliding door.

"That should do it." Tori surveyed the bed they had made for the boys.

"Thanks again for keeping us tonight."

"You're welcome. Is there anything else to do at your house?" They had all waved good-bye to the moving van this morning, then spent the day cleaning and doing yardwork.

"No. I'm just going to walk through it one last time." Linda headed toward the sliding door.

"I'll come—"

"No, Tor, wait here. And don't look so scared. So which have you decided, to rush into his arms or ignore him?"

"I shall be cool as a cucumber. Then the next good-bye won't be so hard."

"Could we negotiate that decision?"

Tori turned to see Erik across the room. At the sight of his lopsided grin, tousled hair, rumpled white polo shirt and khakis, her determination to remain aloof vanished. She ran to him.

He caught her up in his arms with a laugh. "Whew, I am a good negotiator."

"You are such a pompous snob!" Her giggles ended abruptly when he kissed her. "Oh, Erik, how can you make it easier and more difficult all at the same time?"

He raised his eyebrows.

She just shook her head. "You look tired. Let's sit in the front room. There's no space in here. The boys are sleeping on the floor tonight. Tim and Linda and Kelsey are using the bedrooms. Do you need a place to sleep?" They sat down on the couch.

"I reserved a room at that motel just off the freeway. What's the schedule?"

"We're eating dinner here. Everyone will leave about 8 tomorrow morning. They're taking Danny and David to Phoenix to visit Grandma Jeffers. They usually spend a couple weeks with her in the summer. I'll drive over for a few days when it's time to bring them home. Will you eat with us?"

"Yes, thanks. I'd like to spend some time with Tim."

She touched his forehead, gently smoothing the furrows. "This was such a long trip for you to make. You didn't have to."

He smiled. "But is it all right that I did?"

She squeezed his hand. "More than all right. How are things in Hanoi?"

"The office is set up. We can't have official delegates there yet, so my unofficial services fit right in. And I was able to visit Ho Chi Minh City and check on some business." His eyes brightened. "Tori, I found an underground church. We met in a home. Something happened there . . . I made my peace with God, Tori. I gave my soul to Jesus."

She studied his face and saw beyond the tiredness. She smiled, thrilled at what had transpired in the heart of Erik Steed. "You're not angry anymore, are you?"

"No."

She hugged him, then put her hands on his shoulders and looked up at him. "But an underground church—that had to have been dangerous, for you and for them! And for the MIA efforts. Oh, Erik, what if . . . ?" She noticed his mouth twitch, one corner lifting, then straightening out as the other one went up. "You're not listening."

"Why are you so surprised at what I did? People have been praying for me."

"Now I suppose you'll want to take up smuggling Bibles." His blue eyes danced with a familiar restless energy. The first time they had ever spoken, at the gas station, she recognized it. Why couldn't she have loved Allen instead? "You probably already have." She wanted to ask more but felt it wasn't the time.

He shook his head and smiled. "Not yet."

"I know who might want to help."

His eyes widened. "What?"

"You said you would spend tomorrow with me? That we would do whatever I wanted?"

"I told you that on the phone. It hasn't changed. Who might want to help?"

"Tomorrow." She stood and walked toward the kitchen. "There's too much commotion right now. Tim's in the backyard. The boys should be here any minute. Kelsey's on the phone. I have to put dinner in the oven. Why don't you just relax awhile?"

"Tori?"

She hesitated in the doorway, looking back over her shoulder at him.

"I love you."

"I know," she whispered.

Tim let out a low whistle. "God sure does work in strange ways."

For a few moments the two men were quiet, the silence broken only by the muted sounds of distant freeway traffic. The nightly low clouds of early summer had rolled inland, hiding the stars from view. The friends sat on padded lawn chairs in a corner of Tori's small backyard, in the damp grass, away from the open screen patio door. Their conversation was private.

Elbows on knees, Erik sat hunched over. He peered up now at Tim, trying to make out his features in the darkness. Lights from the house cast shadows across his eyes. He couldn't read his thoughts. "You really think God was in on this?"

"Buddy, you can be sure that whatever Joe, or Goldie as we called him, was in on, God was in on. The guy was constantly talking to his Father. He figured that by keeping the communication lines open, he was always right where he should be, doing what God had planned for him."

"Then you think this whole scenario is feasible?"

"Feasible?" Tim chuckled and held out his hand, lifting one finger at a time as he reviewed Erik's story. "When you throw in Goldie's faith in Christ, his aircraft carrier in the South China Sea, the U.S. government, and the Navy, what you've got isn't just feasible, it's a sure thing."

What felt like a fist twisted in Erik's stomach. He shook his head. "I'm sorry."

"There's nothing to be sorry about. Which is exactly what Tori will say."

"I can't tell her."

"Do you love her?"

"Yes."

"Then you have to tell her. She can handle the truth, Erik. Even when it's painful. Look, she's Linda's best friend. She's the widow of my best friend. I love her, too, and before we accepted this transfer I had to consider how it would hurt her. We can do our best to take care of her, but in the end we can't protect her from life. God doesn't give us more than what we can handle."

Erik nodded. "I read that somewhere."

"Well, she knows that's true. I mean she really knows it. After Joe died, sure, she fell apart. But God put her back together again, with a stronger faith. Now, I can't guarantee her initial reaction. You know how she is." They smiled at each other briefly. "But she'll be okay."

"Tim, I love her, but I can't give her what she wants in a relationship. There's too much to be done in Hanoi and for the church there."

"Linda's right. You're a lot like Joe."

"The whirlwind aspect, as Tori calls it, maybe, but not the spiritual. He reminds me of Phil in that respect."

"Did your brother's faith take him to Nam?"

"Yeah. He thought Jesus needed another Marine, not another college student. He didn't know why, but he said he didn't need to know why, because God was taking care of him. I think I'm just beginning to get a glimpse of what he meant by that."

"Faith grows over time. Like love." Tim paused. "She needs to hear the truth now, no matter what your future plans are."

"What if Washington doesn't confirm my suspicions before I leave San Diego?"

"I think she should know where you're coming from. Personally, I don't need Washington to confirm anything. There was something about Joe. I mean, I know Christians die in storms, but it just never seemed quite right that Joe went home that way."

Everyone arose early despite the fact that they had all talked late into the night. Erik, too, arrived in time to eat pancakes and help load the car. At last, the quiet, tearful hugs completed, Linda and Tim and all the children drove off.

Tori and Erik stood at the end of her driveway waving at the empty street. The sky was a gloomy gray.

"Do you need to cry now?"

"No. I've done enough to last for a while." She wiped tears from her face and sniffed. "Well, you'd better get ready."

"For?"

"The zoo. And it's July, so the sun will burn off this gray gunk soon. Wear shorts, but bring that sweatshirt because it might be cool tonight."

"Why don't I help you clean up and put things back in order?"

"That will give me something tangible to do when you leave. Do you leave tomorrow? Oh." She closed her eyes and shook her head. "Never mind, don't tell me. I just need thirty minutes."

An hour and fifteen minutes later Tori pushed the silver bar of the entrance gate at the zoo, pocketing the pass she'd just shown to the attendant. "Hurry up, Erik. They're waiting by the flamingos, just ahead." Bright, warm sunshine and a pungent eucalyptus scent enveloped her as she walked out from the covered entryway.

"I don't see any flamingos." He strode up beside her, looking ahead at a large group of people milling about. "But I think I just landed in Vietnam."

She smiled up at him. "It's just a small church. Our church is their sponsor, kind of like a parent. We get together every so often for outings like this. I've never been on one, but, well, I volunteered you to stay with the group of older adults around the zoo. Their English isn't very good. Can you talk to them? Do you mind?"

Laughing, he put an arm around her shoulders. "Yes. And no, I don't mind."

After introducing Erik to the man in charge, she watched him meet the group of seniors. She wondered if she'd only imagined an arrogance about him. There was no hint of it now. He seemed almost oriental in his demeanor, so obviously respectful in the way he stood and spoke, the strange words flowing without hesitation in his husky voice.

They spent most of the day apart. Tori walked with a group of elementary-age children and young mothers, mostly Vietnamese, but a few from her church. Their contagious excitement was the antidote she needed.

When it was time to leave, a caravan of cars and vans formed in the parking lot to take everyone to the Vietnamese church where they would eat supper. Noticing some boys eyeing

Erik's truck-like vehicle with interest, she invited them to ride with him while she rode with others. He winked at her.

They parked in a poor neighborhood of three-story apartment buildings and walked to what appeared to be a sort of clubhouse. It was well-manicured outside, with lush flowers and magnificent bougainvillea climbing the walls. Inside, a pleasant cooking aroma filled the main room that contained long tables and chairs. Tori learned that on Sundays the chairs were placed in rows, so the congregation of about seventy-five could meet here. She estimated that well over a hundred people filled it now.

"Try this." Erik had found her at the serving table and began filling her plate with unknown foods. "And this. I think you'll like it. How was your day? You don't look so uncomfortable anymore."

"I wasn't uncom—" She clamped her lips together. She had been extremely uncomfortable at first.

"Tori, you can separate these people from your father's experience. The older ones fled the Communist regime in search of a better life for their descendants."

"I've had a great day. I didn't think I could relate to them, but it seems that kids and mothers have a universal language."

He smiled. "Don't be afraid of the food. It's delightful, too. Excuse me, I'm in the middle of a discussion about smuggling Bibles."

She didn't know if he was teasing or not but followed him to where he sat with a group of older men. Since they spoke in Vietnamese, eavesdropping didn't help, but she watched their earnest faces. Erik spoke gently, leaning slightly forward. She sensed he was asking the questions.

The sun was setting as they headed north on the freeway. Erik was subdued. "I learned so much today. Oh, will you write this down? There's paper in that compartment." He recited a name, a town in Virginia, a date—1968, and spelled two Vietnamese words for her. "I met a young man. I promised to get this information to the right people, to help locate his American father who hasn't seen him since he was two."

"Having a good friend move just one plane trip away doesn't seem so devastating now."

"Is that why we went today?"

"I didn't have that in mind. The guy in charge read the article I wrote about you and called me, hoping you would be available to interpret. It happened to be on the day you were here . . . It seemed the right thing to do."

He reached over and squeezed her hand. "It was."

"Yes, it was."

When they pulled into her driveway, Tori spoke, rushing her words together, wanting to quickly get over with the inevitable. "What time do you leave tomorrow?"

"I have to start driving to San Francisco tonight."

She tightened her hands into fists on her lap.

"I—" He cleared his throat. "I couldn't work out any other schedule. I have to get my car back there, pick up some files, catch a flight out on Wednesday."

No need for a car here, eh? "Will you see Nicky?"

"Yeah."

"I'm sure he'll be glad to see you. Well, this makes for less hours in the good-bye countdown. It's better that way." *I won't ask when he's coming back.* "You need to go then. Thank you for today." She leaned over and kissed his cheek. "For everything." *Dear Erik.*

"May I come in?"

She took a deep breath. "Prolonged good-byes are just so horrendous. I'm really all right. And exhausted. I'll sleep well. Erik, I understand, truly." *Same tune, verse 137.*

"Please, I have to clear the air about some things. Tim told me it would be best. I promised him."

The look on his sober face filled her with dread. As they walked in silence, she breathed a prayer for grace to accept what she was sure would be his final good-bye. Inside the house she flipped on two lamps, and they sat at opposite ends of the couch, facing each other.

"Tori, the government has offered me a full-time position in

Hanoi. That would allow me to devote all my time to the MIA situation."

She squeezed his arm. "That's wonderful. Did you accept?"

He nodded.

"What about your company?"

"Well, these past six months have turned into a trial run." His eyes brightened. "We learned I don't need to be physically present at the office and meetings. I can function as a long-distance consultant. And with the possibility of Vietnam opening up again, I'll be in good position for laying the groundwork there for trade."

His mind was already made up about future plans. "It does sound perfect for you."

"It does, Tori. It's best for us, too, if I just stay there." He looked at her.

His words sank into her heart. "Don't I get a say in that decision? Erik, I did a lot of thinking these three weeks you've been gone. I'm not looking for a full-time commitment anymore. When I'm with you, even for a short time like today, I remember why I chose to live this way before. It's just a lifestyle. You get used to it. You make the best of it. I can handle it because I love you."

"Tori, please . . ." He moved closer to her and grasped her hands between his. "Hear me out."

She saw his handsome features contorted in anguish, and she felt afraid. "What's wrong?"

"I'm—" He tightened his grip on her hands. "I'm responsible for Joe's death."

"What are you talking about? Joe died in an accident, in a storm, Erik."

"That was the official report."

She heard his slow, measured words whispered hoarsely. She felt so cold.

"Ten years ago I was twenty-six. I had only two reasons for getting up each morning: to find my brother and to expand our company. We had numerous political contacts, and through them I found other people interested in getting back into Vietnam, either for financial reasons or because of personal interests in the POW/MIA situation."

He lowered his eyes. "I knew the Far East, and I knew the language, but it's money that buys power, and I had that. I became part of an inner core that was in a position to secretly negotiate with the Vietnamese government." He squeezed her hands and looked up at her again. "Five years ago on September 19th, a group of us flew into Da Nang."

Her body was shaking now. His voice droned on.

"We knew there were factions within that country that would prevent any effort toward normalizing relations with the U.S. We knew China would be watching. We needed an escort. Fighter pilots in the area volunteered. They protected us. We got in and out, but before we crossed the border, an attack was made. One of the jets was shot down." He stopped.

For a few moments their eyes locked in silence. Then Tori whispered, "How do you know it was Joe?"

"Everything, of course, was so secret, we never met the pilots. It was the date. The location of his carrier. The body not recovered. The fact that there was no storm in—"

"That's all coincidence."

"The intercom was left on by mistake. I heard—I thought I heard—'Cody's been hit.'"

Cody . . . or perhaps Goldie. "Maybe that's what you did hear. But it was the 18th, not the 19th."

"It was the 18th here, the 19th there. It didn't storm until the 20th." He closed his eyes for a moment. "When I was in Washington last month I started procedures to open the records. It's still highly classified information." His arms were around her now. Still she shook. "It's too much to be coincidence."

"Did they eject?"

"What?"

She raised her voice. "Did they eject?"

"No. No parachutes were sighted. It was a . . . a direct hit. Reconnaissance spotted nothing in the following weeks."

She pushed him aside and walked to the darkened window. "Tori, I am so sorry."

She covered her face with her hands. The pounding of her heart echoed in her head. Thoughts agitated through her mind. Joe's RIO had been single, without a wife or children. Should she tell his parents? Was this still so secret that they couldn't know? But what difference would it make now?

Of course it was Joe. He would have been first in line to offer to fly such an assignment. Of course he was there. He was just like Erik. No, Erik was just like Joe. *Oh, God!* Tears trickled through her fingers.

"We shouldn't have been there. It was too soon. The monsoon should have delayed things but didn't. Maybe later it would have been different."

She wiped her eyes and turned to find Erik close beside her.

He repeated, "It was too soon. The timing wasn't right. We shouldn't have gone."

She took a deep breath. "But was it groundwork for what you're doing today?"

"Yes, but it could have come later, and Joe would still—"

"No! You had to go, and he had to go."

"Tori, sit down. You're white as a sheet."

"I'm all right."

Grasping her elbow, he guided her back to the couch. A wave of nausea rolled through her. She buried her face in his shoulder, and he wrapped his arms around her. "Why didn't you tell me before?"

"When you told me about Joe, that night after we came back from the hospital . . . it sounded too crazy, too coincidental." She strained to hear his husky, anguished voice. "It was before I understood that there is no coincidence with God. Still, I suspected the truth, but I didn't know what to do. I felt you had a right to know, even if the government didn't think so. I just couldn't bring myself to hurt you. You'd already been through his death once. What difference would it make now?"

He took a deep breath before continuing. "Since then, I've

tried to ignore it, hoping it wasn't true, convincing myself you didn't need to know. But I couldn't shake the responsibility, the guilt. I kept waking up in a cold sweat, thinking about what I've done to you and the boys. I had to find out if it was true. And so . . . I've no right to ask, but . . . can you forgive me?"

Sitting up, she touched his cheek. "Oh, dear Erik, it's not your fault. You said it yourself. He volunteered. I know he would have been the first in line. There's nothing to forgive. Please don't blame yourself."

"That's what Tim said. He told me you'd say that, too, but you can't deny there's a connection. Can you live with the fact that you're a widow because of a situation I was responsible for?"

She wrapped her arms around his neck and held him for a moment before responding. "I think it makes you able to share my grief more than anyone. And that I can live with."

"Oh, Tori . . ." He hugged her. "I'll make it up to you, I promise. You know, I'd give you anything in the world."

Make it up . . . ?

"I've set up trust funds for the boys, for college. And one for you. Is there something you need or want? A car? A house?"

Blackness swirled in her head. She pushed herself away from him. "You don't have to make it up."

"Let me try—"

"You *can't* make it up. And that's okay, except—" She took a deep breath, searching his eyes. "I think that's all you've been doing—trying to make it up, working out your guilt."

They stared at each other.

"No, that's not true. I love you."

"I don't think so. Our friendship has been based on your guilt. You felt guilty when I got hit in the head with a baseball. Before that I was only someone you had to put up with because my sons happened to be your most valuable players. Then you realized who I was and the guilt just multiplied."

"Tori—"

"I don't want your pity, Erik." She stood and strode to the front door. "Or your trust funds. You have your work to do. I have mine. There's no reason for any long-distance relationship, so just go." She opened the door and turned. The sadness on his face grieved her. Her breath caught in her throat. "Please. It's all right."

Slowly, he made his way to the door. He kissed her forehead, just above the right eye, then whispered, "Take care, Torinado."

When the door closed, Tori became sick to her stomach. Near midnight, she finally fell into a dreamless, exhausted sleep.

Most of Sunday she slept, waking only to eat a piece of toast, drink a cup of tea, and give the boys a brief call. That evening Linda phoned.

"Oh, Tor! Tim—" She hiccuped. "Tim just—"

"Just told you, right? Where are you?"

"Amarillo."

"Please don't cry, Lin. There's nothing to cry about. I mean, it's a shock, but isn't it just so typical of Joe?"

"You do forgive him, don't you?"

Tori closed her eyes. "Who? Joe or Erik?"

Linda wailed.

"No wonder Tim waited until Amarillo to tell you. It's definitely too far to turn around."

"I should be there with you."

"No, you shouldn't. I'll be fine. I'm just numb now."

"Is Erik still there?"

Her friend wasn't helping much. "No."

"But everything is settled? It won't interfere with your relationship? You do forgive him?"

"Yes, of course."

"What about the long-distance issue?"

Tori sighed. "There isn't one, because there isn't a relationship. Don't you see, Linda? His feelings, everything he did, was based on his guilt over Joe. I never was his type, Lin, and he can't give up his work. And his work is halfway around the world."

After twenty minutes of consoling her friend, Tori
exclaimed, "This is costing a fortune!"

"Oh, dear."

"Sweetie, I can't handle any more guilt from a friend. I'll be
fine. Good-bye."

"Tor, what about Joe? Do you forgive him?"

She thought a moment. "I'm working on it."

On Monday she phoned the office to say she was ill and then
slept until late afternoon. That night, with her body rested, she
cleaned, scrubbed, and reorganized the house from top to bottom. On Tuesday she went to work and tried to think again.

By evening she concluded that she needed to think through
Erik Steed and then forget him. She sat at her desk in her room.
Nothing tied them together but a peculiar string of events that
she needed to shelve in the past. Just as she had shelved other
events, other emotions.

Joe's letter.

She found it in the box of his things in her dresser drawer,
separate from his other letters. Sitting on the bed, she fingered
the worn, blue envelope. Its arrival five years ago had disturbed
her because it came such a short time after the naval officer and
a pastor she didn't know had stood at the front door, avoiding
eye contact with her.

"Mrs. Jeffers, it is with deep regret that we must inform you
that your husband . . ."

She now realized Joe had written the letter knowing the
very real possibility that it might be his last.

The familiar slanted printing tugged at her.

*I love you more than ever, Tori. I thank God for your faith because I
know that's what makes you strong and able to let me go and do this job.
That gives me freedom and courage to do what I'm best at, serving our
country. We make a good team, baby!*

He'd often told her these things. She agreed that they were good together, even when thousands of miles lay between them. Growing up a military brat had taught her the importance of living a moment at a time, and she brought that to their marriage. In each other's presence, she and Joe lived intensely, always aware that separation waited just around the next corner. When apart, they poured those intense energies into individual responsibilities.

His last paragraph, though, contained thoughts that had pierced her heart. These he had never shared until this final letter. Now, five years later, the words twisted a double-edged sword.

> *Deep down I really do regret our lifestyle. I know we're in the Lord's will, and I know you understood what you were signing up for when you married me, but still it isn't fair to you. I've prayed that if anything happens to me, God will bring along someone who will take better care of you and stick close beside you all the time. Hug the boys. See you all at home.*

At home. Well, he was Home, and they would see him there.

Tori carefully folded the pages and tucked them back into the envelope. She didn't want to live that way again. She couldn't, and her husband wouldn't want her to. And so it was best that things turned out as they had with Erik.

Pent-up bitterness and anger flowed now with her tears. It was as if the healing had finally rounded third base. The end was in sight.

— *Eleven* —

"OH, FRAN, he still makes me so mad."

Joe's mother reached across the kitchen table and patted Tori's hand. "I know, honey, but like you said, it was so typical of Joe. He was always jumping into situations to help others, and he depended on those of us who loved him to just trust him and keep on loving him."

"And not try to change him." Tori smiled at her mother-in-law. "That's why I loved him in the first place."

"Exactly. He was confident in who he was and in what he was supposed to do for others. And he loved you because of your strength. He regarded you as his helpmate, even when you weren't physically with him. You were as much a part of this mission as he was."

They looked at each other for a few silent moments. Fran's blue eyes welled. Only the gray strands that streaked her short, blonde hair hinted at her age. Widowed a few years before her son married, she had just completed her third year as an elementary school principal after many years of teaching. She was the wise, comforting counselor Tori knew she could turn to.

"Lord," whispered Fran, "forgive my prideful boast, but it somehow seems fitting that our Joe should not have died in a storm."

"Mom!" Danny burst through the back door ahead of David. "We saw the car. What are you doing here?"

"Hi, Mom!" David added.

Tori stood and hugged the boys. "Oh, I missed you three. I thought it'd be fun to stay with Grandma, too, so I took some extra days off work."

"We don't have to go home yet, do we?"

"Of course not. How's the pool?"

"Great!" David said.

"Can we go back? It's not dark yet."

"Sure."

The boys raced back out the door and across the patio toward the apartment complex's pool area.

"Fran . . ." Tori sat at the table again, somewhat tired from the six-hour drive to Phoenix after a morning at the office. "Do we tell the boys?"

"In time." Fran poured more iced tea into their glasses. "They seem to like this Erik Steed a lot. They've talked incessantly about him."

"That's been going on for months."

Fran eyed her over her glass. "You never said much about him. He's quite handsome. They've shown me pictures. And Linda was rather ecstatic about him during their short visit on Saturday." She sipped her tea.

Tori turned sideways and stretched out her legs, slipping bare feet out of her sandals. "Uh-hunh."

"Do you blame him?"

She looked up. "Goodness, no. You don't, do you?"

"No, not in the slightest."

"Fran, does it make sense why I ended our relationship?"

"Y-yes, it makes sense . . ."

"But?"

"But I think you love him."

Tori looked down at her glass and slid a finger up and down it, wiping away the water beads.

"It's written on your face, honey. And don't think for a minute you're betraying Joe or me."

Tori swallowed and still did not look up.

"What I think we need here is a change of pace, a change of scenery. Let's take the boys up to Durango."

Tori cleared her throat. "Colorado?"

"Yes. We'll ride that train up into the mountains. Breathe fresh, thin air." She stood. "Eat beans. Hike. Buy cowboy hats. Give me a day to get organized, then let's take two weeks. They'll let you off at the paper, won't they?"

"Sure. There isn't much going on during July and August."

"That settles it then. And I think afterwards I'll run over to San Diego with you for a bit, if you don't mind. It's been too long since I've ridden a wave."

Tori laughed. "You don't have that kind of time available, Mrs. Principal."

Fran walked around the table and gave her a hug. "Oh, right now the world can be put on hold, but my family can't."

It was the time off that Tori needed. Responsibility for the boys was shared with Fran, and Tori was able to relax more and just enjoy them. They laughed and sang, and she grew calm inside. The nagging thought of Erik diminished in the mountain air. As promised, Grandma accompanied them home.

On the morning of July 30th, Tori lingered in her bedroom. This was Joe's birthday, and it would be a difficult day. The memories were more poignant than the day she'd received news of his death because this was the day she last touched him. He had reported for duty at midnight. Usually she and the twins were in Phoenix at this time, but because of Linda and Tim's move, they'd visited earlier than usual this summer and were now already back home.

Well, at least she wouldn't have to face it alone. The four of them planned to spend the day at the beach. The boys knew the significance of the date. As in the past, she and Grandma would tell them stories of their dad and in that way celebrate his life. Linda would call and send her love. Nighttime would arrive and then sleep, and tomorrow life would normalize again.

The doorbell rang, and she walked out to see Fran holding a large crystal vase that contained what looked like at least two dozen white roses.

"There's no card, Tori." She turned toward the front door. "I'll catch the delivery boy."

"No." She folded her arms across her stomach. "They're from Erik."

"How—?"

"Well, obviously Joe didn't send them," she snapped. "It must be nice to be able to afford to pay off your guilt."

Fran walked past her to set the bouquet on the coffee table. A thick rose scent trailed behind her. Tori stood still, tightening the grip around her middle, fighting down the feeling of nausea.

"Honey, it wouldn't be nice at all." Her mother-in-law faced her. "It would make it extremely difficult to understand the free gift of Jesus if we could buy off our guilt. But what must be nice is to be cared for so deeply by a man. Now, I'm going to butt in here. I don't think I've done that too often through the years, have I?"

Tori shook her head.

"When Joe's father died, I was fifty-one years old. My son was in college with plans to become a Navy pilot after graduation. I didn't think I needed a husband or he a father. I buried myself in work. I don't regret anything I've done, and I've enjoyed it all. But there's a loneliness in my life that is not appropriate for the twenty-nine-year-old mother of my young grandsons."

With the palm of her hand, Tori wiped tears from her face.

"Now, do you have his address? We owe him a thank you note. And that's all I'll say on the subject. Oh, and that the neighbor told me the waves are really good this morning."

Nothing more was said. Fran stretched her visit to ten days. Tori sometimes wondered if it was to prevent her from throwing away the roses. She considered doing so but thought that might provoke Fran into discussing the subject again, and that she couldn't bear. It was easier not to talk about him. So instead she endured the thick floral scent and delicate purity of the white petals until at last she admitted to herself there was love in his gesture.

Tori enjoyed Fran's companionship and help with the boys. Grandma took them to swim lessons and soccer practice, while she worked and scheduled sitters for the remainder of the summer. Together they welcomed the new neighbors who moved into Linda's house and were delighted to meet a Navy family with two boys close in age to Danny and David.

As the August calendar began to fill up with various committee and board meetings, last spring's conversation tugged at her heart. *"Mom, maybe you should get married. Then our dad could take care of us when you had meetings."* She loved those activities and knew she was good at them. She also realized that she used the busyness to keep loneliness at bay. With a prayer for the ability to cope with that inevitable consequence, she began rehearsing the word *no* before answering the phone and spent hours recruiting others to fill her upcoming, time-consuming positions. The boys deserved more from her.

When the time came for her mother-in-law to leave, Tori felt stronger and energetic again. Only one thought remained to be communicated. After all the good-bye hugs were given, Tori leaned through the open car window.

"Fran, I do love him."

She smiled and patted her cheek. "It's good you can admit it."

"But I will not write or call him."

"Just leave it up to God then, honey. He'll do what's best for you."

"I know."

Dear Erik,

Thank you for the lovely roses. It was so thoughtful of you to remember Tori on this day. I hope your work in Vietnam is progressing well. Your dedicated service to our country is much appreciated.

Sincerely,
Fran Jeffers

Fran Jeffers? Erik set down the card dated a month ago, addressed to his San Francisco office. It must be Tori's mother-in-law. Joe's mother. Tori had mentioned once or twice that they were friends. She hadn't been alone then. Good.

He hadn't really wanted or expected acknowledgment of the gift, which was why he requested no card be attached. The story of Joe turning thirty on the thirtieth and leaving the next day had stuck in his mind. An ache to comfort her had prompted him to reach out in some tangible way without pressuring her into two-way communication. That decision would always be hers, and he had no right to ask or even hope for it. That Tori knew who sent the flowers was no surprise. It was his typical *modus operandi* that covered thanks, apologies, love . . . and guilt.

He read the note again, searching for a hint of the woman he tried each day to forget. There wasn't much in the polite phrases. The roses were pretty and had arrived on the correct date. Obviously she had told her mother-in-law that he worked in Vietnam. She had probably told her everything, if they were friends as she had indicated. She would feel Joe's mother had a right to know. The note didn't say "Tori sends her appreciation." But perhaps his gesture was a comfort to Fran anyway. He hoped so.

Your dedicated service to our country is much appreciated. There was no condemnation in her words.

"Now that, Fran Jeffers," he said to himself, "is what is much appreciated."

The only word from his contact in Washington was to not count on receiving information that would confirm or disprove his suspicions. It was still too soon to begin declassifying government secrets involving Vietnam. U.S. sanctions remained tight against that country. If peace talks with Cambodia became fruitful, perhaps the situation would change.

Did he need to know, really? It seemed a given with everyone who had known Joe that it was him. Even if it weren't, Tori's interpretation of Erik's actions would not be affected. She would still view his motives as based on guilt, rightly or not.

Erik heard a step in the outer office and looked up from his desk to see an American in the doorway. The man was dressed as he was in a white cotton, short-sleeved shirt and khaki slacks, both in the inevitable wrinkled condition of the humid climate. His close-cropped hair was gray. Sharp gray eyes surveyed him through wire-rimmed glasses.

The man grinned and limped toward him. "If you're an American, I must be in the right place."

Erik stood and shook the outstretched hand. "Michael Carter?"

"Reporting for duty."

"Welcome to Hanoi, Dr. Carter. I'm Erik Steed. Have a seat. We didn't expect you for a few more weeks, not until late September."

"Call me Mike. Oh, I can only sit around a Pentagon office for so long. DIA's not going to teach me anything more about identifying bone fragments."

He referred to the Defense Intelligence Agency, now officially overseeing the POW/MIA research. Erik said, "Ah, but did they tell you that the real technical difficulty is digging holes through sixteen feet of mud?"

Mike chuckled. "That's my specialty."

"You must have served here."

"Just short of two tours with the Army, in '70 and '71." He stretched out his left leg. "Couldn't keep digging those foxholes with shrapnel in my thigh, so they made me go home. How about you?"

Erik shook his head. "I'm the civilian on board. I've been in on the unofficial negotiating end of things for years. The other guys here are military—specialists in the history of the war, locations, etc. They're down in Vinh right now, following a lead."

"I hear the Vietnamese are receptive."

"They sincerely want to help. They find their way here, tell us about a crash site, where the pieces of a jet were buried. Sometimes they remember correctly, more often it doesn't pan out, but we keep on going. They tell us about sightings from years ago. It can get pretty discouraging. It'll be good to have your fresh insight. What brings you here?"

"God. More specifically my job, my interests. Some of my buddies died here. My wife's cousin is an MIA. Twenty years ago I learned about God here. And I love the U.S. and want to help fix what happened. So," he gave a thumbs-up sign, "here I am. How about you?"

"My brother's an MIA. We lost him in '72."

"I'm sorry to hear that."

"Thanks." Erik liked his easygoing manner that seemed to offer immediate friendship. "So how did God get your attention in Vietnam?"

"I was in the hospital, in Saigon, for quite a while before they shipped me home. There was this Marine kid who'd come by every day or night, depending on his duty. I remember waking up, coming in and out of the morphine, and he was always there, talking real quiet or reading to me. Thought he was the nurse at first. He'd just keep me company. Trying to keep my mind off the pain. After a while, I didn't notice the physical pain anymore, but a different kind of pain took over."

Mike tilted back in the chair and folded his hands behind his head. "I'd seen enough horrors. I had my undergraduate degree, but there wasn't anything to live for after 'Nam. This kid just kept telling me about how Jesus loved me. If he hadn't given me that hope, I would have died or spent these twenty years since out of my mind. Just when I caught on, he gave me a Bible. Then the next day he didn't show up. The nurses figured his company moved out." He stopped talking. His eyes seemed focused elsewhere.

"Did you ever meet him again?" Erik asked.

"Sorry to say, no. His name was Flip Stevens. I tried looking him up back in the States. He had mentioned growing up in San Francisco and playing basketball on scholarship at the University of Arizona, but those leads didn't pan out. That guy was special. I owe him my life."

The small office reeled around Erik. His hands gripped the

arms of his wooden chair. "Are you sure you've got the name right?"

"Well, like I said, I wasn't too coherent. He didn't talk much about himself, just those few things. And something about his dad being in the trading business and his Heavenly Father being in the business of trading His Son's life for lost souls. His first name probably wasn't right. Flip sounds like a nickname for something."

Erik let out a deep breath. "It was. His little brother couldn't say Philip."

The other man stared at him. "What was your last name again?"

"Steed." Erik smiled, and his fingers relaxed their tight grip. "Not Stevens."

Mike's chair came down with a thud. "You gotta be kidding. No, of course you're not. He was in Saigon, in November '71?"

"Yeah."

"Wow."

"He joined the Marines while he was in school in Arizona."

The two men sat in silence for a moment. Erik asked, "Do you know why he spent time with you?"

"Oh, I wasn't the only one. The nurses told me he visited a lot of guys at the hospital. And the way he was, like he was on a mission, he must have shared God with everyone he met. You can bet all kinds of men owe him their lives. Do you know what happened?"

"The last we heard from him, he hinted at being near Cambodia. The government gave us different locations." He rubbed his burning eyes with his fingers. "Mike, I can't tell you how much I've needed to hear what you just told me. It's the answer I've been waiting twenty years for."

"What was the question?"

"Why Flip insisted on coming here."

"Your accent is really lousy, Carter," Erik fired off in rapid Vietnamese.

Mike laughed. "Tell me something I don't know."

A camaraderie had developed quickly between the two men in the week they'd known each other. They sat now on a park bench where they could see the immense gray tomb of Ho Chi Minh looming through the trees. The hot noonday sun drew steam from puddles on the sidewalk.

"It's your flat Midwestern speech. Nothing you can do about it," Erik said, reverting to English.

"You know, your brother never complained about any learning disability on my part, Steed."

"He always was a more patient teacher than I'll ever be."

"Did he teach you about Christ?"

"He tried. I wouldn't listen. I only wanted to learn baseball."

"So how come he had such faith at the age of twenty and you guys grew up in the same house?"

"As children we did the usual Sunday school bit when we weren't traveling outside the States. When Phil went away to Arizona, he got hooked up with a group of Christian students. It just seemed to click with him. He never seemed satisfied with life until then. Of course what I saw was he got religion, quit school, baseball, his girl, and signed up for Nam. It didn't add up for me, especially after he was listed as missing."

"Understandable. But things seem different for you now. What happened?"

Erik stared up at the blue sky. "I met Tori."

"From the look on your face, I'd say that was good and bad."

The sense that Mike was as close as a brother had been almost instantaneous for Erik. He knew it stemmed from the fact that he was the last link he'd had with Phil. The story spilled now from his heart.

His new friend was silent for a few moments and then asked, "Will you take me to Saigon?"

The question yanked Erik from his reverie. "Sure, but you're supposed to say Ho Chi Minh City."

"Whatever. I want about another week with you, to learn all I can about the situation here. I need you to re-familiarize me with Saigon and introduce me to Pham Xuan. I'll do what I can business-wise there for you, and I have some Bibles he can have. And then, Erik, you can go home."

He met his friend's eyes. "Home?"

"Yeah, you're through here. The peace treaty with Cambodia could be signed by October. Things'll open up more then. We can get along without you. I'd say you've come full circle, buddy."

"Full circle?"

"You've done what you can here. Let somebody else take a turn. Five years ago is forgiven. You know God, and you know that Phil served a purpose. Go home."

Erik shrugged. "I don't know where that is."

"Yeah, you do. Just leave Tori's number with me."

—Twelve—

A FEW WEEKS after school resumed, David commented, "Hey, Mom, you're not going to so many meetings this year, are you?"

She kissed him on the forehead. "Nope. Are you almost finished with that book? It's getting late."

"Aww, it's Friday."

"And the soccer game isn't until noon. I know, I know. Good night."

As had become her nightly habit no matter what the day of the week or the day's activities, she curled up on the sofa in the front room to read until sleepiness eventually caught up with her. The phone rang, and she went to the kitchen to answer it.

"You weren't asleep, were you?"

"Linda! Hey, it's my turn to call you."

"I couldn't sleep. Are you reading?"

"You know my routine. What are you doing? It's after one o'clock there. Is everyone all right?"

"Yeah, fine. It's just one of those nights. What did you do this week?"

They chatted for a bit about daily details. "Oh, I saw Allen yesterday. He took me to lunch. He asked about you all. He's busier than ever. And," she chuckled, "he's engaged."

"No! To whom?" Linda giggled. "Did he break it to you gently?"

"To a client, and of course. Stop laughing."

"You were so funny about him, Tor."

"Don't remind me. I'm surprised I can still look him in the face without turning red."

"But he didn't realize, did he?"

"I don't think so. The thought of us marrying was so off the wall, he wouldn't have imagined it, but I know what I was plotting. Do you think I'll ever learn to be still and wait for God without barging ahead of Him?"

"I think you've probably learned it now. After all, you gave up all those boards and committees. I know you're more still than you were last spring. The real reason I called, Tori, is because I woke up thinking about you and couldn't get back to sleep. So I'm glad to hear nothing's wrong."

"I suppose things are right with me, except for not being too interested in eating or sleeping."

"Healing takes time. You are making yourself eat, aren't you?"

Tori laughed. "Yes, Mother! Now, good night. And thanks for checking on me, sweetie."

"Good night, Tor. Hug the boys."

She was still reading on the couch after midnight when a soft knock on the door startled her. She didn't move until she heard it again. "Who is it?" she called through the door, tightening the belt around her robe.

"It's me."

A rush of ambivalent feelings bombarded her. Almost three months had passed since she'd last heard that instantly recognizable voice. She leaned her forehead against the door, taking a deep breath to still the pounding in her chest. She switched on the outdoor light, then slowly unlocked the door and opened it a few inches. The sight of his half-closed eyelids, stubbly jaw, and rumpled suit tugged at her.

"Tori, I apologize for barging in like this, but, please, I just didn't know where else to go."

Wordlessly she backed out of his way. He stooped to pick up a large suitcase, garment bag, and attaché case before stepping inside. She shut the door behind him as he dropped his luggage. "How did you get here?"

"Cab . . . From the airport." He glanced around the room. "I, umm . . ."

"Do you want to sit down?"

In a halting manner he moved toward the couch, turned to a chair, then slumped onto the couch, raking his fingers through his already disheveled hair.

"Erik?"

He stared toward the empty fireplace.

"Can I get you something to drink? Some tea?"

When he didn't respond, she walked around the coffee table in front of him. He glanced up at her.

"Erik, what is it?"

Leaning forward, he propped his elbows on his knees and massaged his forehead. "I just need to be here awhile. Please."

Tori heard pain in his raspy voice, saw need in the hunching of his broad shoulders. Memories of him holding her as she cried flooded her. "Of course."

"I remember sensing it the first time I walked through your door. When we had that team meeting."

She dimmed the lamp, then sat down beside him, close enough to hear his husky words, but not close enough to touch him. "Sensing what?"

He lowered his hands. "A safe harbor. I didn't know what it was for a long time. I just felt like everything was all right whenever I stepped foot inside this house. It's in the air in here. What do you do to it? It's like a mixture of oxygen and comfort that everyone can breathe in. I knew you couldn't stand the sight of me and yet you gave me cookies. Twice."

She studied his profile. "Why do you want a safe harbor?"

He turned his face toward her. "Because the whirlwind needs to stop."

Even in the soft light she could see the deep creases around his eyes, the dark circles, the drawn mouth. "What's happened?"

"I guess I succeeded. We have determined fates. And that's

my job." Breaking eye contact, he shifted his gaze about the room. "Only 2,236 to go. We keep digging and digging. So few remains. Just fragments of bone. Shreds. And then there's the wreckage. The twisted metal. And the rain that never stops."

"Phil?" she whispered.

Erik rested his face against his hands. "Not yet." His shoulders heaved. "Sometimes I don't want to know. Just call it KIA/BNR. Like Joe."

She slipped her arms around him and laid her cheek against his shoulder. *Killed in action, body not recovered.* For a long time they sat in silence. At last she felt his body relax.

He combed his fingers through his hair again and took a deep breath, turning his face toward her. "One good thing, though." He attempted to smile.

"What's that?"

"I met someone who knew him. He says he owes him his life because he told him about God."

Her hand flew to her mouth. "Oh, Erik." They stared at each other in silence. "You look exhausted. When did you last sleep?"

He shrugged. "A little on the plane. Maybe yesterday."

"Where did you come from?"

"D.C. New York. Chicago. Los Angeles. It was the quickest route for a last-minute flight to San Diego."

She stood. "Do you want some tea? Something to eat?"

"No. I—" He stood also. "I'll just call a cab and go to a motel—"

"Nonsense. You can sleep here." She strode toward his luggage. "Take Danny's bottom bunk. Nothing wakes him."

"Don't lift that." He moved to her side and took the suitcase from her hand. "I'll sleep on the couch."

"The boys would disturb you in the morning. *Early* in the morning. Now go." She shooed him toward the hallway. "I insist."

After a few steps, he paused and looked back at her. "Why are you still awake?"

She smiled softly at him. "The forecast said whirlwind arriv-

ing tonight. Thought I'd better stay up and make sure the harbor was ready. Good night."

Tori turned off the lamp and sat back down on the couch,
too full of Erik to close her eyes. Erik Steed, the complicated
man who complicated her life. He did care for others. He gave
his money and energy to help them. Did no one care for him in
return? Did no one offer him a safe harbor, a time and place of
quiet? She loved him.

But it wouldn't work. He took the safety from her own
harbor.

In the morning she'd let him go. With that determination
and a quick prayer, she fell asleep.

"Mom . . ."

"Hmm?"

"Can we watch cartoons?"

"Umhmm."

"How come you're out here?"

Tori opened one eye to see Danny leaning over her. It took
a moment to remember where she was. And why. "Coach came
in late last night. Guess I fell asleep on the couch."

"Coach came? Dave!"

"Shh. He's sleeping in your room."

"He's here? Why didn't he go home?"

"He doesn't live here anymore." She sat up.

"Oh, yeah. Is he gonna stay here?"

"Danny, I don't know! Ask him . . . Later."

"Gee, you sure are grouchy when you wake up." He raced off
to the family room.

She allowed the twins to watch an inordinate number of
cartoons before mustering enough presence of mind to send
them to play with friends down the street. She spent the morning pulling weeds, trimming bushes, sweeping the driveway,
working Erik Steed from her mind—trying to anyway.

"Good morning."

She looked up from her kneeling position in the grass to see his long legs beneath khaki shorts. "Hi."

He smiled at her. "Or is it afternoon?" His jaw was clean-shaven above a white shirt. His wet hair glistened in the sunlight.

"Not quite. Did you sleep well?" Removing her garden gloves, she stood.

"Very well, thank you. I used the shower. I hope you don't mind?" His eyes reflected the summer sky.

"Of course not. Come inside. I'll fix coffee for you."

"I don't want to interrupt . . ." He followed her.

Tori rolled her eyes. *You've interrupted my entire life, Mr. Steed. A pot of coffee is nothing.* "Are you hungry? The boys had pancakes. I saved some batter."

"No, thank you." He sat on a stool at the counter while she washed her hands at the sink on the other side, slightly turned from him. "Your hair looks good."

She glanced at him. Was he serious? She was long overdue for a cut. Brushing aside her bangs, she reached for the cof-feemaker. "It's a little on the shaggy side."

"You've lost weight."

With a shrug she held the carafe under the running faucet, wondering how he could tell. She had noticed loose waist-bands . . .

"I hope you're not dieting?"

"No." *I just haven't been interested in eating lately.*

"You're perfectly beautiful just the way you are."

She dumped a spoonful of coffee grounds onto the counter-top, then, with great deliberateness, finished the task of making coffee. "You really should eat something. How about some toast?" Turning her back to him, she reached up into the cup-board for a mug.

"Tori, I love you."

She stared at the cup in her hands.

"I think I started loving you the first night we met at the Little League meeting. You were so feisty, so independent, so determined to keep things orderly and proper. I'll never forget those amethyst eyes blazing up at me. I think that deep down I drafted the boys just so I could see you again."

She strained to hear his low voice through the rushing sound in her ears.

"Oh, you exasperated me to no end, but I watched you with the team, with the parents. You were influencing, making an impact, and you weren't even trying. You didn't even realize you were doing it. You taught me so much. Like change and progress don't mean a thing if individuals aren't cared for."

The mug blurred before her eyes.

"I knew I loved you when I saw you lying on the ground, bleeding. I couldn't handle seeing you hurt. When I learned you were a widow, I only admired you more. When I learned who your husband was, who he might be, the guilt devastated me. But my love multiplied; it began to grow very complex. Tori, I would have loved you anyway."

She sensed him rise from the stool and walk around the counter. Blinking rapidly, she set down the mug, then clutched the edge of the counter.

"I know you don't need me." His voice was right behind her. "And the boys don't either. You've done a fantastic job of raising them so far, and you'll continue to do so." He turned her around and, cupping her face in his hands, looked steadily into her eyes. "But I need you. You're my home. The greatest peace and happiness I've ever known has been with you and with coaching the boys. Will you marry me?"

Last night's resolution, honed to clarity this morning, wavered at his touch, at the inevitability of hurting him. But . . . "I can't."

His eyes closed.

"Erik, our worlds are too different. I can't do it again."

He looked at her. "Can't do what, sweetheart?"

"I can't make your safe harbor at home and then send you off to change the world." Placing her hands over his, she lowered them from her face and held them tightly beneath her chin.

"I don't have any more good-byes and welcome homes in me. It wouldn't work."

"I'll make it work. I could spend just six weeks at a time in Hanoi, come home for four—"

"No, Erik. I've thought about this a long time." She took a deep breath. "I love you, but please try to understand . . . I lived that life once, and I'm still working out traces of bitterness. Here . . ." Dropping his hands, she brushed past him and opened the pantry closet. Inside hung her apron. From a pocket she withdrew Joe's letter where she had placed it earlier in the morning after reading it one more time. "Read this. It might help explain what I'm trying to say." She handed it to him, then hurried through the family room and out the sliding screen door.

In the backyard she grabbed the hoe and attacked the garden weeds, choking back a sob with each vicious swing.

Some time later, Tori ventured inside the family room. The house felt quiet. With hesitant steps she walked through the house. A faint scent of his spicy cologne lingered in the hallway. His suitcase lay open on Danny's floor, last night's clothes strewn across it. Her throat tightened as she noticed the lumpy bedspread, his obvious attempt to make the bed. In the bathroom his hairbrush, razor, shaving cream, and toothbrush sat among her array of cosmetics. His damp towel hung over the rack beside her dry one. Water droplets still clung to the glass shower doors.

I miss this.

She bit her lip.

But I'd miss it more if he were only here part-time.

She determined to get out of the house as quickly as possible. The boys needed shoes, didn't they? She'd bribe them with new shoes and a McDonald's lunch after the soccer game. While they were out, they might as well shop for clothes and groceries. That should take care of the afternoon. That would give Erik enough time to return and pick up his things. She'd leave a note on the door and a key in the flower pot.

Five ulcer-producing hours later the boys whined from the back-seat of the station wagon.

"That's enough, guys! We're almost home."

"We can't help it, Mom," David insisted. "Shopping is the biggest drag in the world! And you still didn't tell us how come we can't see Coach."

A weary sigh escaped Tori's lips. "I told you, I don't know. He had things to do and then he had to leave. Right away." *Please let him be gone.*

"I don't understand why dads always have to leave," David commented in a quiet voice.

Tori eyed his sober face in the rearview mirror. "Dads?"

The boys glanced at each other. Danny explained, "We thought he'd be a good one for us."

Rubbing the back of her hand across her tired eyes, she focused on the street. "He works with the government. He really has a lot of important responsibilities that keep him busy."

"Kinda like our dad?"

"Kinda." The car slowed. "Oh—" She pounded her fist on the steering wheel.

"Mother!" the twins reprimanded in unison.

Tori pulled hard on the steering wheel, pointing it toward the curb. It coasted to a stop.

"Why are we parking here?"

"We're out of gas."

"Mom!" David scolded. "We just passed three gas stations!"

"I know that!" she yelled. They were on a wide stretch of road that saw little weekend traffic. Red and white oleanders lined the sidewalk along fenced backyards. Their turnoff was only half a block away. From there it was about four blocks to the house.

Climbing from the car, she took a deep breath. "Come on. We have to get some of these groceries home."

The boys must have respected her frayed nerves because they responded without a word. Opening the back door of the wagon, she sorted through the brown paper sacks, filling three with refrigerator items and other things she needed for dinner. They each took a bag and trudged in silence down the sidewalk.

Rounding the corner, they crossed to the left side and began walking up the slight incline. At the sudden noise of squealing tires they all turned. A shiny apple-red minivan screeched to a halt beside them.

"It's Coach!"

A grinning Erik leapt from the car. "Find a new parking spot?" He grabbed the boys in a bear hug. "What do you think of the van? I'm test driving it."

"It's cool!"

"Boy, this bag is heavy."

"Well, climb in." He opened a door.

"No!" Tori commanded. "They're not heavy, and we're walking." She turned on her heel.

"Guess you better do what your mom says, guys."

"Gee, Mom!" The boys complained, but they followed her.

The van followed her too. Erik drove slowly beside the sidewalk, on the left side of the street, leaning through the open window. "You know how she is when she makes up her mind about something. There's no changing it."

Tori shot a piercing glare at him.

"But she might change it if I change the situation."

"You're an expert at that, Mr. Steed, but I've had my fill of your changes." She walked faster.

"How about just a couple more?"

"No." She shifted the bag to her right arm, blocking her peripheral view of his grinning face. That lopsided grin was back. She turned the corner and spotted the boys a few feet behind her, jogging to keep up. Beads of perspiration dampened her forehead.

Erik swerved around some parked cars, then pulled beside her again. "What if I changed my line of work?"

She ignored him.

"Mom, we quit!"

Tori peered over her shoulder to see the defiant looks on the boys' faces as they set their bags on the sidewalk. "Thank you for your influence, Mr. Steed. Now they blatantly disobey me." She continued her brisk pace.

The van stopped, and she heard doors open and close. A few moments later they drove past her, horn honking, arms waving through the windows. She walked on, her breath labored. What was he talking about? His line of work didn't matter. It was the way he was—an incessant changer who would always be occupied with scattering his energies around the world.

I love him.

I know it wouldn't work, but I love him. He's so good with the boys. His toothbrush even matches mine.

The van was parked in the driveway. Why was he making this more difficult? Why didn't he just leave?

The front door was unlocked. They must've found the key. She trudged through the silent house and set the bag on the kitchen counter where the other two lay emptied and neatly folded. No one was in sight. She quickly yanked out a gallon of milk and shoved it into the refrigerator. Now what was she supposed to do? Invite him to dinner? Suggest he leave?

Tears of frustration bubbled near the surface. She pulled at the neck of her cotton blouse in an effort to fan herself. It was so hot. A shower would help her think more clearly.

Thirty minutes later the warm water still pelted her face as she mumbled aloud to God.

"Lord, I can't hide in here all night. What am I to do? What if he proposes again? This is not an answer to Joe's prayer! You know that. Even if he does love me. And why did You let me love him? Oh, why did You bring him here in the first place? I didn't have to know the truth about Joe. I could have lived without that."

She turned off the water. "That's it, isn't it? You did bring him here, didn't You?"

Her monologue continued as she dressed and blow-dried her hair. "But I can't, Lord. Six weeks is not such an unreasonable amount of time, I know. It's nothing compared to six or eight months. But all the going away and coming home times. It's too hard. He would feel guilty over that. He's like that. He'd wear himself out trying to take care of us until he wound up just resenting me. Us."

Shadows lengthened across the bedroom. The sun had dropped behind the hills. She sat on the edge of her bed and stared at the closed door. Erik was a special man. She liked his lopsided grin. The gentle way he held her face between his hands. The goose bumps when she heard his husky voice. The surprise gifts of flowers that always threw her off guard. His attentiveness. His relationship with the boys. His deep concern for the MIAs. His whirlwindness.

Yes, even that. "But, Lord, but . . . Oh!"

With a sigh she opened the door and walked down the hall. They could be friends. She'd invite him to stay for dinner, which was obviously going to be rather late tonight.

At the front room, she halted. The brass candlesticks were on the coffee table with lit candles. A bouquet of purple flowers sat in a crystal vase between them. Soft strains of Mozart reached her ears.

"Hi, Torinado." Erik was standing in the kitchen doorway.

"Where are the boys?"

"At the new neighbors. I said it was okay."

"Would you like to stay for dinner?"

"Dan and Dave already invited me. They've offered to cook hot dogs and macaroni and cheese for us. They'll be home soon. So," he walked toward the couch, "have a seat. I'd like to finish this morning's conversation."

She eyed him warily. "Please, Erik, don't do this to me."

"Don't do what?"

"Light candles and give me flowers and look at me like that. I was just getting used to not having you here."

He smiled. "Will you give me just five minutes? After that, if you want me to go, I'll go."

She walked around the opposite end of the couch from where he stood, then sat in the wing chair. Her alarm increased as he came toward her, then knelt before her.

"I find that kneeling is the most appropriate position for serious negotiations. Tori, I love you. Did you mean it when you said you loved me?"

She broke eye contact with him, looking down at her hands twisted together in her lap.

"Because if you didn't, there's no reason for me to continue."

After a moment, still avoiding his eyes, she whispered, "Yes."

"All right. Then I understand the only thing that remains a difficulty between us. Joe's letter helped me see it clearly. He was a better man than I am, I know. I hope to have a fraction of his faith someday. But I don't understand how he could leave you."

She looked up at him.

Erik loosened her hands and held them, his forearms resting on her knees. "I don't know how I imagined leaving you for six weeks or whatever at a time."

Her stomach flip-flopped.

"Sweetheart, I will never ask you to live the kind of lifestyle you did with him. I resigned my position in Hanoi today."

"Why would you do that?"

"So I can live in San Diego and coach Little League."

"The season's over."

"I've always been kind of interested in soccer. The boys tell me their team needs an assistant coach. Then there's basketball before baseball starts up again. And in my spare time I want to work with the Vietnamese church here and the local veterans' groups. I may have to visit Washington once a year. It's a great place to teach kids history."

"What about your family, the company?"

"They don't need me more than for occasional consulting."

Tori blinked. "How can you give it all up?"

"I love you that much." He reached into his jeans pocket,

then laid a tiny white box in her hand. "And I told you, this is home to me. I don't see any reason to leave it on a regular basis. It's not like I need the jet lag. What I need is a wife and twins and maybe a baby or two."

She stared into his blue eyes. "But what about Phil?"

"I can let him go now. Others will continue the work. I think he went to Nam so I would follow, so I'd take our knowledge and resources to strengthen the MIA negotiations. They were gifts I could give." He took a deep breath. "And I think I went to Nam so Joe would follow, so you and I would find each other. Does God work that way?"

With a shrug, she smiled through her tears. "Maybe."

Brushing bangs from her forehead, he leaned forward and kissed her right eyebrow. "Will you marry me, Tor?"

"There you go again. Barging in and making all kinds of changes. Babies? Working with the Vietnamese church? Is there anything else I should know before I say yes, Mr. Steed?"

He stood and, pulling her to her feet, wrapped his arms around her waist. "Well, I plan to keep your car filled with gas."

Their laughter subsided as she slipped her hands around his neck. "I do love you, and I want you here, but I don't want to hold you back."

"You won't." He softly kissed her lips. "Do you remember when we first met and I had a cast on my leg? I had spent years pushing myself to the point that when I skied down that slope, I didn't care if I lived or died. That's all you're holding me back from, sweetheart."

In their deepening kisses she sensed a release of her fears and bitterness and loneliness. A freedom to love Erik replaced them, along with a freedom to accept the changes he would inevitably bring into her life.

She felt small arms hugging her from each side.

"Did you say yes?"

"Where's the ring?"

Tori looked at him.

He grinned. "I had to propose to them first! And Linda and Fran are waiting for your phone call."

Her eyes widened.

"I needed prayer support!" He slid her arm from his neck.

She had forgotten the ring box was still in her hand. "I'd say you were pretty sure I'd change my mind, Mr. Steed." She lifted the lid and gasped. A diamond set in a circle of amethysts on a gold band twinkled back at her.

Erik slipped it onto her finger. "With all the changes that took place today, I figured anything was possible!" His arms enfolded the three of them.

Tori knew then that the only constant she would ever need was his love.

Epilogue

September 1994

"On behalf of the President of the United States and a grateful nation, I hereby award this Purple Heart in honor of Lieutenant Commander Joseph P. Jeffers, who was killed in action on September 18, 1986, while serving his country. The President sends his belated condolences, Mrs. Steed, and his heartfelt gratitude."

The solemn admiral, in his starchy dress whites, presented the medal to her, shook her hand, then Dave's and Dan's. The short ceremony was over. Erik thanked him and, pushing the double stroller before him, followed his family out the conference room door.

"Hey, Dad . . ." Dan broke the silence a few minutes later as they walked through a parking lot at Miramar Naval Air Station. He squinted in the bright noonday sun. "Will we get to do this for Uncle Phil? Will they give him the Purple Heart post— . . . postum—"

"Posthumously. They might. Maybe next year."

Dave, walking next to his mother, turned around. "I'll push Sara and Philip. They missed the whole thing. Babies sure sleep a lot except in the middle of the night." He nudged Erik aside and, with eyebrows raised, cocked his head in the direction of Tori whose back was to them.

Erik stepped forward and placed an arm around her shoulders. "Are you all right, sweetheart?"

She smiled up at him, her amethyst eyes sparkling with unshed tears. As always, he felt a rush of gratitude that those most uncommon eyes would look at him in that way. "It was lovely," she whispered. "And so significant for the boys. Thank you."

"For what?"

"Oh, Erik, for arranging it."

"I didn't."

She studied his face. "Really? You didn't?"

The roar of two jets flying low overhead drowned out his voice. He shook his head.

"Wow!" Dan yelled as the noise subsided. "Hey, Dad, Mom! Did you see that?" He pointed skyward. "The shadow of that jet's wings just crossed over us!"

The author's E-mail address:
sallyjon@aol.com